A Brilliant Match

The Earl's Sisters

JENNIE GOUTET

Development edit by Jolene Perry @ Waypoint Authors

Proof edit by Theresa Schultz @ Marginalia Editing

Cover Design by Shaela Odd at Blue Water Books

To my son, Gabriel.

CHAPTER I

March, 1805
Grosvenor Square, London

Sounds of the bustle of opening up a long-dormant residence erupted in all corners of the late Earl of Poole's London house, most favorably situated on Grosvenor Square. Lady Dorothea Rowlandson, eldest sister to the next earl in line, sat at the Hepplewhite writing desk in a bedroom she'd only once had occasion to use and sifted through the stack of letters she had brought to London with her. Every one of them was addressed to The Right Honourable the Earl of Poole.

Two letters were covered with the spidery handwriting of Lady Cowper and the more youthful scrawl of Lady Jersey, both of whom she had learned were London's arbiters of the *ton* in their role as patronesses of Almack's. It should be a natural thing that Dorothea and her sister be accepted into Society because of their father, but such a conclusion was not foregone since they had never been introduced to any of the patronesses —nor anyone else of consequence, really.

Other letters sported more masculine scrawls—some names with which she was familiar, such as Lord Berkley, but most with whom she was not. More than one letter was written by the hand of a certain Archibald Stanley, but she could not tell from the contents of his letter if he was a gentleman or a merchant, and therefore could not be sure if he would be a useful person to know. Amidst the more usual correspondence were also scented letters from women with the names Mrs. Grace Plummet and Mrs. Rosalie Kavanaugh, but the letters dripped with more intimacy than was proper between a married earl and a woman betrothed to someone else. Dorothea had not troubled her mother with the task of looking through any of the correspondence from her late father and had certainly not made her privy to those letters.

Once again, she sorted the correspondence into stacks, hesitating over certain names whose consequence in the *ton* she could not immediately divine. Then, smoothing her hand over those letters more pertinent to her quest—all of them softened with age and rereading—she allowed her gaze to roam around the unfamiliar room. Behind her, a fire crackled in the grate of the marble fireplace. On the opposite corner of the front-facing bedroom was a bookcase filled with books on history and agriculture she was unlikely to read, not a novel to be found among them. The four-poster bed was made up with a white and blue counterpane and pale blue bed curtains. And the dressing table held a mirror that seemed to have been recently replaced, as the glass had not yet blackened with age.

She looked down at Mr. Stanley's name again, puzzling over the contents of one letter, which mentioned investments but no gentlemen's clubs. It included another one of his invitations to a "cozy evening's entertainment at his house," which left her none the wiser about his importance to her late father.

But now was not the time to ruminate on things she had no answer to—or to wonder again at their father's neglect in bringing them to Society's notice. Time was running out before her first London event that evening, and she must learn as much as she could about its members so she might take her place among them without faltering.

"Dorothea."

Her mother stood at the bedroom door, her hand on its post as though to prop herself up. Lady Poole was a faded version of her second-eldest daughter, Sophia, although very little of the beauty she had bequeathed her remained in evidence.

She cast a pleading glance at her daughter. "I do believe we should send our regrets for this evening. We have only arrived in London this morning. It is all too much to contemplate going out again so soon."

"We shall not stay late, Mama," Dorothea soothed, coming over to take her mother's arm. "There are several hours yet in which you might rest. Let me take you to your room, and I'll have Mrs. Platt bring you a tray with tea."

"I fear I shall need *days* and not hours to recover. I was already worn through from worry over Tilly."

Her frail mother fussed in that way back to her room but allowed herself to be persuaded of the necessity of attending the opening ball, adding only how regrettable it was that such a thing must be undertaken without the escort of their father, who had been most attentive to family duties up until his death.

At such a fictitious tribute, Dorothea pinched her lips together to prevent a wayward retort and went over to tug on the bell pull, returning to settle her mother comfortably into a chair. After giving the orders to Mrs. Platt and reassuring her mother as well as she could, she strode back to her room.

"Dorry!" Her third youngest sister popped her head out of her room when she passed it. "You forgot to tell Betty to pack my braided riding crop. You know 'tis the one I prefer. I should not like to use a borrowed crop. Perhaps you might send for it?"

"You were to oversee your own trunk, Joanna," she answered without pausing in her steps. "You are fifteen, for heaven's sake. See if Miss Cross remembered to have it packed."

Miss Cross had served as governess to the three eldest daughters—and their brother before he went off to Eton—and now had charge of the youngest two. Contrary to her name, she was a sweet, plump woman who managed to teach the basic arts essential to any young lady, but without any real authority.

"Found it!" Joanna shouted a moment later. "It was at the bottom of my trunk."

Miss Cross hurried by, her sewing kit in hand. "Oh dear, is anything amiss? I was quite sure we'd thought of everything."

Dorothea reentered her room, her brows constricted. They most assuredly did *not* have everything. As the eldest daughter, she was embarking upon her season an entire year after she was supposed to have done so. And rather than being in a position to help Sophia establish her place in Society as her older *married* sister, Dorothea was to come out at the same time as her. Besides that, the two gentlemen she had decided were an interesting catch last year had both found a bride in that same season. There might not be such eligible options again this year.

Alas, her coming out last year had had to be pushed off. The Fourth Earl of Poole fell off his horse after imbibing too much at a country party, and a letter with the news of such arrived at the manor two days later. Dorothea ordered new black gowns for every one of them, mourning attire for the servants, and a black coat for young Everard, her brother of twelve, who was now the Fifth Earl of Poole. She had the servants drape the windows in black crepe and set a hatchment upon the front door. Then, in the weeks that followed, she received any number of callers with the support of her sisters Sophia and Camilla, since her mother found the effort beyond what must be asked of a woman prostrate with grief. Dorothea had carefully wrapped every one of her newly made gowns in silver paper—and with those, her hopes—to be thought of only the following year. And now the season was once again upon them.

Her eyes fell on the discarded stack of correspondence on the desk. From it, she pulled a letter from the hand of a Mr. Plummet, less than friendly in nature, and attempted to see through what was written and discern if this was indeed the Plummet of the *scented letter.*

"I know I am not to attend any of the parties this year," her second youngest sister announced, entering Dorothea's bedroom without ceremony. "But I am convinced I do not have enough gowns even for the occasions I *am* to be part of. I must have grown a full head since last year and none of my silk gowns fit."

Dorothea set down the letter and raised her eyes to her sister, releasing a silent breath. As her sister's words registered, she pursed her lips and refrained from stating the less-than-flattering truth. Camilla had not just grown in height.

"You cannot have grown a full head. Besides," Dorothea assured her, "I have taken care of the matter, just as I promised I would. Pen is letting out the seams of my old gowns that have enough fabric to allow it. I've written ahead to secure an appointment with a *modiste* as soon as one might be arranged, and your gowns will go to Joanna."

Camilla gave an unladylike snort. "*She* will not wear them."

"To Tilly, then," Dorothea said, striving for patience with the sister who held the unfortunate place of middle child, and who combatted a lack of confidence with a grating bluster that must be refined out of her before she was to come out next year. "But do give me some time alone to think, dear. I have much to see to before we leave tonight."

Camilla made a face and left the room, sparing Dorothea a few minutes of peace before it would be stolen from her. It always was. She carried the letters over to the armchair, placed near the warmth of the fireplace, and dropped half of them when she went to tug her shawl back over one shoulder. With a hiss of frustration, she bent down to collect the letters.

"Let me help." Sophia hurried into the room and collected the letters that Dorothea had not yet reached, handing them to her without a word. Her sister was aware of her preoccupation with the letters, although she had expressed her opinion that such preparedness was unnecessary.

As Dorothea resumed her seat, Sophia sat on the edge of the bed. She folded her hands and met Dorothea's regard with a wistful smile she interpreted to mean her sister had nothing else to occupy her at the moment.

"I have asked Margery to lay my evening gown out on the bed." Sophia wrapped one slender arm around the bedpost and leaned against it. "Are you certain we must attend tonight, Dorry? We have only just arrived this day. It all seems so hurried, and it worries Mama to be rushed like this."

Dorothea had thought nothing remained in the way of preparation, but at Sophia's reminder, she went over to the wardrobe and pulled out the gown she had planned to wear that evening. It had been carefully hung and was not wrinkled, but that might change with a couple of hours stuffed amongst her other gowns.

"Of course, we must attend. Lady Berkley's ball opens the season, and it's the only one we have been sent an invitation to

6

so far. It was unfortunate that Tilly should have taken ill and delayed our arrival in London, but we must not miss tonight."

When their youngest sister Matilda had fallen ill the day before their scheduled departure, their mother refused to leave the manor until she was quite certain she had not caught the vicious cold from her daughter. It would be unbearable to travel from Surrey to London with a head cold, she'd affirmed.

Sophia swiveled in place to watch Dorothea lift her gown high and examine it for any signs of imperfection. "Still, I fear it will be uncomfortable for Mama. And I don't know why you insisted I come out the same year as you. I would have been perfectly content to have waited until next year. Camilla and I could have had our season together."

Dorothea paused in her actions to stare. "You cannot mean that. While last year you might have stayed behind in the schoolroom, though that's hardly usual for a young woman of seventeen, you simply cannot delay your being out again. Not at your age. You shall have every opportunity I have to make an eligible match."

She raised an eyebrow, adding with the glimmer of a smile, "I believe you'll need it, too. It will take time for any gentleman, much less the right one, to win your regard."

As the words left her lips, Dorothea fell prey to a hitherto unthought-of dread. It was true, her sister was shy and would not give her heart to the first suitor who presented himself. This was one of the reasons Dorothea wished for her to have as long as she needed to win a gentleman's heart before her sister could be considered on the shelf. But what if it did not all go according to plan? What if her sister was the toast of the town and she, Dorothea, was cast into the shade? It would be the height of unfairness, when she was the eldest and deserved to secure her husband first.

Unaware of these jealous and fearful intrusions upon

Dorothea's mind, Sophia regarded her openly.

"In truth, I am in no hurry to be married. I shall not consider a match if I am not motivated by love." She cast her eyes down to her lap and leaned back on one hand before lifting them again to Dorothea. "I could not tie my lot to someone who must be nothing more to me than a stranger."

"I would expect no less of you," Dorothea replied, fighting back her fears over all that was at stake with efficient movements to ready her attire. Satisfied that her evening gown was flawless, she laid it over the bed and went to the jewelry box to choose something to go with it. It served to remind her, and she turned to Sophia with a crease in her brow. "What accessories have you chosen for tonight?"

"I had not thought of it. I have the longer strand of pearls from Mama. I suppose it must be that."

Dorothea was already shaking her head. "No, that will be too long for the bodice of your gown, and the pearls have an ivory cast to them. I think you should wear my triple strand of miniature pearls. Their rosy hue will go well with your gown and complexion, and they are of a perfect length. Those will suit you admirably."

Sophia stood and came to hug her. "You are always thinking of others. I hope you will also make a love match this season. You deserve as much."

Uncomfortable with praise that she knew to be unwarranted, Dorothea gave a short laugh.

"A love match—I? No, sister, I do not seek a love match. I seek an advantageous match—a *brilliant* match. Only with that will I be content."

"Well, I think you shall miss out with such low expectations of happiness." Sophia's scrutiny was too sharp for Dorothea's comfort. "Think of having a marriage like Mama and Papa, may God rest his soul. It is not to be borne."

"I *do* think of it." Dorothea slipped out of her sister's embrace. "Our mother married very well. And, although I wish to observe every filial consideration to our dear mama, unlike her, I have been raised the daughter of an earl. I shall be an asset to any peer who chooses me for a wife. I am not overly given to tears or fainting spells, and it would take much to overset me. No, I believe none but my choice to marry for position will suit me, and it is what I am determined to do."

Sophia looked unconvinced, but she let the matter drop.

At precisely nine o'clock that evening, Dorothea was tugging on her gloves as Sophia pulled her cloak around her gown. Their mother had yet to come down, but her lady's maid assured them that Lady Poole would be ready at any moment. The surprising sound of someone knocking at the front door caused Dorothea to pause in her movements. Her sister returned her stare, perplexed, then moved toward the door to the drawing room. When it opened, she threw up her hands in surprise.

"Evo! Whatever are you doing here?"

Their brother, in London? Dorothea went stock-still. This was not what she had planned. She had specifically arranged for Everard to arrive the day after the Berkleys' ball so they need focus only on one event at a time. There must have been an error in communication for Evo to have arrived today. When their younger brother walked in and gave her a jaunty bow accompanied by a grin, she put her hands on her hips and sent him a dark look.

"Everard, why are you here a day early? Where is Mr. Sands?"

"Surprised, are ya? I knew you would be." Everard looked

around the drawing room. "By gad, I'd forgotten what this place looked like."

"Surprised—and also in expectation that you will answer my question," Dorothea replied.

Her brother still had the look of a boy, even at the age of thirteen. He was on the short side and had not hit any noticeable markers that would lead one to believe he was on the cusp of manhood. He marched into the room and flung himself down in one of the chairs as both Sophia and she sat to hear his story.

"Well, it was a stroke of pure luck, I tell you, but I ran into Harv who was also heading into London. Only he was traveling with his cousin in a chaise and four and was making double the time on what we were doing with that rental pair of bonesetters. So when he invited me along yesterday at breakfast, I told him I'd come. I ditched Mr. Sands, who was sleeping still."

"You didn't," Sophia said, looking at him in wounded reproach.

"Evo, did it occur to you that Mr. Sands might be distressed at having lost his charge?" Dorothea asked him in a voice of awful quiet. "Or that it was a shameful thing for you to have left him without a by-your-leave?"

"Not a bit," he replied, cheerfully unaffected. He stood as their mother entered the room. "For you see, I left him a note."

"How nice that you are here, Evo," Lady Poole said, tilting her cheek so he could come to kiss it. "I am ready, Dorothea."

Her mother's response was so placid, so unsurprised, that it caused a wave of irritation to rise up in Dorothea. But then again, it fell to her to handle everything untoward or surprising, so why should her mother worry about anything unforeseen?

In the next instant, to her dismay, her irritation turned and she was blinking back a surge of tears. Her carefully laid plans now tumbled about like Friday's washing—or so it felt to Dorothea. She sent instructions to the butler to have Mrs. Platt see to Everard's room and adjured him to behave himself until they could talk the next morning. And they *would* talk, she'd assured him.

She was soon seated on the rear-facing seat for the short distance to the ball, then standing in the receiving line before she could realize what was happening. Sophia stood behind her, one arm around her mother to offer protection from the cold March air that drifted in with each new arrival. Dorothea attempted to recall everything she needed to ensure that evening's success.

Her prospective husband must have a title; he must be wealthy; he must be respected in Society; there could be nothing in him to disgust... It was a simple list, really, and anyone who did not meet the requirements must quickly be dispensed with.

Ahead of them, several people waited, and as Lady Berkley was in no hurry to rush the guests into the ballroom, Dorothea had time to look around at her first London ball. The glimpse at the elegant decor caused her nerves to fray in dreadful anticipation, although it *was* beautiful.

The Berkley house was known for its ballroom of an impressive size, and indeed, one wall was lined with six tall windows, and its opposite wall had a matching number of columns. The room was lavishly decorated with hothouse flowers, candles, and white silk cloth draped artistically. It was easy to take in the room at a glance as the crowds were yet sparse, and Dorothea made a mental note to arrive a little later at the next ball. It would not do to appear as though they were desperate.

She peeked around the gentleman in front of her to the couple who was now standing before Lady Berkley and exchanging greetings. Her eyes drifted back to the gentleman, and she took a moment to appreciate the fine cut of his black coat and the broad shoulders that filled it. The agreeable height, thick head of curly dark hair, and athletic build from his slippered feet upward hinted at a fine specimen of the male race. She wondered if his features were as handsome as the back of him seemed to promise.

Perhaps it was because she was admiring him that her ears were unnaturally attuned to the audible whispers that came from behind her sister and mother.

"The gentleman just there in the black coat has the appearance of Mr. Shaw, your brother's friend. Is that he?"

She stilled, straining to hear what the response would be and wondering if he had heard them, too. She didn't think so, for he was now greeting Lord Berkley.

"Yes, it is he. I haven't seen him in London before. I shall have to tell Robert that he has come if he doesn't know already," the second voice murmured.

"He is a handsome devil. Perhaps he will ask me to dance." This came out in a playful giggle that made Dorothea long to turn and see who was speaking. She resisted the urge.

"Perhaps he will, but have a care. His estate is heavily encumbered from what my brother says—"

The rest of her words were lost as Dorothea greeted Lord Berkley, smiling at his compliment and conveying her gratitude for the invitation. In truth, it was his kindly wife who'd sent it, expressing her desire to help any daughter of the deceased Lord Poole have a successful début in London.

As Dorothea moved ahead to greet Lady Berkley, the magnitude of the moment struck her, and a sudden surge of contentment leaked out in her smile. She was having her season at last, and she would find a husband befitting her station—a husband who would provide her security from poverty and spinsterhood. A husband who, by his distinguished title, would be at the head of the perfect family she was about to create. Then her real life would begin.

CHAPTER 2

Miles Shaw was possessed of everything a fortune could not provide him. A glimpse at his smiling reflection in the mirror of his rented lodgings had told him as much. His coat molded to his broad shoulders as closely as a coat could without the help of a valet—a necessary economy. His neck-cloth was crisp and folded in an elaborate knot that he himself had learned to tie. His eyes were an unusually brilliant blue that had encouraged more than one young lady to look his way twice, if the deep matching dimples in his smile hadn't done the trick. Only his hair reflected the stubborn personality of its owner with a cowlick on the left side that sent his dark brown locks in two different directions, no matter what he attempted with a comb. But he must be satisfied with what he could not, after all, change.

As he moved forward in the receiving line at Lady Berkley's ball, Miles wondered if this evening would bring better luck than the past few weeks had afforded him. It was early in the season, that much was true. But he had yet to meet a single woman who had inspired in him the desire to begin a courtship in earnest. Every one thus far had either been too shy to respond to his flirtation with anything but crimson blushes, or was so bold he feared to charm them lest he be snared before he was certain.

But his time was running out. He had received that very day a letter from his mother communicating that the black mold in some of the unused rooms of their ancestral home had grown at an alarming rate in the past weeks, and she feared the damp was causing her to be unwell. He had no choice but to find a wealthy wife and to woo her as quickly as his natural gifts would allow.

He had a view past the receiving line into the ballroom, where strains of music filtered out. The musicians had not begun the livelier pieces that would invite guests to dance as it was early yet. Candles were lit in both grand chandeliers above the dance floor, and their flickering lights reflected on the glasses of champagne and other sweet drinks that servants carried on trays as they wove their way around the guests.

It was a mood ripe for romance, Miles thought with a flicker of wry humor, knowing it would require every ounce of his skills in flirtation to direct a romantic courtship rather than a mercenary one. He had come to London to find a wife with a portion—one whose dowry would remove the necessity of further drudgery of the kind he had experienced for the last four years. One whose dowry would make his poor mother more comfortable.

He required this, but he was not of a cold, avaricious mindset. Not he! Along with his determination to marry well, he would seek out a woman he truly had affection for. And what was more, he wished to find her before he had grown very much older. He had an unaccountable fancy to live long enough to see his grandchildren into adulthood.

At the head of the receiving line, Lady Berkley turned from the couple in front of Miles and held out her hand to him.

"Mr. Shaw, I must tell you how pleased I am to see you in London at long last. Your mother is well, I hope. Is she here?"

He bowed over her hand and rose with an engaging smile that coaxed one from his hostess in return.

"Most well, I thank you. Mother bid me give you her warmest greetings and regrets that her health did not permit her to journey to London at present. She promised that a letter was forthcoming."

Miles omitted the part about how his mother did not possess a wardrobe suitable for an entire season in London and would be coming for only one month later this spring.

"Well, I do hope you enjoy your evening," Lady Berkley said. "And come and visit me one of these mornings, for I am generally at home to friends." She turned to meet the next guests, and the look of hesitation on her face led Miles to believe she did not know them.

For the first time, he turned to look behind him and met the eyes of a tall woman with burnished curls, intelligent eyes, and the most flawless complexion he had ever seen. Her gaze was curious before she whisked it away and smiled at their hostess. It seemed she was explaining something, or presenting herself to Lady Berkley, whose face then lit up in comprehension. He paused to stare, unable to help himself, intrigued by both her situation and her beauty that was not in the common way.

Although she drew herself up into what seemed like a posture of haughty condescension, her eyes sparkled with warmth as she spoke with Lady Berkley. Her thick brown hair framed a handsome face with elegant, mobile brows, and her chin, which leaned toward the obstinate, made him certain she could not be persuaded to do anything she did not like. A challenge if ever he saw one. Perhaps *this* might be a woman worth courting. From the look of her jewelry, she did not subsist on the edge of poverty.

Lady Berkley caught sight of him still standing there and motioned for him to return.

"Lady Dorothea, I must introduce you to Mr. Shaw, whose mother was a particular friend of mine in our youth. Mr. Shaw, this is Lady Dorothea Rowlandson, eldest sister to the Earl of Poole."

She paused her speech to wait for the older woman behind them, who was still talking to Lord Berkley, before concluding her introductions.

"Lady Poole appears to be taken up in conversation with my husband, but this is Lady Dorothea's sister, Lady Sophia."

Miles bowed deeply and smiled at both as he lifted his head, allowing his gaze to linger on the eldest. As an earl's daughter, she must certainly have a dowry worth considering. And she was excessively fine to look upon. Perhaps his hunt might provide him with an early reward.

"Lady Dorothea, it is a pleasure. Lady Sophia," he added, turning to her sister.

Lady Sophia responded by averting her eyes as she curtsied, much like the shy women he had frequented since arriving in London. As for Lady Dorothea, all signs of curiosity had been replaced with cool assessment, as though she had decided he wasn't worth her time. After a brief curtsy, she turned away when Lady Berkley spoke again.

"Far be it from me to be overly managing, Mr. Shaw, but I would be remiss as a hostess if I did not encourage you to invite Lady Dorothea and Lady Sophia to dance. It is their first season in London, and it is an object of mine that my floor be packed with dancing couples from the very first set."

Miles lifted an inquisitive eyebrow in invitation, and Lady Dorothea's icy mask grew more pronounced at the suggestion, which struck him with the urge to laugh. So, she did not think him an eligible *parti*? Briefly, he wondered if kissing her would thaw the ice—after he had worked his charm, of course. He did not kiss unwilling maidens.

"I would be most delighted, Lady Dorothea, if you would dance the opening set with me?" he offered, after these thoughts had passed through his mind in rapid succession. "And if you, Lady Sophia, would accept an invitation for the second?"

Lady Dorothea's face revealed little of the warmth she had shown their hostess, but no fault could be found in her gracious acceptance. Lady Sophia murmured her consent as well, but in such shy tones her response could barely be heard. Miles brought his eyes back to the elder sister, speculating on whether she were truly as cold as she seemed. He suspected she could not be from his brief glimpse of her conversing with their hostess. It would be amusing to find out.

"I shall seek you out then," he said with another bow, then descended the three steps that led to the sunken floor where the guests congregated.

A cursory glance around the room revealed only one set of familiar faces. His sister and her husband.

"Mary," he said when he reached her side, before turning to shake his brother-in-law's hand. "Albert. I understood from Mother that you both would arrive next week. Something about your house still being rented out until then?"

Albert Penworth was a gentleman with wealth enough to give him consequence and access to certain select circles where investments rather than titles were given prominence. A portion of his wealth had also been derived from such economic gestures as renting his house out when it was not needed. Miles was glad for his sister to have escaped a life of scrimping and saving, but sometimes wondered at her complacence in accepting a man who rarely had anything of interest to say.

"Our tenant did not wish to stay once Parliament brought

the London crowds back in droves, but as the contract stated they must pay through to the end of March, I am the one who benefits in this round." He chuckled heartily and—spotting a gentleman of his acquaintance—left them abruptly to go shake his hand.

Mary's warning glance communicated clearly that while she knew he thought her husband obtuse, it was not a discussion she would enter into again. She then followed that look with the one subject upon which she and her brother were in common accord.

"Did you leave Mother well?" she asked.

He nodded, adding after a moment's reflection, "I suspect she would have liked to come to London for the entire season, but...well, you know."

Mary sighed. "I attempted to prevail upon Albert to purchase some gowns and accessories for Mother, as you suggested. I'm afraid he thought it a shocking waste of money, considering we might one day have daughters of our own."

She leaned in and imitated Penworth in uncharacteristic reproach. "Why, Mary! Would you give away the fortune of your own unborn daughters, preventing them from making an eligible match, in order to clothe your mother in style—an old woman who is no longer on the hunt for a husband? Surely no wife of mine could conceive of such a thing!"

Miles sent her a sympathetic smile, and she returned it before adding loyally, "But he means well. He is a good man. I think he truly does care about our daughters—"

"The daughters you have yet to bear him," Miles clarified in a look heavy with irony. A chuckle escaped her, and she lifted a shoulder.

His gaze drifted around the room, seeking acquaintances of his own and extending his search to Lady Dorothea. He found her with little effort as the room was not yet full. She was still near the entrance, standing with her mother and sister, and they did not appear to know a great many people—or, at least, not anyone who was present. Somehow, this reassured him. He might make progress with his suit before any other gentleman attempted to woo her. Of course, this might only be wishful thinking. She was, after all, the daughter of an earl, and if anyone knew how particular those of the peerage were about titles, it was he.

Mary stepped away to speak to a woman in a jeweled turban as Albert returned to stand next to Miles. But by then, the musicians had picked up their instruments again. This was his cue.

"Albert, I beg you will excuse me. I am promised for the first dance." He took a step, then as the thought occurred to him said, "You will perhaps wish to ask Mary to dance."

"Wouldn't do, my boy," Albert answered, though he was only five years' Miles's senior. "A man never dances with his wife in public."

Miles offered a polite smile and made the circuit of the room toward his first partner. He would certainly dance with his wife when he had one, though it was not a fashionable thing to do.

If he had expected, upon arriving at Lady Dorothea's side, to see a look of relief at being rescued from sitting the first dance out, he was doomed to disappointment. Upon bowing to Lady Poole, then extending his hand with the words that he believed this set to be his, Lady Dorothea merely graced him with that same bland smile and set her hand on his arm to join the couples congregating. He was not a man easily daunted by a little resistance, however, and he was determined to coax her out of her shell.

One of the musicians seemed to be dealing with a broken string, so they took their places on the sidelines and waited.

"Is this your first season in London, my lady?"

"It is." The soft blue eyes that turned his way were at odds with the decisiveness in her voice and the obstinacy of her chin. After a brief hesitation, she added, "It was intended that I come out last season, but my father died three weeks before we were set to leave. We naturally had to postpone it."

"My condolences," he replied promptly, surprised and touched by her admission. It made her seem more human. "I was not attending to any news coming from London last year, otherwise I might have heard of it."

Then again, the news of an earl leaving this earth would not have made an impression on one who had not known any of the bereaved.

When the conversation stalled, he seized on the one thing they had in common.

"I, too, lost my father, although it is not of recent date. He fell ill of pneumonia four years ago and did not recover."

"My sympathies," she answered in turn, then took a silent breath and let it out. He wondered if she were nervous, or reserved...or simply bored.

He cudgeled his brain for something to say that wasn't quite so morbid a topic as death. Usually the women he made an effort to charm thawed more easily than she did. But Lady Dorothea had offered him something more than commonplaces, and he would not give up in trying for more.

"Your sister...am I right in assuming she is out at the same time as you?"

"Yes." Lady Dorothea looked as though she would say more, but the strains of the cotillion had begun, and her eyes lightened in anticipation. He hastened to lead her into the first circle that was forming before they lost their place.

The music began, putting an end to their conversation. He bowed before her, with one arm behind his back and one extended in front, and she curtsied in return. Then they began to dance in a circle, clasping the hands of those around them as they moved, nodding and bowing to each partner in turn.

As he rejoined Lady Dorothea, clasping her hands in his and advancing, side by side, he was filled with the pleasure of dancing with a woman who required little effort to lead. She might have an obstinate chin, but she was made for dancing. It caused him to direct an appreciative regard her way more than once, and he was given at least one truly authentic smile in return. Each time they drew near, her fresh scent muddled his senses, causing his admiration to increase. He bit his lip to keep from grinning. She was delightful!

At last, the music to the first dance came to a close, and they stepped off to the side to wait for the next dance of their set. Miles held out his arm, and when she set her hand on it, he drew her near.

"You dance elegantly, my lady. I've rarely danced with a partner who gave me more pleasure."

Her cheeks were rosy from effort and her eyes bright as she pulled away slightly to create more distance between them.

"I take pleasure in dancing. It is the one time we are allowed to cast off restraint and enjoy the felicity of the moment."

She seemed to check herself, a furrow to her brow as though she had revealed more than she wished. It was exactly the sort of thing Miles desired to know about her, as it confirmed his suspicion of a warm heart that beat underneath the ice.

"That is very true. I like it myself for that reason."

After a beat, she ventured, "You also make a fine partner, Mr. Shaw. You make dancing seem effortless. The gentlemen I've danced with in Surrey have not been so talented."

He responded with easy gallantry, although his smile was genuine. Despite the fact that it was not a high compliment to compare favorably to local country gentlemen, its authenticity had touched a chord in him.

"You honor me. I am sure my feet will be even lighter now from your praise."

"And you, I hope, will not repeat my words," she cautioned, lifting her brows almost playfully, "for I have cast aspersions on other gentlemen, although no names have been mentioned." The warmth he had caught glimpses of reached her eyes for the first time since she had turned them his way, and he received it like a laurel wreath.

"I give you my word as a gentleman," he replied, easily matching her lighthearted tone and exalting in having pierced her façade. "But then, I have forgotten to ask if you are thirsty. Next I shall hear it said that a certain gentleman pays all the most proper observances, such as fetching a drink for the lady in between sets, unlike *other* gentlemen she has danced with."

This time she laughed outright, and the suspicion she did not give up her laughter easily sent him another flush of triumph. A grin tugged at his lips. By George, he *did* like her! A woman with character, who was beautiful, and whose fortune must not be despised.

"Let not *that* be said," she replied, mercifully unaware of his thoughts. "And I would be most grateful for a cup of lemonade —cold if it could be had."

"If I have to go down to the kitchens myself to find it, I will do so." Miles began to walk off to fetch the glass but then turned back. "Shall we go together? I should not like to leave you unattended, even for the minute it would take to fetch one."

By way of answer, she set her hand on his arm, and he led her forward, dodging a couple as the ballroom had begun to fill.

"Are there just the three children of the late Lord Poole? You, your sister, and your brother, the young earl?"

She shook her head, slowing as they reached the table that held the refreshments. "You are missing the three sisters who are still in the schoolroom. Or should I say, two are in the schoolroom. Camilla is old enough to be out, but we all thought that three Rowlandson ladies making their débuts at once would not be quite the thing."

Miles spoke a few words to the servant standing near the refreshment table and procured two glasses of cold lemonade for them both.

"Camilla, you say? With the Ladies Dorothea and Sophia… dare I guess that each one of the daughters has a name that ends with an *a*?"

"You might guess, and you would be right," Lady Dorothea said before lifting her cup to her lips, her smile revealed only in her eyes. "My father must have given way to my mother's insistence on that score, for he was not at all sentimental. There are still Joanna and Matilda to bring out at some distant date."

"And the Earl of Poole? Does his name end in an *a* as well?" Miles teased. "Roberta? Fredericka?"

"It does not," she replied primly. The twitch of her lips convinced him that for all her chin's signs of stubbornness, she did not lack humor. "His name is Everard."

He accepted this with a nod and let a natural silence fall. He watched her drink and look around the room. She seemed to take naïve pleasure in the sights. It was refreshing.

This time she turned to him to ask, "Do you have… Where is your estate located?"

The question caught him off guard, and he fought the natural wariness that rose up in response. He'd always maintained he would be completely honest about his financial situation. He might go about wooing like a hunter with his sights on the prey, but no one would be deceived. The woman he chose would know what she was getting into when she accepted him. That was what he had told himself.

"My estate is located in Lancashire, near Manchester," he

replied. "It is not immense, which I must suppose to be a blessing at the moment, for I am in the process of restoring it to solvency."

The look in her eyes led him to suspect she already knew it. Miles had not thought his situation to be so generally known.

He gave an involuntary laugh and said the first thing that came into his mind. "You must not worry, however. I am not on the hunt for a wealthy wife. I plan to restore it without the help of a dowry."

As soon as the words were out, his insides froze. He had just dissembled to the point of dishonesty. But before he could modify his claim, she visibly relaxed as though her mind was relieved of one worry—that he would not go on the hunt for *her* —and he found he could not utter the words to correct what he had just said. His guilty conscience tapped at him. Had he not decided he would be open about his situation?

But then, he actually liked this woman. How could a man openly admit he was on the hunt for a wealthy wife if he was in the early process of trying to charm her? He could not, and must hope that her feelings developed naturally in a way that would forgive any pecuniary considerations that accompanied his pursuit.

Lady Dorothea's reaction made him aware of his situation's precariousness as a man whose estate did not pull in any income to speak of. He could not let it circulate that he was hanging about for a rich wife. Besides losing his chances with her, such a thing would be the death of his social prosperity in London. And without invitations, there would be little chance of crossing paths with her or any other eligible lady.

He struggled with how to turn the conversation from there and was thankful that, after his last disclosure, it was she who opened her lips next.

"It is noble of you to attempt to restore your situation

without resorting to the age-old ways of men and women." She smiled at him kindly, expounding, "To try to better your situation by attempting a favorable alliance."

Miles had lifted his glass to his lips and was in the process of swallowing when her words caused him to breathe in the liquid. It was therefore through bouts of coughing that he managed his reply.

"You are very kind, my lady."

He looked away and attempted to marshal his thoughts. It was not well done of him to intentionally mislead her. Perhaps this was something he ought to remedy.

But that was something to think about at another time.

CHAPTER 3

Dorothea peeked at Mr. Shaw, then slid her gaze away. She had never met anyone as attractive as he—both in physical appearance and in allure. But what in the world had come over her to share her circumstances so openly with a man she had only just met? First, she had gone on about her father's death and the subsequent delay to their season, and then she was effusing about how much she loved to dance. Encouraging him over his skills as a dance partner in a way that could only be described as flirting. *Flirting!*

Dorothea could almost be disgusted with herself for her lack of restraint were it not for the fact that she recognized in Mr. Shaw a man who possessed an unnatural abundance of charm. With his piercing blue eyes settling on her in that expectant way, and his focused smile directed at her as though she were the only woman in the ballroom, such attention was nearly impossible to resist. Her sheltered heart responded to it like a wilting flower whose roots had just been drenched. After all, the only people who paid her any mind at all were family members, and then it was only because they required something from her.

In an effort to break free from Mr. Shaw's power of attraction, she used the excuse of drinking her lemonade to turn and stare at the other guests. As she thought of her uncharacteristic behavior in Mr. Shaw's presence, so out of line with her goals for the season, she silently admonished herself with creased brows and firm lips. She should not bestow her affection so cheaply! Had not her first reaction to his invitation been one of dismay, although she credited herself with hiding it? The fact remained that he was simply ineligible.

It had taken very little effort on his part to worm his way in, and she wondered at her ill luck. How could she have come all this way to London seeking a most brilliant match, only to begin her search by being paired for the first dance with a penniless man of no title?

"Lady Dorothea?"

Mr. Shaw interrupted her thoughts, and when she turned, he was holding out his hand for her empty cup. She handed it to him, and he placed it on a tray.

"The next dance is about to begin. Shall we take our places?"

She nodded and allowed him to lead her to where the couples assembled, her mind still wary but her heart not immune. More than one set of female eyes were turned his way.

One's first ball should have a more auspicious start. She had a respectable fortune, was associated with the peerage, and had a pleasing face—at least she believed it to be so, although she couldn't hold a candle to Sophia...and both Joanna and Tilly were looking to turn out quite fair.

Dorothea did not ask for much. She merely required a match due to one of her station. Mr. Shaw could not set his hopes so high, and she was glad he owned as much, for she should not like to have to snub such a nice man as he.

The dance was another cotillion with different figures, and

the simple pleasure of dancing overcame her, already causing her to forget her good intentions to keep a proper distance. She had never danced with anyone who'd brought her more pleasure, for he danced with a flourish she thought quite in keeping with his modish appearance. The firm grip of his hand whenever the steps brought them together, coupled as it was with his attractive smile and agreeable scent, alerted her to the particular danger he posed. She could not let down her guard lest he slip past her defenses and fool her into declaring him eligible.

And yet, these resolutions flew away when he danced the steps with such grace. It was not only his skill in dancing. He was also an excessively handsome man—a perilous combination for one possessing so engaging a disposition. There was only the way his hair sprang from his head as though it wished to run in two directions...

Forgetting herself, Dorothea laughed at the image she had conjured, and Mr. Shaw, pivoting around her at that point, glanced at her, startled, before an answering smile played about his lips.

"Do tell me what it is you have found to amuse you."

She did not think herself prone to the blush, but how could she answer him? Tell him she was laughing at his hair? No, that was impossible, but her usually agile mind betrayed her, and she could not come up with a thing. When his steady regard persisted, she merely bit her lip and shook her head.

"I beg you will not press me. I assure you it was a silly thought of no consequence."

"Far be it from me to press a lady," he replied promptly before the steps of the dance led him away again. But his penetrating, speculative gaze, combined with the hint of humor around his mouth left her feeling guilty. It was not fair to poke fun at handsome, impoverished men.

Truly, he would make any lady of a lower station a fine

husband. She should keep her eyes out for one such lady and introduce the pair of them. It was the least she could do, for a gentleman as agreeable as he merited a degree of consideration. Perhaps she could even find him a wealthy wife. Now *that* would be a kind thing to do. Despite his noble intentions not to marry for wealth, his life would be made a great deal easier by his wife's portion if such were large enough.

Their dance ended at last, and although she could not feel completely satisfied with the fact that her very first partner in London society was a man of no consequence, she could appreciate his way of bowing over her hand. And she might admire the frank appraisal that caused a few unexpected sparks to ignite in her belly. Those, she quickly snuffed out.

After Mr. Shaw had brought her back to her mother's side, Dorothea found her luck improved. Her sister had not sat the first set out after all, and her mother was sitting beside Lady Sefton. Fortunately, the august patroness of Almack's did not seem to require scintillating conversation, for Lady Poole could offer no such thing. She did inform her daughter that Lady Sefton would provide them with vouchers for Almack's. Dorothea tried not to let her relief show as she thanked the patroness.

Lady Sefton watched Mr. Shaw's retreat before bringing her gaze back to Dorothea. "Who is he?"

"It is Mr. Shaw, my lady. I know very little else about him, except—"

She had been about to say that he had no fortune but thought it would be ill-bred of her to say so, besides being unkind. "—except that he is a fine dancer."

Lady Sefton made a noise in her throat before saying, "I've been expressing my condolences to your mother over the loss of your father. Lord Poole was appreciated by many in the *ton* and graced nearly every social event."

"Thank you, my lady," Dorothea said. *'Twas unfortunate his own family should have seen so little of him.*

"And I was telling your mother I've a mind to introduce you to some of the more eligible men of the season. You will be wishing to make an advantageous match, if I am not mistaken," she added.

Lady Sefton was *not* mistaken, and Dorothea hid her eagerness when one of the gentlemen in question came in response to Lady Sefton's summons. She turned to receive the bow of Lord Peregrine, whom Lady Sefton explained was a baron.

"A pleasure," Dorothea said as she curtsied, bringing her gaze to his in anticipation.

His smile lacked the warmth that Mr. Shaw's held, but she supposed that was only normal. After all, he was likely courted and hounded by eligible females all across Society, poor man. He would not receive such treatment from her.

However, she must not be behind in showing him how well she might suit as baroness were she to stand a chance at gaining the role. Of course, a barony was not the highest in the peerage, but it was a peer. And if Lady Sefton knew him, then he must certainly have the right connections. As long as he was solvent, she would not mind it.

His eyes flicked from the dance floor back to her. "May I have the honor of leading you out in the next set?"

"With pleasure," she replied, realizing too late she had just used the word "pleasure" the last time she opened her lips. She must gather her wits about her if she did not want Lord Peregrine to think she had no conversation. To be deemed uninteresting was the kiss of death in London society, she'd heard.

"I will come back to claim your hand as soon as this set finishes then," he said. His frosty smile was back, along with another bow.

Dorothea watched him walk off, nonplussed. She had quite

thought he would stay and make conversation with her while this set finished. It was not as though he could dance with someone else since the current set had already begun. And it would give them a chance to know each other better. It would behoove her to be wittier than her first interaction had made her out to be. She knew she could do better than that.

Her mother and Lady Sefton resumed their conversation, so Dorothea was left to watch the dancers. Mr. Shaw was now dancing with Sophia as he had promised. That her sister was smiling at something he'd said showed that Sophia had opened up to him more than she generally did. It was unusual, for charming men usually came up empty-handed when they tried to ply said charm on Sophia.

Concern pinched Dorothea's brows. She certainly hoped her sister would not develop a *tendre*—and an ill-chosen one, at that—so early in her career. Her sister could look higher than Mr. Shaw. As the daughter of an earl, Sophia must marry well, for all she had declared she wished for a love match. She had no talent for surviving a life of poverty. Such a gentle creature as she must be pampered. In truth, if anyone in the Rowlandson family was capable of surviving poverty, it would be Dorothea herself. Who ran the entire household in an efficient manner, sometimes putting on an old dress to go among the servants and oversee that the tasks were done properly? It was she.

Crowds of lavishly dressed people milled in front of her, blocking her view of the dance being performed in the center and bringing her back to her objective. Not that she had any intention of living in poverty. No, she had known her objective since she had been old enough to assess her worth and situation. She was destined for greater things.

The world came back into focus as the music and dancing ended. Dorothea stood on her toes, peering around the room to see where Lord Peregrine was, eager to begin her dance with him. As it was after eleven o'clock, there was now a throng, and she barely made out Mr. Shaw leading her sister toward them. He must not find her without a partner when he arrived. That would be too lamentable and perhaps even give him the wrong idea. As it stood, he must know himself to be fortunate to have danced with her and not think that the shoe was on the other foot.

She bit her lip and began tapping her foot underneath her gown. If Lord Peregrine did not come to find her now, Mr. Shaw would have the audacity to think *her* fortunate to have been partnered with him.

Mr. Shaw drew near, wrapped up in conversation with Sophia, when Dorothea felt a touch on her arm. Lord Peregrine murmured something about this being his dance and led her over to the sidelines as the music was beginning. They slipped into place just in time and were deprived of the chance for conversation as the music signaled an energetic Scottish reel.

Although she enjoyed the dance itself—it had always been a favorite of hers—Lord Peregrine did not show best in the reel. He stepped on her toes twice and went in the wrong direction three times. She could not help but compare him to plain Mr. Shaw and own that in this, at least, Mr. Shaw must be declared the better man.

Deprived of her usual pleasure in dancing, Dorothea began to wish for some conversation other than the continual monologue that ran in her head. It was not mere dancing that made a man, and perhaps he might be a skilled conversationalist. At last, before her feet were thoroughly bruised, they stopped for the break between sets, and Lord Peregrine held out his arm.

"We must have something to drink," he proposed and without waiting for her answer, led her over to the refreshment table at a near gallop.

She had a chance to observe him while they waited for their

turn to be given a drink. His fair skin had turned red at the exertion from the dance, and she sympathized with him. He must not think she would hold it against him, though. When she allowed herself to dwell on his appearance, she thought he could be handsome, despite the very pronounced widow's peak and a nose on the longish side.

"I owe you an apology," Lord Peregrine said. "Had I realized it would be the Scottish reel, I would have sat that dance out. I do not show to advantage in reels."

"It is of no consequence," she replied, hiding her disappointment over his lack of skill. The table cleared of people, and she waited while he stepped forward to retrieve two glasses. At least he could own he did not excel in the art of dancing. Honesty certainly had value in a potential suitor.

"Are you in London every season?" she asked him when he handed her a lemonade and took a glass of champagne for himself. Did he enjoy society or did he prefer his estate? As his wife, that would determine where she would be spending most of her time. These were the questions she had decided in advance she would ask in order to know which gentleman might suit her best.

"I have done so for the last three seasons," he replied, then drank his champagne in one go and set the glass on the tray of a passing servant. "I am following the parliamentary sessions, but besides that, there is nothing of interest happening anywhere else. All the families who organize country parties wait until summer is in full swing before they send invitations."

"That is very true," she replied, although she had nothing to compare it to. She had never had a season, and the only summer party she'd gone to was when she was still in the schoolroom. Not for the first time did she realize that her life as the daughter of a peer was unusually sheltered. And not for the first time did she wish her father had cared enough to make more of an effort to bring them into society.

She waited, watching the people circulating the floor as she sipped her lemonade. Her eyes drifted over to Sophia, who had been asked to dance immediately after Mr. Shaw had released her and whose eyes were now glued to the gentleman's waistcoat as he spoke to her, despite him appearing to be a very agreeable partner. Sophia's brief spell of openness was over, causing Dorothea to worry again over her sister's feelings for Mr. Shaw. It must not be allowed that she take a fancy to the man simply because he could make her smile. Dorothea would have to put more gentlemen in Sophia's path.

Lord Peregrine stared around the room as she did, not contributing to the conversation. Surely he could not find her so uninteresting. She tried again.

"Where is your estate located?"

Oh heavens. She *was* uninteresting. That was exactly what she had asked Mr. Shaw.

"It is near to Cambridge." Lord Peregrine took a step forward, his eyes on the couples congregating on the sidelines. "Shall we ready ourselves for the next dance?"

"If you wish it," she said with hesitation, remembering his aversion to the quicker-paced dances. "Or if you prefer to sit this dance out, I do not mind."

"By no means. I should not like to deprive you," he replied in tones of distraction.

Dorothea was thirsty, so she drank the rest of her lemonade and held out the glass to her partner, but his eyes were still fixed on the couples near the dance floor. A servant collected her glass instead, and Dorothea followed Lord Peregrine's gaze to the gathering couples. It suddenly dawned on her that his unaccountably obtuse behavior must mean that his heart already belonged to another lady—although Dorothea could not divine which one it might be. She set her hand on his arm, and he moved forward automatically.

Her heart dipped with disappointment at the realization that Lord Peregrine would not find her interesting no matter how much effort she put into it. Then she drew herself up. If his heart was lost to another, there was no point in considering him as a potential suitor any longer. She would treat him kindly and wish him the best in his suit.

But she would be less than human if she did not hope that her whole evening—indeed, that her entire season—was not doomed to repeat the cycle of ineligible charming men and eligible distracted ones.

CHAPTER 4

The following morning, Dorothea woke up with a headache that gave her no relief, even when she took medicinal powder and sipped coffee, which Miss Cross had told her was more effective in counteracting headaches than tea. She was not sure it was so, and she could barely stand the bitter stuff, but she needed to try everything she could to prepare for the eventual visits that would follow attending a ball.

Oh, and the flowers! The flowers that arrived at a young lady's house the morning following a ball were legendary. The only doubt that assailed her was the fact that, although she did end up having better luck for the remaining dances the night before—she scarcely sat one out and counted among her partners more than one titled gentleman—she had not seemed to make a connection on a deeper level with any of them that could lead her to believe they would call. Regrettably, neither did she find one as attractive and engaging as the unsuitable Mr. Shaw. Fortunately, the season had only begun.

She was still in the breakfast room when Sophia entered. Her sister liked to stay abed as long as she could, but Dorothea had warned her that she must be up and about early so they might read the notes on the flowers and welcome the morning callers, although those would not begin until early afternoon. As it was already noon, they had no time to waste.

"Dorry, you look a fright. Is it one of your headaches again?" Sophia asked in her soft voice as she turned to take a plate and fill it with the offerings from the sideboard. Her words could not have pierced Dorothea's confidence any more if she had attempted to wound on purpose.

The door clattered open and Joanna entered, followed by their youngest sister, Matilda, whose pale appearance showed the unwisdom of being up so soon after her illness.

"Tilly, what are you doing out of bed?" Dorothea asked. "Joanna, you should not encourage it."

"I encouraged nothing. She followed me," Joanna said, going over to the sideboard. She was in riding dress, with the mud still caked on her habit from her ride with the groom.

Not to be distracted from the earlier topic, Dorothea ignored the mud and instead signaled to Sophia for the milk.

"What do you mean I look a fright?" She added more milk and sugar to her coffee to make it drinkable, although their governess had clearly stated that only black coffee would work.

"Joanna, you took all the eggs, and now there are none for me." Tilly dropped her plate on the table with a muffled thud and sat with a pout, punctuated by folded arms.

"Here, take mine, Tilly. I don't want them." Sophia pushed the plate over with one hand and paused in the act of bringing her teacup to her mouth. "Forgive me, Dorry, I did not mean for the words to cause pain."

Dorothea closed her eyes to the chaos that had erupted in the breakfast room. She knew what her sister meant. It had taken one look at her puffy face and dull eyes in the mirror that morning to know she looked her worst. Like someone who had endured incessant banging on the right side of her head all night, which was exactly what her headache felt like.

When she opened her eyes again, Sophia continued. "It is just that I cannot bear to see you suffer."

"I know you meant well," Dorothea said, swallowing the waspish urge to fight pain by inflicting it.

Of all the days she should have a headache! She might easily have one later in the season when she had secured her future husband. Once the contract had been drawn up, he would already have counted the costs for better or for worse on the weaknesses of his betrothed. And she could assure him that the headaches were only a few times a year, although they did sometimes last for more than one day. And she could promise him that she would continue to run the household without any hindrance. After all, look at her today. She had risen at her habitual hour, had clothed herself with the help of her maid, and here she was, the first of the family to take breakfast.

"Perhaps you should think about retiring to your room. It is not such a shocking thing to turn visitors away," Sophia reasoned. "The important thing is that you get your rest and are quickly returned to good health. Who knows but that we might be invited to some other event you would not like to miss and would be forced to do so, only because you are being obstinate today."

Her sister could be quite loquacious when she was with family only. Why in the world did she clam up so spectacularly when others were around? For it wasn't simply the gentlemen. She fell silent even when there were other women present outside of the family or her one close friend in Surrey.

"I cannot think of going back to bed. You must know as much." Dorothea rested her elbows on the table and leaned forward to rub her temples with her fingertips. She opened her eyes wider than mere slits to the most amiable view of her sister sitting hunched over her breakfast as she shoveled the eggs in.

"Joanna, your mouth should be nowhere near your plate. Kindly sit straight and spare us that sight."

Tilly giggled at the remonstrance that wasn't directed at her, and Dorothea turned back to Sophia.

"We must begin the season properly, right from the beginning, and with the correct behavior." She glanced at Joanna, hoping she was listening to that last bit. "If we begin turning away callers before the season gets fully underway, people will label us conceited. You and I will find ourselves without a husband."

She closed her eyes, adding in little more than a mumble, "And then we shall be in the suds."

"Dorry!" Sophia chuckled at the unexpected slang coming from Dorothea's mouth. Joanna began telling Sophia about her ride that morning, and Tilly asked when she might be allowed to ride out, prompting a hearty refusal from both Sophia and Joanna.

Leaning her face into her hands, Dorothea tuned out the chatter and hid the bright light streaming through the windows of the breakfast room, which of course was situated to receive the sun coming in from the east. She allowed herself a few moments to rest like that, knowing she should be up and doing something. For instance, was Cook preparing the cakes for their visitors as Dorothea had instructed her yesterday? Had the housekeeper overseen the drawing room arrangement to make sure it was ready to receive callers? It was still too early in the season for them to go without fires in the chimneys. There was much to prepare, but she couldn't seem to move.

"Joanna, Tilly, have a care for Dorry's head and keep your voices low." Sophia turned to Dorothea. "Is there anything I can do to help?"

Dorothea kept her face in her hands. "Will you go and see that Mother is out of bed? She must be in the drawing room with us to receive callers, and you know as well as I that she does not perform that duty unless she is brought to do so. If I had to guess, I would say she is still sleeping."

"Of course," her sister replied, adding after a pause, "Is that all?"

Dorothea looked up at her, blinking to bring the world into focus. Her sister was dressed properly at least. Dealing with her mother was what Dorothea liked to do least of all. She could oversee the household matters, but not cajole her mother to be up and doing. Not when her head pounded so.

She shook her head, immediately regretting the movement. "No, I need to see Cook and Mrs. Platt. And do warn Camilla, if you please, that breakfast will be removed soon. If she wants any, she must come."

"Camilla never misses breakfast," Joanna said with a smirk. "I am sure she has been down to the kitchen already."

Sophia frowned at Joanna, then stood and placed a soft kiss on Dorothea's head before leaving. "Very well."

Miss Cross entered the breakfast room, followed by Camilla, and bid everyone good morning. Dorothea stood. It was time to see to everything that needed doing. She must conquer this weakness.

With her steps steady and head lifted high, she went to the kitchen where Cook was pulling a pan of fairy cakes out of the oven. *Blessed woman!* Mrs. Platt was coming out of the stillroom, and Dorothea conferred with her on the details of the drawing room and the appropriate time to bring the tea tray, once the knocker sounded on the front door.

After that, she went upstairs, holding her head still with great care. Perhaps she did have some time to rest before people arrived. Perhaps there were even flowers waiting for them now, although she had not heard the promising sound of anyone knocking at the door. That happy noise would surely chase away any headache.

"Turton, has anything been delivered?" she asked, hoping against hope, as soon as she saw him standing by the door.

"Nothing, my lady." He waited a moment, then turned his face away again, stoic and ready for the deluge of visitors that would arrive at any minute.

Slightly disheartened, she considered taking to her room but feared that if she did so, she would inevitably fall asleep and appear in front of their guests with lines on her face. It would be preferable to suffer an hour of discomfort rather than that.

When Sophia finally joined her in the drawing room, promising that their mother would soon follow, Dorothea was feeling very much the worse for wear. And the pitying looks her sister shot her let her know she *looked* very much the worse for wear as well. There was little conversation as both were tired. Dorothea noted the continual absence of their mother but was too weary to go in search of her, especially since there was at the moment no need to do so. In the second hour of sitting—at last—the first knock on the front door sounded through the entryway.

She sat up straight, her heart beating painfully. Her season should not be like this. It should be filled with visitors and laughter and flirting—with the right gentlemen, of course. There should be no headaches, or empty drawing rooms, or absence of floral arrangements with little cards tucked into them. It was humiliating!

"Where is Mother?" she hissed as the sound of their guest's entrance reached her.

"I will go and fetch her," Sophia said before Dorothea could protest at being left alone.

Her sister did not have time to open the door, for it opened on its own and was followed by their brother slipping through and closing the door behind him.

"I've come to lend you countenance, sister," he said, his expression far too innocent.

Dorothea's head gave a particularly painful throb, and she could not give him the fine trimming she longed to, not when Turton's footsteps were already sounding in approach. The door to the drawing room opened again.

"Mr. Shaw to see you, my lady."

CHAPTER 5

Miles entered Lady Dorothea's drawing room, struck first by the grand size of it and then by its emptiness, save for her sister and a stripling of a boy. He tucked the flower arrangement he had brought into the crook of his arm and bowed, as the two ladies curtsied.

"Mr. Shaw, you know my sister," Lady Dorothea said, her eyes flicking to the flowers he'd brought. "May I present my brother, the Earl of Poole."

He handed his flower arrangement to Lady Dorothea, which contained carefully selected freesias, violets, and ferns. If he was going to begin a proper suit, he needed to start well and hoped she would read the message he intended to send her in his choice of flowers.

"These are for you, my lady."

Without waiting for her response for fear of forcing a reaction, he turned to her sister and brother. "How do you do, Lady Sophia? A pleasure to make your acquaintance, my lord."

Miles's gaze rested on Lord Poole and stayed there. His frame was still small and slender, showing him to be not yet on the cusp of manhood. His facial features were elegant and as yet absent of any whiskers on that obstinate chin so similar to his eldest sister's. The young earl's eyes held a hint of mischief as he gave Miles a measuring stare. Then, he turned and shot a wicked glance at his sister before returning the bow.

"And I you, Mr. Shaw. As the head of the family, you will naturally be addressing any discourse to me." He slipped his hand into his waistcoat, underneath his small twist of a cravat. "And should you aspire to the hand of one of my sisters, you will not find me unreasonable."

"Evo!"

"Everard!"

Miles's laugh turned into a cough as Lady Sophia slipped her arm through her brother's and led him unceremoniously out of the drawing room, leaving the room empty but for him and Lady Dorothea. She turned to set the flowers on the side table, but not before he caught her dipping her nose into the freesias and inhaling. *So she likes flowers, does she?*

The gesture also partially hid her face. Last night, her complexion had been a beautifully even tone, despite the vigor of the dance, but it was now flushed a shade he had not thought possible of her. Given her embarrassment, he would not mention her brother's impertinence.

He had hardly expected to find her drawing room empty of guests, much less find her completely alone. In fact, it was odd that no one else was here. He had expected to have to tussle with other suitors, and even women callers, in order to coax another glimpse of that tightly veiled personality he'd been witness to last night.

"Mr. Shaw, will you sit?" she asked, her smile strained.

Any musings on the luck of finding her alone vanished when he studied her more closely. She was as lovely as always, but the fine lines about her eyes gave evidence to her fatigue and let him know this visit must be more of a trial to her than a pleasure. Her eyes seemed smaller somehow than they had last night. He wondered if it would be too cruel to remain when she was clearly feeling under the weather. But he had come all this way and might not have another such moment to claim her undivided attention.

He narrowed his brows. "Please allow me to ask how you are faring, my lady?"

"I am very well, I thank you. Did you enjoy the rest of the ball last evening?" Every word was spoken in a low, carefully chosen tone, and he was not deceived by her assurance.

"You appear to be suffering from a headache, I believe? It is not that you look anything other than...perfect..." That much was true, despite how obvious her discomfort. "But you seem not to be yourself this afternoon, and I wondered..."

He fell silent. This was an unusual approach for him when engaging in any sort of flirtation. He rarely touched any topic but the most superficial, finding that most ladies appreciated the light banter. Either his honesty would backfire, or she would welcome it and open up in return.

After a quick glance his way, she trained her eyes at some distant point in the room. It gave him a chance to enjoy her profile with its high sculpted cheekbones, straight nose, and full lips.

"You are correct, sir. I believe the combination of the journey and last night's ball has fatigued me, and my head pains me a very little today." She attempted a smile, which he was sure must have cost her.

"If you are indeed unwell, it is a fortunate thing your drawing room is not packed with noisy crowds trying to draw your attention. I feared it would be." His soft chuckle died away quickly, when he saw that his observation had not pleased her.

Of course it had not. What lady liked to be reminded that

she had not every suitor upon her doorstep? Good heavens, where was that charm he worked so hard to cultivate?

Although, truthfully, he could not have been more thankful to be spared having to compete for her attention. How much of that attention would have been directed his way now that she knew of his circumstances?

A knock echoed in the entryway, and Lady Dorothea sat up in anticipation. He had counted his luck prematurely.

"Well, it appears I have spoken too soon, and hordes of London society are this very moment at your door," Miles said lightly, and in the next instant decided to launch his objective for coming. "I may not have another chance to present you with my request, so please allow me to ask if you would be free to drive with me in Hyde Park tomorrow afternoon?"

"I...*um.*"

Lady Dorothea glanced at the door, and he feared it was in hopes that the announcement of guests would save her from having to answer him. He hoped she would say yes, for then he might pursue his courtship without competition—at least for an afternoon.

"Thank you for your invitation, Mr. Shaw. I am free," she returned briefly before bringing her eyes toward the door.

"Excellent."

Her hard-won agreement caused his heart to beat with happiness. This was not something Miles had experienced since he was a green lad newly discovering the delight of a female smile turned in his direction. The way the sun seemed to come out at her acceptance made him think that maybe he would pursue this woman in earnest. If he could win her heart, she would not mind his lack of fortune.

The butler opened the door and announced, "Baronetess Lady Milton, and her daughters Miss Bernice Milton and Miss Abigail Milton."

Lady Dorothea's face seemed to fall slightly at the announcement. Miles knew it because he was watching her. He wondered if she had been hoping for other suitors, or if she simply did not like the baronet's wife very much. She stood to receive them, and he leapt to his feet at her side.

Lady Milton moved forward with both hands outstretched, her daughters trailing behind her. "Lady Dorothea, how delighted I am to find you at home." She gave the barest clasp of hands, then turned to observe Miles with an air of studied surprise before turning back with an arched brow. "Why, where is your mother?"

Lady Dorothea flushed in embarrassment for the second time, and although she opened her mouth, no ready answer left her lips.

Miles could not bear for her to feel uncomfortable and went against his nature to provide an answer to a question that was not addressed to him about an issue that did not concern him.

"Lady Sophia left us a moment ago. Did I understand correctly she wished to see that your mother was coming?"

Lady Dorothea smiled at him gratefully. "You did indeed." Then, to Lady Milton, "My mother is unaccustomed to the late nights so early in the season, and my sister went to make sure Mother had everything she needed. They will both be joining us in a moment."

Before the introductions could be performed, there was a tap on the door, and servants entered carrying a tray laden with a variety of cakes and a slender china teapot. Not an instant later, Lady Sophia and their mother arrived. Miles was glad for Lady Dorothea. He was given the impression the household ran a little haphazardly.

"Lady Milton, I apologize for my delay," Lady Poole said. "Have you already had your tea?"

"We have not had time, Mama," Lady Dorothea said, and

Miles noted the distinct look of relief in her eyes. He was glad he had been able to do his small part to help her manage the guests in a way that would not cause tongues to wag.

She performed the introductions, and they all sat. Sophia prepared a plate for her mother as Lady Dorothea opened the lid to the teapot, then set it back again, allowing it to steep longer.

Lady Milton glanced around the empty room. "Well, I called upon Lady Berkley before coming here. Apparently, all of London has become smitten with Miss Maryann Stanley, who has taken the *ton* by storm with her fifteen thousand a year."

A friend had pointed Miss Stanley out to him the week before, mentioning her wealth, but Miles had not seriously considered pursuing her. Yes, she was wealthy and beautiful, but she seemed too conscious of her attributes to tempt him.

"Miss Stanley, you say?" Lady Dorothea seemed arrested by the mention of the name.

"I've heard the gentlemen are congregating in her father's drawing room as we speak," Lady Milton went on. "There is even a line out the door, although there were a fair number of callers at Lady Berkley's, too. I assured Lady Berkley that her ball must be deemed a success. It had even more people than I'd expected for so early in the season. I am sure our daughters enjoyed themselves immensely, didn't you, girls?"

"I am sure I did," the younger Miss Abigail said, who was by far the fairer of the two. "I cannot say the same for my sister, who did not dance more than two sets the entire evening."

At her words, Miss Bernice flushed to her roots and sent a vicious look at her younger sister. As for Lady Dorothea, her face registered shock at the unnecessary cruelty, and she exchanged a look with Lady Sophia.

"Well, you have always been the fair one, my puss," Lady

Milton said complacently as she nibbled on the cake she had taken. "You must not dangle that over your sister's head."

Again, Miles did not miss the widening of Lady Dorothea's eyes at this absence of maternal rebuke that would surely have restored sisterly harmony, and he liked her the better for it.

Lady Dorothea set her lips in a straight line and picked up the tea pot. "How do you take your tea, Lady Milton?"

"With milk and two spoons of sugar. Thank you."

She poured her a cup, then repeated the process, asking each guest what they preferred. At last she came to Miles. He took his with just milk and told her so before turning to the elder of the Milton daughters.

"Miss Milton, I was present last night and wished I had known you had dances to spare. I would surely have asked you. I hope you will do me the honor of standing up with me at the next event, which..."

He frowned suddenly. He never kept track of his invitations, despite not having a great number of them. If he'd had more wealth, he would hire a secretary to manage them, among other things.

"The Answorths' ball, I believe is the next event that much of London is being invited to, although it's not for over two weeks." Lady Milton looked at him approvingly.

"Ah." The name was unfamiliar. "I don't believe I have been invited to that one, but you may be sure that I will dance with you at the next ball in which we both attend."

Miles needed to stop there, lest everyone including Lady Dorothea think he was here to court Miss Milton. It was only that he could not bear for a woman to be humiliated by her own sister, and before strangers. He wished to teach the younger Miss Abigail a fine lesson. He would not be asking her to dance.

Miss Milton sent a grateful smile his way, which vastly improved her features. "I would be delighted, Mr. Shaw."

Miles quite thought Lady Dorothea looked upon him approvingly as well, if her smile toward him was any indication. If he could continue to rise in her esteem in this manner, it might not be such a difficult thing to win her regard.

"Mr. Shaw, I don't believe we have met before," Lady Milton said. "Is this your first time spending the season in London?"

"It is, yes. I have come before for brief spells, and earlier when I was freshly out of school. In general, the affairs on my estate occupy me, but this year I have left them in the hands of my steward and plan to spend all of the spring months in London."

"How fortunate for us. I am sure I can convince Mrs. Answorth to send you an invitation for her gathering," Lady Milton replied with a glance at Lady Poole.

The latter was a slight woman with a faded look about her, who had fallen into silence after the initial greetings. Lady Poole nodded her concurrence when she saw what was expected of her.

"That is most kind of you." Miles finished his tea quickly. He must not overstay his welcome. Besides, he wished to avoid an overly inquisitive conversation about his estate that might disrupt his peace. He would not hide his financial condition, but it did not mean he had to announce it to every person in London.

"Well, isn't this lovely?" Lady Milton said, just as another knock on the front door sounded.

The lull in conversation grew pronounced as the sounds of the butler's footsteps approaching the drawing room reached them.

"The Earl of Hastings." The butler stepped aside to allow this august gentleman to enter the room. Lord Hasting's hair and whiskers could still be called blond, though he was exiting the far side of his youth.

Miles glanced at Lady Dorothea and did not miss the pleased expression on her face. He wondered if she had particular interest in Lord Hastings or if she just considered his visit a coup because of his title. Neither were very flattering to Lady Dorothea.

Neither were very promising to him.

Her dull eyes told him she was still suffering from a headache, which was likely worse by now. He would at least remove himself from her presence and be one less visitor to pull upon her attention. As soon as the introductions were made, he used the opportunity to excuse himself.

"Ladies," he said, bowing to each of them in turn. He shook hands with Lord Hastings.

"Lady Dorothea." He caught her gaze from across the room, unable to keep from singling her out. "I will call for you tomorrow at five o'clock if that suits you."

She nodded, her lips prim, although they still curved in a polite smile. Then she turned to their newest visitor, leaving Miles to show himself out. As he crossed the drawing room to the entranceway, where the butler fetched his coat and hat, his mind was filled with speculation. He thanked the butler, put both coat and hat on, and exited onto the broad flagway of Grosvenor Square. Outside, it was sunny and cold, the skies tinged with gray and with no clouds in sight. He hoped tomorrow would be warmer when they went out driving.

Had he mistaken his initial impression of her? Lady Dorothea had not seemed to warm to him upon further acquaintance today. He reminded himself that there were many other women in London, and that she was merely the first one who had truly caught his eye this season. He required only wealth in a future wife—not even a title was necessary—and beyond that, a woman with conversation whom he found attractive. Surely there were others...

He strode down the street, his mind working, as he weighed his commitment to the pursuit of Lady Dorothea. It was unlike him to show this sort of partiality for a woman who offered so little encouragement. In fact, it had never happened before, as women generally responded to his attempts to please. He pursued this line of thought for a while then abandoned it. Even if he willed himself to open his mind to other possibilities who might be easier won, his mind seemed to go back to Lady Dorothea of its own accord, as though she were a mystery he had to unravel.

As Miles walked on, he finally shook his head and gave it up. He would take her to Hyde Park tomorrow. They would come to know one another better. Either she would begin to thaw toward him and show him more of that warmth he had seen glimpses of, and he would pursue her in earnest. Or he would see clearly that he had been misled in his attachment to her, and their budding relationship would dwindle to nothing.

Having come to this conclusion, he decided to think of it no more. And he did not. He merely thought of that crease between Lady Dorothea's brows and wondered how to remove it.

CHAPTER 6

Dorothea could not bear another minute of entertaining callers and when contemplating the disappointment that it had merely been Mr. Shaw, the Milton ladies, and Lord Hastings, her relief at bidding them all farewell was tangible. Her chagrin was tempered by Lord Hastings's visit. As a wealthy and titled widower who was not yet in his dotage, his decision to follow their dance with a visit was no small coup.

Their conversation had been slow in between the set at the ball, and she'd feared they had formed no real connection. She was glad to see she had been wrong. Now, if only her mind's enthusiasm over the victory of Lord Hasting's flattering attention could impress itself upon her heart. Alas, her heart beat its same steady rhythm whenever he was near.

The only thing to truly mar her afternoon—besides Evo's horrible, impudent display of embarrassingly bad manners—was the knowledge that Lady Milton had caught her alone with Mr. Shaw. The Miltons were one of the few families they knew in London, as they too hailed from Surrey. Lady Milton was a notorious gossip, and Dorothea was afraid news would spread all over town that she was developing a *tendre* for a gentleman whose station was beneath hers and that it would chase all offers away. This fear was somewhat mitigated by the fact that he had offered to stand up with Bernice at the next assembly. Perhaps that would redirect Lady Milton's thoughts from associating Mr. Shaw's name with hers.

It had been kind of him to do that. To offer to dance with Bernice when her sister humiliated her. Dorothea had no patience with Abigail. She never crossed a line into being overly flirtatious or lacking respectability, but she crossed every line when it came to unkindness. Mr. Shaw had stepped in nobly without even knowing Bernice.

And he was the only gentleman to bring them flowers. Or rather, bring *her* flowers, as the short note was addressed to her alone. She adored freesias. How in the world did he know that?

He had also noticed her headache, which she could not quite so appreciate. Mr. Shaw would have done better to remain silent when she was not in good looks. But then, one must give him credit, for he showed her every consideration apart from that ill-chosen comment. He rescued her when she could not think of a single thing to say regarding her mother's absence or why she was receiving gentlemen callers alone. He saved her from Lady Milton's censure with that comment. For that reason, she must like him a very little bit.

Dorothea left the remnants of the tea, trusting the servants to clear it, and wearily climbed the stairs to her room. There were fortunately no invitations for that night, and she would be able to retire without needing to perform for society—for if there had been invitations, she certainly would have gone. Her maid helped her to undress and prepare for bed at an unseasonably early hour. Indeed, it had barely turned dark and it was still early in the spring. She could not bear any more movement or sound and needed to be in bed.

Surely, Mr. Shaw entertained no hopes in her regard, she

worried as she closed her eyes. Simply because Lady Berkley had introduced them, he need not pay her any special attention. But there he was, calling on her the very next day and carrying an elegant arrangement of flowers symbolizing just about every finer emotion except love. And then to request to take her driving a day later. What would everyone whisper when they saw her sitting next to him in Hyde Park? Why, they would assume he had begun courting her.

Her thoughts were muddled, and she tried to think of Lord Hastings to elevate them. True, conversation with him was stilted, but *he* was wholly eligible. After all, a wife need not spend any time conversing with her husband except for the few evenings he tried to spend at home. And that was something she fully intended to discourage. She must think of his finer points. He was titled. He had all of his hair and teeth, and he was known to live comfortably. That was all she needed to make her decision.

Her thoughts, however, were most contrary. They refused to stick to Lord Hastings and drifted back to Mr. Shaw. He really did not think to court her, did he? If she'd felt well enough, she would laugh at such a notion.

No, no. He could not think it. Besides, he said he was not hanging out for a rich wife. Perhaps he merely wished to be her friend. The notion of having him for a friend was a pleasant one. How nice it would be to have a gentleman friend who expected nothing in the way of marriage. Unbidden, the memory of his blue eyes appraising her flooded her mind, and along with it those sparks she had experienced. Sparks which leapt and whirled inside of her. Was that what it was like to...to have a *tendre*? To love?

She nipped the wayward thought in the bud. Absolutely not. He was the last thing she was looking for in a match, and she was not one to grow weak in the knees from one glowing look. Besides, he had said he was not looking for a wealthy wife. His objective was simply to play the gallant, she concluded. Or perhaps he thought her consequence might attract others who would be a suitable candidate for himself.

Still, she could not entirely shake the feeling, despite all, that she might be misreading his intentions. It would be too bad when she was attempting to think well of him to have him overreach and strive to court her in earnest. It would force her to put him in his place, and she could not like to do that to a man who seemed, if nothing else, to have a great deal of kindness for what one might find in a gentleman.

The next morning, Dorothea awoke and felt better than she had in the days since they'd quit Poole Manor. She looked at the clock, finding the hour was already advanced at two o'clock. She generally took her breakfast well before noon and must have needed the rest.

Stepping out of the bed, she stretched her arms high and lifted on her toes. A smile came to her face. It was wonderful to feel well again, and she was thankful her headache had only lasted the night. Perhaps they had rushed things by going out to a ball the very day they arrived. Perhaps the season did not require the frantic pace she'd thought to successfully secure a husband.

A knock came on the door to her room, and her maid entered. "I've come to help you dress, if you should like it, my lady."

Margery knew Dorothea well enough to sense what she would like to wear and pulled out the very day dress Dorothea would have chosen if she were riding in Hyde Park with Lord Hastings or a man of his ilk. But she supposed she need not wear something so fine for Mr. Shaw.

"I shall wear the brown cotton," she instructed and sat to have her hair dressed.

Margery showed her surprise only by the lift of her eyebrows and paused in her path toward the wardrobe to answer the door when someone knocked. It was another maid bringing chocolate and toast for Dorothea. She'd missed her dinner last night, and her stomach growled at the sight.

"Thank you," she told the maid. "I *am* hungry."

She alternated her sips of chocolate with her toast that was buttered to perfection, giving into the sensation that all was well in the world as Margery tugged at her hair and pulled it up.

There was another knock on the door.

"Come in." Dorothea glanced at herself in the reflection, pleased to see that her eyes were much clearer than they had been the day before. Mr. Shaw would have no occasion to call her haggard. She sniffed.

Sophia entered, and as soon as she saw Dorothea up, she came over and planted a kiss on her cheek.

"I came to see you last night when you did not come down for dinner, but you were so sound asleep I did not wish to wake you. It is good to see you up and eating something. Are you feeling much improved?"

"Very much," Dorothea said, greeting her sister with a smile. "Did Mother give Evo a severe scolding for leaving Mr. Sands behind after our guests left yesterday?"

"Oh, you know Mama," Sophia said, which meant she had not, proving that if Dorothea didn't curb his wayward tendencies, who would? His bouts of mischief had only started to get worse in the year since Father had died. She had not yet had the chance to give him the promised talking-to, but she could not put it off.

"Mr. Sands did arrive at an early hour this morning, and I apologized to him for Evo's stunt, then sent him to Mr. Reams for his compensation."

"Well done, Sophia," Dorothea replied with a look of admiration. "You are in a fair way to being ready for the role of mistress of your own house."

Sophia's scowl made Dorothea laugh, when even yesterday she would have begged to know what was behind it. But her heart was too light for worries today.

It was unlike her to feel anything akin to happiness. The only emotion she usually felt was a vague sense of anxiety. But here at last they were in London for the season. True, her first ball had not been a resounding success. There had been other ladies more beautiful and wealthier than she, who had stood out among the crowd. She wished she had met the Miss Stanley who apparently had all of London at her feet. It could only be the daughter of the Mr. Stanley of her father's letters. Miss Stanley—clearly a diamond of the first water—seemed to lead the *ton*, though she had no title.

Dorothea wished she could be compared to a diamond of the first water and have her pick as easily as any of them.

She wrestled the jealousy into its place. It was not such a hard thing to do when the sun shone, especially feeling as well as she did. She took another bite of toast then looked up at how Margery was arranging her hair.

"I will wear a simpler style today. You need not add curls on the sides. Just pull it all back." She stared up at the maid through the reflection and thus caught the second look of surprise. Never before had she requested to be made plainer in appearance.

Sophia apparently wondered at it too, for she pulled back from the armchair she had sat upon to peer at Dorothea.

"Why would you not want the curls? You know they suit you so charmingly when they frame your face that way. I hardly know you not to wear them."

Dorothea averted her eyes as she sipped her chocolate. "I am riding out with Mr. Shaw today, and I do not wish for him to think I desire anything other than friendship. I plan to dress simply, so he does not imagine I've made any special efforts for him."

"Dorry!" Sophia stood, her brows pulling together. It was as much censure as Dorothea had ever heard in her sister's voice. "What do you mean by such a thing? Mr. Shaw is most gentlemanly. You should honor his invitation by attempting to look your best."

Her sister's strongly voiced criticism had merit, but Dorothea was not in the humor to listen to it. She shook her head as she chewed her last bite of toast. The thought that her sister might have developed a sudden *tendre* for him returned in full force.

"Sophia, you must know that Mr. Shaw is ineligible and set your sights elsewhere, if that is what you are thinking. You have the whole season ahead of you, and I certainly hope you have not pinned your hopes on the very first man who asked you to dance."

"Oh, for heaven's sake," Sophia replied in what was a most unusual expression of exasperation for her. "I have no thoughts for him. Besides, he spent more time asking about you during our dance than he did attempting to win my regard. I merely think you do him a disservice by not attempting to appear at your best. It is beneath you," she added in a voice of quiet dignity.

This almost turned Dorothea from her path, but she remained staunch as she sipped the last of her chocolate. However, Sophia's next words had the effect of convincing her.

"All of London will be in Hyde Park this afternoon. You cannot afford to look less than your best at all times, even if you do not favor the gentleman you are riding with. What if people begin to whisper you are a dowd?"

Dorothea flushed at that and sat up straight. It was humiliating to have this conversation in front of their maid, but her sister's advice was too pertinent to be ignored.

"Very well. You may add some curls, Margery. And I will not wear the brown dress." She darted a defiant look at Sophia. "I shall wear the gray."

"Good," Sophia said brightly, ruining Dorothea's attempt at gaining ground. "Your gray gown is the prettiest day dress you own, in my opinion. It is simple, but you look well in it."

Dorothea glared at her sister, who remained supremely unbothered by her remonstration and returned an innocent smile. She did not know why Sophia could not show this side of herself to suitors. They would be lined up at the door if they saw it. When she smiled like this, her eyes lit with playfulness, her dimples came out in full force.

Dorothea allowed Margery to finish her hair and help her to slip on the gray gown. It was made of a light linen cloth that flattered her form. It would be best if she focused on her own suitors for the moment. As soon as she had secured one, she would be able to focus on arranging matches for each one of her sisters. Appraising herself in the mirror, she had to agree with Sophia. The soft gray gown with the pleated bodice, as simple as it was, lent an appearance of purity and youth that she knew was already fleeting. It softened her stubborn chin and made her more approachable.

Well! She would have to make sure she kept her eye out for other gentlemen once they reached Hyde Park. Not only for other gentlemen, but even the ladies. It was not until they were at Lady Berkley's ball that she realized how much their family had slipped out of Society. She knew so few people, and that factor would not put her in the way of the most acceptable candidates. She desperately needed friends in the right places.

CHAPTER 7

Dorothea went looking for Evo as soon as she was dressed and eventually tracked him down in the library. He was spinning coins on the table and looked up when she came in. He dropped his gaze and slapped his hand on the coin as it neared the end of its turns.

"Evo, we need to talk." She went and sat opposite to him, clasping her hands on her lap.

He flicked a glance upward but remained silent as he sent the coin spinning again. Behind him, the diamond-pane windows let in little of the light from the outdoors, causing Evo's face to rest in the shadows.

"Have you nothing to say for yourself for leaving Mr. Sands behind?"

"I am certain you have enough to say for the both of us," he answered and flashed her a smile. There was an attempt at lightness in the tone, but the smile was unfriendly.

She frowned at his careless attitude so unlike the boy he'd been, when he had wanted to tell her everything. Was this what it was to lose her brother? Would he simply grow into a man like their father once he reached adulthood? Detached, hardened, with no family loyalty. Evo had always been such a joy to the family—to her. To think he might end up like his sire caused her heart to grow heavy.

"And the stunt you pulled in the drawing room with Mr. Shaw. I should hope you will never do such a thing again. It was humiliating for both Sophia and myself."

"It was spoken in jest," he mumbled. "Mr. Shaw knew it. He laughed—or nearly laughed," he amended.

"Mr. Shaw's behavior is no concern of mine. Yours, however, is. I want to see you grow well, Evo."

"Has it never occurred to you that it is not your responsibility to see that I do?" he shot back. "If you will remember, my mother is still alive."

"But she—" Dorothea clamped her lips shut. She would not voice what she knew to be true. Her mother would never direct the steps of any of her children. That was left to Dorothea. She had to try again.

"It is not good to ditch a man in your employ simply because it suits your pleasure. You have a responsibility to those underneath you. It matters not that you no longer need a tutor. Mr. Sands was to see that you made it safely back to London, and you deprived him of fulfilling his role. It was badly done of you."

Evo didn't look up again, but answered with cloying sweetness. "I'm an earl and can do what I like. Did you not know?"

"Perhaps. But a *gentleman* keeps his oath, even when it hurts," she replied gently.

When he didn't reply, or even look at her, she stood to leave the room. Her words had not penetrated his heart, not even a little bit.

AT FIVE O'CLOCK, the sound of a knock on the front door alerted Dorothea to Mr. Shaw's arrival. She put down the embroidery she was working on, thankful to have an excuse to leave it behind and go where there were more interesting things to see. Even if that was in the company of Mr. Shaw. Sophia did not appear to begrudge her the afternoon out and was content to stay with their mother.

Dorothea's nerves quivered inside of her as the sound of the butler's footsteps neared to announce their visitor. It couldn't be from nervousness at seeing him, so she could only assume it was because she would join the fashionable crowds in Hyde Park, where she would be under the scrutiny of the *ton*. She stood as soon as he entered, as did her mother and sister.

Mr. Shaw looked hale, having come in from the outdoors. His cheeks were ruddy, his eyes bright, and the combination of those colors only made his teeth shine all the whiter when he smiled. He came to stand in front of her and bowed.

"Lady Dorothea." He then greeted her mother and sister. When he turned back to her and glanced at her gown, he hesitated. "It is rather cold outside. I fear to take you out if you are not covered well."

A flash of annoyance went through her. He was right, of course. As soon as she saw his red cheeks, she realized she had not thought about the weather when she'd chosen her gown. It was not yet close to summer, and she was not going for a quick ride in a closed carriage, only to sit inside for a visit. She would be riding out in his open carriage, exposed to the elements for a sizeable length of time.

"I will be fine," she assured him, unwilling to change or admit she had not thought everything through. "My redingote is quite warm."

He did not appear convinced and looked to her mother and sister for assistance. But as she suspected, they were of no help to him. Her mother did not trouble herself with matters that did not concern her so nearly, and Sophia was too shy to speak out in public. She merely managed a whispered, "Enjoy your ride."

Mr. Shaw thanked her and seemed to feel his case was lost. He held out his arm for Dorothea. She had not expected this courtly gesture in her own drawing room and thought it quite unnecessary, but she could not snub him. That was to be unkind for no good reason. She placed her hand on his arm and allowed Mr. Shaw to escort her out.

In the entryway, the butler helped her with her redingote, which was indeed lined and went to her ankles. It might have been smarter to change her dress for a thicker cotton and to have added a pelisse underneath, but she did not wish to prolong the moment. She tied a bonnet under her chin and allowed Mr. Shaw to lead her outside, where a street urchin was holding the horses. The handsome pair of chestnuts were connected to a phaeton finer than what she had expected of him. Perhaps he was not so impoverished as he had led her to believe.

After he helped her to a seat, she wrapped the skirt of her gown and redingote around her and tried to tuck the fabric under her knees for additional warmth. Mr. Shaw climbed up and reached behind him where he pulled out a blanket. He shook it out, keeping the reins in one hand as he spread it over her, leaning his arm against hers as he did so and causing a sensation of shock at the intimacy of the movement—and the kindness of it. Her breath grew unsteady until he pulled away.

"I can't quite tuck it around you in the manner that would keep you most warm," he said, "but I hope you will make free use of it."

"Thank you," she said, touched by his thoughtfulness, as the carriage started forward.

It was indeed colder than she had anticipated. She feared that even with the blanket it would not be long before the frigid air seeped into her and made the outing uncomfortable. The blanket was a nice gesture.

But then, she reasoned, any man who had the merest gentlemanly notion must think of such a thing. Mr. Shaw's gesture was not so very out of the ordinary.

Would Father have thought of it? she asked herself. The answer required no deliberation.

Mr. Shaw was skilled at driving. He easily wove the carriage around the traffic and did not seem perturbed when another carriage drew too near to his. She allowed him the quiet he needed to focus and looked around her instead as they approached the park. It was pleasant to be in London and would be pleasanter still when it began to warm up.

As they drew near to the gates of Hyde Park, he glanced at her. "Not too cold?"

"No," she replied, although her teeth had the ridiculous urge to chatter as though to prove her wrong. She clenched them.

It was not quite so cold underneath the blanket, but the blanket did not reach up to her chin. Or at least, she refused to pull the blanket up to her chin and so humiliate herself.

"You have a nice phaeton." She had to clamp her lips shut to refrain from speaking the rest. *I did not expect it.*

"It is not mine," he replied, cheerfully unaware how he must appear to others at such an admission. "I convinced my brother-in-law to lend it, which required a bit of ingenuity. He does not lend out his possessions easily."

"I see," she replied, attempting to keep the censure out of her voice.

Never had she had a conversation with someone who spoke without embarrassment about his financial situation, despite needing to borrow the most basic necessities. Strange that he did not seem at all shy about it, for it hardly recommended him to her. This was what made her think her sister had been misled in thinking he was interested in her simply because he'd asked about her. He certainly put no effort into displaying his most brilliant feathers.

"I did not ask you the night of the ball, but when did you arrive in London?" He did not appear to notice they had just entered the famous Rotten Row and that there was so much more to see there than the ends of their noses. How could he think to hold a conversation with all this around them?

She had to refrain from swiveling in her seat to catch sight of everyone who congregated there and barely managed to return a reply.

"We arrived the day of the ball, as a matter of fact. Lady Berkley had sent us an invitation in advance and we accepted it, but our delay in arriving had to do with Tilly, who had caught a cold."

Mr. Shaw gestured discreetly with his gloved hand, out of sight of the public. "That is the celebrated Miss Stanley that Lady Milton had spoken of."

Dorothea followed the direction of his gaze with great curiosity. Miss Stanley rode an impressive mount, and she was flanked by a gentleman on either side of her. Petite, with sparkly eyes and a chin that came to a dainty point, whatever Miss Stanley lacked in title and position, she made up for in vivacity and a most charming countenance. Dorothea was certain she must be related to the gentleman her father had been corresponding with. If she was accepted by the *ton*, she might prove to be a valuable asset. There was certainly no shortage of eligible bachelors in Miss Stanley's orbit.

"It is no wonder you were exhausted the next day," Mr. Shaw said, picking up the thread of their conversation. "To have traveled all day, then danced all night. Not many women could be so stout."

She wasn't sure if she appreciated being called stout. But after a brief consideration, she decided not to take offense. It was true, after all. She'd rather be known for her industry than her fainting spells.

"Perhaps not many could, but I must own myself to have been mistaken in my own strength, for it was my sister who was able to face the following day without suffering in any outward way from the exertion."

Lost in observing the other riders in the park, she did not notice that the blanket had slipped from her lap. Without stopping his horses in their sedate walk on the path, Mr. Shaw leaned across her, brushing his arm against her knee as he pulled the blanket back up around her. She was scarcely given time to register the accidental touch when he was back in his seat, except that her breath hitched against her will.

"You are looking very well today, Lady Dorothea," he said, glancing at her and drawing her eyes back to him.

When their eyes met, something flipped inside her belly. That same sensation of sparks igniting caught her off guard. *What in heaven's name...?* Simply because he had pulled a blanket around her and offered a benign compliment. She could not be having any sort of feelings for this man for such reasons. That would be ridiculous beyond permission.

"You are kind, sir." She broke the gaze, turning her attention back to the scene around her.

The ladies and gentlemen riding on horseback or in carriages stopped to greet each other, and she wished she might be acquainted with some of them. How could her father have been so neglectful as to have kept the entire family from visiting London more than once a decade? And why had her mother not insisted they go? Now they were thrown into Society as to the wolves, and with barely any acquaintances.

"Do you have family in London?" she asked when she realized he was waiting for her to contribute her mite to the conversation. At least he was not content to spout off knowledge and bore one to death without allowing for natural silences to develop. But it meant she would have to keep at least part of her attention for him.

"I do," he said, which caused her a momentary pause. He seemed to her to be more of a solitary figure who sprang up out of nowhere with no family or connections. Although, if that were the case, he would never have been invited to Lady Berkley's ball—or have been able to borrow a carriage from his brother-in-law.

"My sister and her husband are in London at present," he said. "My mother is at our home in Lancashire but will likely join us later in the season. And you? Are all of your siblings in London now?"

"Yes, along with the governess," she said. "We are not in the habit of residing in London even for part of the year, so this is novel for all of us."

Mr. Shaw allowed his horses to keep a steady pace down Rotten Row and did not seem at all flustered by the necessity to swerve around carriages as their drivers stopped to talk. Neither did he look for acquaintances of his own. But perhaps he did not have any. In fact, he seemed perfectly content to speak to her as though she were the only person who existed.

"Miles!"

The sound came from a gentleman on horseback headed in the opposite direction. He cut across to the carriage, and Mr. Shaw slowed down to greet him. The gentleman leaned over to shake Mr. Shaw's hand.

"I'm glad to see you, Gerry." Mr. Shaw glanced at her,

including her with his broad smile. "Lady Dorothea, may I present a good friend of mine? This is Mr. Gerald Wilmot."

After they had exchanged greetings, Mr. Shaw glanced to the side, where a carriage was forced to pause. "I believe we are blocking others. Can you send your address to Limmer's where I'm staying? I'll come and find you."

"Will do." Mr. Wilmot tipped his hat to Dorothea. "Good day, my lady."

Dorothea was impressed with Mr. Shaw's friend, but she reserved her judgment. He might be of the merchant class, although he did not appear to be. She knew she had inherited her father's disdain for those outside of the peerage, but she could not be too careful with whom she associated when she was so newly in London. He clicked the reins and let the carriage move forward in silence, which she did not break. Any hopes Mr. Shaw might volunteer details of how he knew his friend were in vain.

"You were saying you were not in the habit of coming to London?" He had not lost track of what they had been speaking of before he saw Mr. Wilmot, and she did not feel she could direct the subject of their conversation back to his friend. What was more, she was not sure she had ever met someone who actually seemed interested in what she had to say, when he added, "Surely your father did not remain at home all season? Unless he was particularly devoted to his family." Mr. Shaw let the statement dangle.

Dorothea laughed. "My father, devoted to his family? Goodness no." She stopped short, realizing she had revealed more of her family's weaknesses than she had intended. "He spent every season in London."

Mr. Shaw compressed his brow as though he found something to censure in the statement, but he did not pursue it.

Dorothea glanced ahead. "There is Lady Berkley. Shall we

go and greet her?" Mr. Shaw murmured an assent, and steered the carriage in that direction.

At last, here was someone she knew. But she could hardly qualify it as a success. Lady Berkley would assume that her introduction was the beginnings of a courtship and would congratulate herself on having been the one to provide it. But she could not ignore the only person in the entirety of Hyde Park who was known to her. Why had she accepted Mr. Shaw's invitation to ride today?

It was beginning to feel as though Dorothea was swept along by the tide to a place she did not wish to go, and she had been given no rudder so she might right her path.

CHAPTER 8

M iles directed his carriage over to Lady Berkley to oblige
Lady Dorothea, combatting the selfish impulse to keep
her all to himself. She was surprisingly difficult to pull out of
her shell, and despite plying her with all the charm at his
disposal, he didn't seem to make any headway.

It was not that she was unfriendly. She answered every
question he had in a natural way. It was just that her expression
remained closed most of the time. That might simply be her
natural reserve, but he had seen glimpses of something much
warmer—particularly when he had leaned over to restore the
blanket to her. The look she gave him was wide-eyed and far
from the cool reserve she usually wore. He had to force himself
to look away.

Lady Berkley's carriage had been surrounded by two
gentlemen on horseback plus a phaeton driven by a third
gentleman. As they neared, the small party broke up with
friendly adieux.

"Good afternoon, my lady," Miles greeted as they pulled up
beside Lady Berkley's carriage. Next to her was a comely young

woman he had not seen before, which likely explained the line of gentlemen who had stopped to make conversation.

"Mr. Shaw and Lady Dorothea." Lady Berkley positively beamed at them. "I am so pleased that my introduction has led to you furthering your acquaintance. May I present my goddaughter, Miss Kensington? This is her second season, and she is staying with me. It is unfortunate she did not arrive in time for my ball, which was supposed to be in her honor."

"Good afternoon, my lady. Mr. Shaw." Miss Kensington smiled. "Yes, Lady Berkley wished to throw me another come-out ball since I did not *take* last year."

She shot her godmother a look of affectionate mischief. Lady Berkley raised her eyes heavenward and patted her goddaughter's hand.

"A pleasure," Lady Dorothea said, laughter evident in her tone. Miles had been sure she had a good sense of humor. "For my sister and I, it's our first season."

"Well," Miss Kensington replied, "if you shall not think it overly forward of me, I hope we might have the opportunity to become better acquainted, especially if you are new to London. I will be happy to show you both about."

"I would like that. We know few people in London." Lady Dorothea smiled at her.

"Few people! How is that?" Lady Berkley interjected, considerably astonished. "Surely your father must have acquaintances everywhere? Or, at least he did."

Lady Dorothea's smile grew pained as she shook her head. "He did, I suppose. But we did not come to London with my father on...on a regular basis, and therefore are acquainted only with a very few, besides the families we know from Surrey, such as the Miltons, the Dewberrys, and the Bradshaws. But other than that..." She stopped and pinched her lips together.

"Well, child. I am so glad you have apprised me of this situation. I, too, will be more deliberate in my introductions now that I am aware of it. I shall have to spend more time with your mother, as well. She must not be finding it easy to go on in society after the loss of Lord Poole."

Lady Dorothea gave a nod. "You are very kind, Lady Berkley."

Miles felt the conversation had come to its natural end, and he gave a farewell before clicking the reins. He had scarcely said two words, but that was not what mattered. He had learned a lot about Lady Dorothea's situation.

"It surprises me that an earl would not have sought opportunities for his family to make more connections in society. Why do you suppose that is?"

"You ask very direct questions, Mr. Shaw."

He darted a glance her way, frowning. "Perhaps. I merely—"

A rapid movement to his left accompanied by a squeal of fright cut off his speech. An instant later, a phaeton barreled by their carriage with inches to spare. Driving it was a young woman who seemed to have lost all control of the reins. In fact, rather than holding the reins, she had her hands clasped over her eyes.

Without thinking, Miles touched the shoulder of his leader with the whip. He caught it in one hand and steered with the other to try to catch up to the carriage. Lady Dorothea held on firmly, but did not scream, for which he was grateful.

"Can you handle the reins?" he asked her, his voice clipped as he focused on the chase. They had gone far enough ahead of everyone that there were few people to pose a threat.

"Yes," she replied, her tone sure but equally short.

The phaeton was still ahead of them but they gained on it until Miles inched up enough to bring his carriage up alongside.

"When we pull abreast, I'll give you the reins and make the jump. The horses will respond to your direction if you give them the sign to slow down gently." Without looking at her, he asked. "Can you do this?"

"Yes," she repeated, and when they pulled up alongside the runaway carriage, he saw she was ready for the reins.

He tossed the leather to her, putting his hand on the side of his carriage and one foot on the seat. In an explosion of movement, he leapt over to the runaway phaeton, which had started to pull away again.

His boot scarcely caught the edge of it, but his hands gripped the sides and he threw himself in. Once seated, he grabbed the reins that hung loose over the front and allowed the horses to grow accustomed to the feel of his control. He reined them in by paces, bringing them to a trot, then a walk. He leaned back in his seat and let out a long exhale.

The girl at his side was sobbing, but he could not think of consoling her. The borrowed phaeton with Lady Dorothea driving it was still barreling forward, now nearly out of sight. The ramifications knocked his breath clean out of his chest.

What have I done?

He had forced a lady whose skill he had no inkling of to take the reins of a carriage pulled by two galloping horses she was not familiar with. If she were thrown, she would almost of a certainty be killed. And he would have to live with that for the rest of his life.

He remained frozen as he watched her, helpless with the horror of it, time stretching until it seemed to stop. Just as he thought she must surely be thrown, the carriage began to slow almost imperceptibly, then by degrees, until at last she had the horses at a walk. She turned the carriage neatly and brought them back in his direction at a sedate pace. He began to breathe again, although he feared he might be sick. He put his elbow on his knees and dropped his head between his legs.

"You all right, Shaw?"

Gerry had come to his aid, and he had never been more thankful for the man in his life. He glanced at the sobbing woman at his side and looked at his friend helplessly.

"I need to..." He gestured ahead to Lady Dorothea then nodded to his side with a pointed look.

Gerry understood at a glance, and although he was not fonder of unknown sobbing females than any gentleman, he showed himself a true friend.

"Miss. Miss, you are all right now. Come. Open your eyes." Gerry had swung down from his horse and was taking the reins of the girl's phaeton.

Miles jumped down and waited until Lady Dorothea pulled up and smiled down at him. Her eyes were bright from the air and exertion.

"Good afternoon, Mr. Shaw. Would you care for a ride?"

He was too sick to smile at her pleasantry. She allowed him to climb up on the driver's side and handed him the reins, after which he turned in his seat to look at her. His heart was beginning to slow as the realization came over him that she was unharmed, but he was still weak from his horror when he thought she would not control the carriage.

"Lady Dorothea," he said in heartfelt tones, "might I tell you what a remarkable woman you are?"

Laughing, she turned to him, revealing a very pretty set of teeth. She had not taken him seriously, but he was deadly serious. He could not but be impressed by her. What woman could take the reins of a bolting carriage led by horses she did not know without a moment's hesitation?

What kind of fool forces her to? He would not easily recover from today. When he gave the signal to his horses to advance, his arm shook.

After a short pause, she touched the wood of his carriage that was painted a fine white along the edges as though admiring it. Then she tucked her hands back under the blanket, pulling it up so it covered part of her arms. He was reminded of the need to get her back to warmth, and he set the horses to a trot.

"You've seen all there is to see in that direction, I believe," he observed.

"And you will need to return the carriage to your brother-in-law," she added.

"Yes, I must."

In the silence that followed, Miles knew that now would be a good time to rectify his comment about not being on the hunt for a wealthy wife. She was aware of his poverty, and he had practically assured her he would not pursue her with that disclaimer. He couldn't bring himself to do it, however. It would likely mean the end of their budding courtship, and he wasn't ready for that.

She faced forward again, then sniffed. Her nose had turned red, and he reached into his coat pocket and pulled out a handkerchief and handed it to her. She shook her head and took one from her reticule.

"I am taking you back home," he said, already chastising himself. He certainly hoped she would not catch a vicious cold because of this outing. "I should not have kept you out as long as I did in this weather."

"I am never sick."

"Good." He drove past the last stretch of trees lining the broad path.

"Are you attending the opera this Thursday?" he asked, in an effort to keep her engaged in conversation. He was still shaken and wondered if she needed it as much as he did.

"I...I believe so. Our plans are not fixed at present. I must confer with my mother." Her hesitation led him to understand that she was afraid he would insist that she accompany him, but he was not such a dunderhead. His was not a suit to press with a heavy hand. And how could he not pursue her? She was simply...remarkable.

He slipped through the gates of Hyde Park as another carriage was entering it. He turned the carriage to the road that would bring her back to Grosvenor, still registering the near run they had just had. Besides his initial fear for Lady Dorothea's sake, Albert would have his head if he returned the man's carriage with a scratch on it. Then again, Miles was not in the nature of driving cow-handedly. He was only cow-handed when it came to putting young ladies in danger.

"Well, I hope you will have some hot tea when you are home, so that you are properly warmed up. I should hate for you to miss any of the pleasures London has to offer simply because I took you out in the bitter cold."

She turned an uncertain regard his way, as though fearful of his insistence on meeting again, but her eyes had thawed when he kept to light topics.

They were very shortly back in front of her house on Grosvenor Square, but there was no urchin this time to stand at the lead horse's head while he assisted her to the door.

"I am sorry I cannot—" he began, but she didn't allow him to finish.

"I am capable of alighting on my own, Mr. Shaw." She gave him her hand briefly, then stepped down from the carriage without help. "Thank you for the pleasant afternoon."

Pleasant? Was it really? He was unsure what to make of this. Was she so eager to leave his presence? Meanwhile, he was starting to think he could not get enough of hers.

"It has been a pleasure, Lady Dorothea. Perhaps we will see each other at the opera."

He received a hesitant nod in response, and then she rushed indoors. Miles drove away, knowing their ride had not gone as well as he would have liked. He had put her in danger, had exposed her to the cold for too long, and had continued to lie about his pursuit of a wealthy bride. That was a disastrous series of choices to make for a lady he was truly beginning to like.

He drove Albert's carriage onto a narrower street in the direction of the mews to return it before hailing a hackney to take him to his own rented lodgings. As he rode, his thoughts turned from the remarkable Lady Dorothea to his own situation. Could he bring his estate in order without the help of a dowry? *Her* dowry? Perhaps...but it would still be a step down for her. And he knew from watching his mother do the same thing that it was not an easy life he would be offering her—especially if they did not touch her portion.

When he'd inherited the estate, too many fields had been left fallow, and the first order of business had been to get them all to the point of bringing in income. The tenants needed to be lured back, and the only way to do that had been to oversee repairing the tenant houses and ensuring that they would receive a fair share for their work.

This was one thing his father had not rectified—the poor returns for the laborers when they were the ones who did all the work. When it had come time for the harvest, he had given them even less than promised, and many abandoned the tenant farms for the city with hopes of a better life working in a mill.

Besides the fields, Miles had set up the process of carding and spinning the wool on his own estate. An overly particular person might accuse him of sinking closer to merchant status with these innovations, but this did not concern him. With the right machines in place to process the wool, he had begun making a substantial amount selling it directly to the weavers.

However, the improvements did not cover the mortgages on the land, and they would not save the house itself, which needed a complete restoration. The house and land held great value to him, for it connected him to his father's memory and to his ancestry. However, only the nostalgic could love the place. The decorations in each of the rooms were antiquated, there was the presence of mold, and not even the roof could be guaranteed to hold for another ten years, according to his steward. His mother contented herself with the use of only a few rooms and never bothered to open up the rest. He could hardly expect a wife to live in such shabby quarters.

But if he had a wife with a large portion, all could be renovated quickly. A lady as reasonable as Lady Dorothea must not think of *that* as hanging out for a rich wife. After all, she would be designing the house just as she pleased. And he would add much to her consequence simply by his easy nature and charm in mingling with the polite world. It would be a match of equal merit. At least, he could almost convince himself of that.

These thoughts preoccupied Miles until he arrived at Limmer's Hotel where he had rented rooms for the season. Or rather, he rented a room. Some might say he was taking economy to extreme measures, but he preferred to put his blunt into his attire, which was actually visible to society. He thus banished those faceless critics to a distant corner of his mind.

As he entered the hotel, a modish gentleman stood in the cheerless coffee room, drawing his attention. Miles started in recognition and could not help the grin that spread over his face.

"Rock!" He wagged his head and strode over to his cousin. They shook hands and he patted him on the arm affectionately. "'Tis good to see you. I understood you would not be arriving until much later in the season."

"And yet, here I am in the flesh."

Robert Throckmorton—or more accurately, Lord Throckmorton, Viscount, and heir to their grandfather, the Earl of

Pembroke—told anyone who became intimate enough that his surname was deuced cumbersome on the tongue and cheerfully went by the name of Rock. He had not been presented to Miles during their childhood, since Miles's mother had been cast off completely after marrying a gentleman of low status.

But when Rock discovered his cousin was attending Harrow, he'd sought him out and let him know he'd be glad enough to recognize the connection considering all he had were sisters. Despite the fact that Rock inherited the title that would have been Miles's own had his mother been born a man, Miles had never begrudged him for it, and they had been close ever since.

"Sit, man. Tell me what brings you to London so early." Miles gestured to the table his cousin had just vacated.

Rock turned up his nose and leaned in. "Are you certain you wish to? This place is filled with the squirearchy. How can you bear to stay here?"

Miles gave him a good-natured shove. "Don't be overly nice in your expectations if you are going to acknowledge the connection. If it's good enough for me, it's good enough for you."

"Very well," Rock grumbled. "To own the truth, I tasted the coffee while waiting for you. It ain't half bad. I just don't think the walls are ever touched by sunlight, no matter how bright outside."

"Or the tables by a wet cloth. I know, I know," Miles agreed. They sat, and he called a servant over, suddenly conscious that he had better watch his tongue when pouring out criticisms if he planned to stay here for an entire season.

"So..." he said as soon as the servant left.

"So, there is nothing really to tell. I grew bored with the house party and decided to leave it." Rock shrugged.

"But it was at your estate," Miles protested, laughing.

"I left word that they might stay as long as they wished, and that I'd have the housekeeper care for their every need. My mother was happy enough to sit with the ladies who came to stay with her and hardly looked at me askance when I announced I was going to leave." His grin brought deep creases to his cheeks.

"I hardly believe that," Miles snorted.

"Oh, very well. She was not above half pleased. But even she had to acknowledge that it was growing deuced uncomfortable for me with the determined pursuit of the young ladies in residence."

"Did you not know of the guest list ahead of time?" Miles asked. "You usually run from these things, and in fact I had come to the conclusion that you were ready to be leg-shackled if you would miss the fun in London for a select party at your estate."

Rock looked uncomfortable. "I had thought perhaps I had found a woman that suited me. But I realized I am not ready to settle down."

"And you told her so in no uncertain terms so she could move on and not wear the willow for you, I suppose." Miles smiled up at the servant who brought them both coffee, along with some rolls and slices of meat.

"Are you daft? I let my mother inform the guests that I had something pressing that required I remove to London." Rock picked up a cup of coffee. "I shall be as jittery as a newborn foal, but I believe I will take another cup."

Miles kept his thoughts to himself over Rock's disclosure. His cousin had a good heart, and he loved him more than anyone, apart from his mother and sister. Where women were concerned, however, he was not the portrait of consideration.

"What took you so long to get here?" Rock asked, breaking off a piece of bread and popping it into his mouth.

"I was riding in Hyde Park with Lady Dorothea Rowland-son." Miles sipped his coffee, remembering the sight of her slowly turning the carriage to come back to him.

"Don't know her. Fresh out? Who's her family?" Rock's dark curls fell over a handsome face, and if they had anything in common, it was their thick head of hair of a similar shade. The difference was that Rock's hair was properly styled and Miles's stuck up in all directions no matter what he did with it.

"She's the daughter of the Earl of Poole—or was. He died last year, and now her younger brother has the title. I like her," he said simply.

"Be careful now, or you will be getting leg-shackled," Rock said, grinning.

"I am not above that consideration," he admitted.

Rock's eyes widened a fraction, then understanding dawned. "Under the hatches again? I suppose it is the most expedient way to settle a failing estate, although I would really have to be desperate to think of such a thing."

"Yes, I'm under the hatches as usual." Miles returned the ghost of a smile at his cousin's remark. "But it is not only for her fortune that I am courting her. I am even questioning whether some of her dowry might not be reserved for any heirs that would issue from such a union, thereby proving I am more noble than she suspects."

"Whatever for?" Rock was truly perplexed.

"A thing called love, coz. I want it. Won't settle for less."

Miles laughed when he saw the look of shock on his cousin's face. They were so dissimilar, but he could not help but be fond of him. Miles's mother had married disadvantageously in the eyes of her family, and Rock would not have been blamed for having cut the connection. But he voluntarily sought him out at school. And Miles would always be loyal to him for that.

"Do you love this Lady Dorothea? Lud, what a mouthful.

Why couldn't they have called her Ann?" Rock held a lump of sugar in the coffee, allowing it to soak through before putting it on his tongue. "Perhaps she has a nickname."

Miles couldn't imagine Lady Dorothea having a nickname, but it would be fun to give her one. "It is too soon to associate the word love with Lady Dorothea. All I will say is that the possibilities are there, and at the moment I have my sights set only on her."

"Well, well. *This* is going to be an interesting season," Rock said. "—or not. Please don't fall in love in earnest and go about moping over unrequited love or some such thing."

"Have you ever known me to mope?" Miles retorted, laughing. "I think you need not fear that."

"Did you tell her your mother is the daughter of an earl?" Rock asked, his look of skepticism showing that he knew Miles all too well.

"I did not, and will thank you for not mentioning it."

Rock shook his head. "I think you've got maggots for brains. If you want to win a lady, you need to use all the tools at your disposal, and your relationship to an earl is one such tool. I've always told you this, but you've yet to listen."

"Technically, I have no relationship to the earl, apart from a bloodline, since he cast my mother off and has never made any efforts to meet me. Attempting to win her that way speaks of hypocrisy," Miles said as he stuffed two slices of ham into a roll.

"You and I are not likely to agree on that subject," Rock said. "But I suppose it doesn't matter."

They spent another half hour *not* talking about earls or courtship, but exchanging stories of all that had happened since the last time they had seen each other. It had been all of two years, with Miles working on restoring his estate and Rock pursuing all the activities of a gentleman of leisure. At the end of that time, Rock stood.

"Well, I came to see with my own eyes that you had indeed come to London. I will put your name up at the club—and pay the subscription this year," he added when he saw Miles about to protest the expense. "It's worth it. London will be vastly more interesting with you here."

Miles smiled at him. London seemed vastly more friendly now that his cousin had come.

"Just don't fall in love," Rock reminded him before leaving.

CHAPTER 9

D orothea stared up at the ceiling of the opera house, where a round painting of Helios driving his chariot on the clouds of brilliant blues, whites, and yellows met her gaze. She stared across to the opposite side of the stage where there were situated four tiers of boxed seats mirroring those in which she sat. Her father's box was conveniently placed in the middle, and she certainly hoped their position and youth would pull the regard of more than one set of male eyes. Of course, any interest they inspired must be attributed to Sophia, for the first glances were always for her.

She allowed her gaze to roam over to the pit, then cast her eyes upward to the farthest box seat on the top tier, where Mr. Shaw was leaning negligently, his elbow over the railing and his head leaning on one hand. At that moment, he glanced her way, and when he saw her looking, he sat up straight, smiled at her and nodded his head in acknowledgment.

Dorothea turned her head, piqued at herself. She had allowed her gaze to linger there for too long. It was not that she liked him. It was just that a person's regard could not help but be drawn to someone they knew in a sea of strangers. After all, she had not seen Lord Hastings or anyone else she recognized from that first ball. They must either have eschewed the opera or were sitting in a box seat on the same side as her.

She had crossed paths with Mr. Shaw twice since their ride in Hyde Park, but both had been brief meetings with no more than a simple greeting. In one, he held the door for her when she was exiting Hookham's with some novels wrapped in brown paper that she'd hoped would bring her hours of enjoyment. He'd glanced at her books and said with his charismatic smile, "We are on the same mission, I see." She had only time to nod and move out of the way for a lady who wished to enter.

The second time was at Gunter's, where she had enjoyed her first strawberry ice in the company of Sophia—and Tilly, who had begged to be allowed to come. The only people of their limited acquaintance they had met there were the Miltons. Afterward, as they gathered in front of the tea shop, waiting for their carriage, Mr. Shaw appeared, engaged in smiling banter with another elegantly attired gentleman. Her heart had stopped, then chugged to life again at the surprise of seeing him. She had to own how well at ease he was for an impoverished gentleman, and how well he carried himself despite that crucial flaw. The other members of the *ton* did not seem to hold it against him.

On that day, Mr. Shaw took a step forward as soon he had caught sight of her. He held out his hand to help her to climb into the carriage, and their gazes met as his fingers touched hers. She murmured a thank you and turned away, aware that her cheeks had heated up. As they had moved forward, she peeked at Mr. Shaw, but he was thankfully not looking at her.

He truly was the most disturbing man she'd ever met. He upset her peace every time he looked at her in that piercing way of his or allowed some casual touch between them. And she would not quickly forget the way he had leapt onto the carriage whose horses had bolted. He moved with athletic grace—no, he *flew* across to the other carriage—in a way that did nothing to still those little flutters in her stomach whenever she thought of it. What was more, he had trusted her to be able to drive the carriage and calm the horses.

In the shadows of their box at the opera, she smiled, recalling his expression of relief when she had at last brought the carriage safely back to him. It had been harder than she'd expected to control the pair, and she was proud of herself for doing it. And it was nice to be lauded for her skill.

She must keep him at a distance, because the simple truth stood. He was *not* eligible. He did not have the position in Society she desired to align herself to, and more to the point, he did not have the funds to set her up in style. With such focused attention coming from him—and with so little coming from other gentlemen this early in the season—she must not allow herself to be vulnerable to his charm.

The tragedy that was being sung below her came to the end of the second act, and she began clapping along with everyone else, conscious that she had not been at all interested in the story or the music. Sophia, on the other hand, had not stopped weeping from emotion at her side. When the audience began to stand and move about in their boxes, Dorothea stood.

"Mama, shall we go and have a glass of champagne?" she asked.

"You two go without me," her mother said, sending them off with a wave. "I cannot bear the crowds. There is only one more act after this, and I long for my bed."

"Are you sure we should take champagne?" Sophia whispered as they walked to the entrance of their box. "I have heard it can alter your senses."

"Not with such a small amount, silly," Dorothea replied, but she was struck by doubt. She had heard that one drank champagne at the opera, and she intended to be like everyone. However, perhaps she should not subject either herself or her sister to that temptation when she truly did not know its effects. Or perhaps she was wrong about what an unmarried lady should drink at the opera.

When they were at last able to secure refreshment, Sophia made no comment when Dorothea asked for two glasses of lemonade. They turned and sipped, Dorothea's eyes taking in the people milling past them with scarcely any opening to cross over to return to their box seats. They pressed their backs to the wall and sipped quietly without speaking, surrounded by a hum of conversation.

Almost immediately, a male voice addressed her from the side. "Lady Dorothea."

She turned, her smile in place, hiding the little dip of disappointment when it was not Mr. Shaw.

"Lord Hastings."

She curtsied, taking in his appearance. He was still handsome, despite having easily passed his fiftieth year, and in spite of his upper lip which seemed to disappear in a smile that was not his most attractive feature. "Have you been presented to my sister, Lady Sophia?"

"I have not had the pleasure, no." Lord Hastings took Sophia's hand and bowed over it. She curtsied, blushing, looking anywhere but at his face.

Silence fell after the initial greetings, and Dorothea strove to think of something of interest. It must not be said that the Rowlandson sisters had no conversation, although she had started to fear that was indeed the case since their arrival in London. The only one she felt at all comfortable conversing with was Mr. Shaw. But he must not count.

"Are you enjoying the opera?" she asked, conscious that it was rather flat in the way of conversational gambits but unable to think of anything better. She waited for him to answer, and he did so after what seemed like an infuriatingly long stretch of time for the simple answer he returned.

"Yes. Very much."

She tried again. "Where do you reside when you are not in London?"

At this, his eyes lit up, and he showed the first signs of life. "My estate is located on the moors of Northumberland, near the border of Scotland. It is there that I prefer to spend the majority of my time."

Dorothea opened her mouth, then shut it again before knowing quite how to respond.

"I see."

This was a daunting bit of information. Although she would not mind an age gap in her quest for a suitable match, she did not relish the idea of spending ten months out of the year in such a cold and inhospitable place as Northumberland.

Just when she thought the conversation was doomed to die for lack of feeding its fire, he spoke again "Lady Dorothea, I am hoping you will do me the honor of walking with me in the park tomorrow."

"Oh, tomorrow! I...would be delighted." Dorothea attempted to mean it as he murmured his pleasure at her acceptance. This was what she wanted, wasn't it?

She was still undecided. As an earl, Lord Hastings would be an excellent match if she could contrive to secure him, and it seemed as though she had caught his attention. But he inspired none of those fluttery sensations that Mr. Shaw seemed to ignite in her. And although Lord Hastings could clearly lead London society if he wished it, he had made his preferences for residing on his estate clear. Perhaps she could convince him to spend more time in London than he had previously done. A wife must certainly be capable of changing her husband's habits, mustn't she?

Sophia cleared her throat delicately and tugged on Dorothea's sleeve.

"I don't think you can have considered," Sophia whispered in a painfully shy voice. "You promised to take Camilla to the *modiste* tomorrow."

Dorothea frowned in annoyance. It was true that none of her middle sister's clothes fit any longer. That was the reason she had not joined them at Gunter's. A trip to the *modiste* was absolutely essential.

However, what no one seemed to understand was to what lengths Dorothea was striving to secure a good match. After all, was she not doing it for her sisters' sakes? She was! For them, and for Everard, too, for it was becoming increasingly clear that he would benefit from the guidance of an older man who could serve as a father figure. Why, only yesterday he had slipped past Mr. Sands again and met up with friends to see a cock fight! She could not seem to get him to mind her.

Attracting a distinguished, worthy suitor would only help them all to achieve more brilliant matches than they might otherwise. But she could not do this while also serving as mother to all of them. The mantle of responsibility lay heavily on her shoulders. All of these thoughts flew quickly through her mind in the time it took her to expel a long, silent breath.

"I don't suppose you could..." Dorothea murmured back to Sophia, hoping she might take Camilla to the modiste in her stead. One anguished, startled look from her sister silenced her. "No, of course you cannot. I did not consider."

Dorothea squared her shoulders and faced Lord Hastings. "I am very sorry, my lord. Tomorrow will not be possible. As you have just heard, I am promised to my sister."

At this news, a frown line appeared between Lord Hastings's eyes. "It is a shame. I shall have to delay the gratification of walking with you then, for I am returning to my estate afterwards for a span of several weeks."

Weeks? A sense of urgency overtook Dorothea. By refusing, she was perhaps missing her only chance, if she did indeed hope to secure him.

She darted a look at her sister. "Perhaps a visit to the *modiste* might be arranged for a different day."

"No, for Madame Fouchard has warned us that her schedule is becoming alarmingly full," Sophia whispered, turning her face away from Lord Hastings.

Dorothea gave it up for lost. "I am afraid it is not possible, my lord."

He did not tarry at their side after that. Somewhat defeated, Dorothea knew they must soon return to their box seats, although she had no inclination to move just yet. As she stood at Sophia's side watching the crowds of people mill by, she wished she might greet everyone as so many others were doing. In all her dreams of coming to London, she had always envisioned a successful entry into Society, not one where she was forced to look on from the fringes.

Dorothea was about to suggest they return to their seats when they were hailed again. She recognized the voice and feared he would notice the agitation of her beating heart that caused heat to stain her cheeks. She turned slowly, coming face to handsome face.

"Good evening, Lady Dorothea, Lady Sophia. I'd hoped I might have the pleasure of meeting you here."

Mr. Shaw bowed before them, sending his clean masculine scent her way as he stood upright. As with each time Dorothea met him, the man was impeccably attired, smiled charmingly, and was altogether too attractive. Her heart seemed to have a will of its own, despite how severely her mind scolded it.

Mercifully unaware of her thoughts, Mr. Shaw turned his winning smile to Sophia.

"You appeared to enjoy the opera exceedingly, for I believe I saw you wiping a tear. Confess it was so."

It was no surprise that her sister blushed hotly, for that's what she generally did around strangers. But what did surprise Dorothea was that she actually responded, and in more than a whisper.

"I've never heard anything like it. The melody was so moving when sung that way, wasn't it? Even though I did not understand the words." She clasped her gloved hands together as though trying to contain her enthusiasm to a level fit for public viewing.

"Alas." Mr. Shaw exchanged a glance with Dorothea. "I wish I could claim being as sensitive to the arts as you are, Lady Sophia. It does you credit. However, I fear I am too prosaic a man to go into alt over the tragedies. I prefer comedy myself. And I prefer it spoken rather than sung."

Yes! Dorothea wanted to say. But she did not like to admit she had anything in common with Mr. Shaw and therefore kept her lips firmly sealed. However, she could not help but appreciate the fact that he was the first man—ever, to her knowledge —who had been able to draw her sister out.

Mr. Shaw glanced ahead at the crowds that were thinning in the corridor. "Will you allow me to escort you to your seats?"

Dorothea was tempted to say not to trouble himself, considering his box was on the opposite side. Before she could do so, Sophia accepted Mr. Shaw's arm. He stepped into the corridor and turned his inquiring gaze to Dorothea. In doing so, he bumped into the fashionable Miss Maryann Stanley, who was walking beside an older woman who might have been her grandmother.

Miss Stanley's startled gaze lit on Mr. Shaw, and then on Dorothea and Sophia.

"Forgive me, Miss Stanley. I did not see where I was going," Mr. Shaw said, turning his charming visage in her direction.

His smile must have worked its magic on her, as Miss Stanley returned, "We have not been introduced. How did you know my name?"

"Maryann, the opera is about to begin," the older lady next to her urged. Dorothea revised her former opinion. It must be the companion and not the grandmother, for she spoke without any convincing authority.

With Sophia still on his arm and Dorothea a step behind, Mr. Shaw bowed before Miss Stanley.

"It is true we have not been introduced, but your reputation precedes you. And although we have not yet been formally introduced, I am Miles Shaw." Casting a look of humor at Dorothea, he added, "Lady Dorothea and Lady Sophia, will you allow me to present to you my new acquaintance, Miss Maryann Stanley? These are two of the Earl of Poole's sisters," he explained.

Dorothea smiled and gave a hesitant nod. Although she was the social superior, Miss Stanley had everything she lacked in Society, except a title. She seemed to know everyone. And she was so vivacious and beautiful that everyone was attracted to her. Even Dorothea herself could not help but be drawn to her. Perhaps it might help to befriend her.

Miss Stanley's slightly aloof expression toward Dorothea and her sister underwent a change. She became all smiles and curtsied.

"Are you indeed the late Earl of Poole's daughters? I am most delighted to make your acquaintance, then, for he was a favorite of my father's."

The bell sounded, alerting them to the end of the pause between acts.

"I hope we shall meet again, now that we have been introduced," Miss Stanley said, before taking the arm of her companion.

"That would be lovely," Dorothea replied, still unsure if she was making the right social move. She thought she was, but despite her father's letters, she seemed to be missing the code that everyone else knew about somehow—of who were the appropriate people to know and how to find them.

This occupied her thoughts as they moved forward and she could not refrain from turning to Mr. Shaw. "I cannot understand how you managed to bring about an introduction when you yourself were not acquainted with Miss Stanley."

He had the audacity to wink at her. *Sparks.*

"It is one of the skills I possess," he said. "I am not overly troubled by etiquette, although I should hope I possess the basics of good manners. If I see the opportunity to further an acquaintance, I am obliged to take it. And in this case, furthering yours, for you have mentioned not having a great deal of acquaintances in London."

Dorothea looked at him askance. She wasn't sure if she liked being his social charity case. And yet, she had to appreciate his skill, since it allowed her to meet Miss Stanley.

"However," he continued, leading them up a set of narrow steps that led to the second tier. He was obliged to drop his arms in order to let some others pass, and he waited until they reached the next level to continue. "I am somewhat in doubt of whether Miss Stanley will be a true friend to you."

Dorothea stopped short and stared at him. "Why?"

He leveled his gaze on her. "She seemed to be interested in making your acquaintance only when she learned you were connected to the peerage."

She left her eyes on him as she reflected on this bit of information, almost forgetting that Sophia was there. "But...isn't that rather normal? Of course she would prefer to befriend someone who could potentially elevate her in Society."

His return smile was inscrutable, and with a glance at Sophia, he ushered them forward to the entrance of their box, directing a questioning gaze as to which one. When they reached their number, he paused again and faced her. Dorothea was breathless from their proximity and his direct gaze.

"I think you underestimate your worth as a friend outside of your title," he said. He allowed her to slip her hand from his arm, his gaze not leaving hers. Then he bowed and turned to leave.

The opera had already begun, and Sophia whispered from behind her as they entered the obscurity of the box, "He said the very thing I was thinking."

Dorothea tightened her lips as she walked down the short aisle toward her seat. That was not a comment worth responding to.

She sat and allowed the darkness to surround her as she meditated on what Mr. Shaw had said. It was not so much what he said, but the fact that he had called her a friend. Surely, using such a word meant he did not intend to attempt a courtship. Goodness knew husbands and wives could not be friends. She convinced herself that his word choice was to send her a deliberate message about his intentions or lack thereof. She was glad it was so. Or...she ought to be glad.

But as the tragedy continued below, she realized that she was rather a bit disappointed.

DURING CALLING HOURS, Dorothea waited for visitors, this time with the support of both her mother and sister. She had learned to accept that making social calls was difficult for her mother, but that she was more than willing to receive them. Even Camilla had joined them, as there had been a gown already made at the *modiste* that allowed her to take her place alongside her mother and sisters.

No sooner were they in place than the sounds of the first visitors reached them, and Camilla sat up straight. It was her first presentation in London. Dorothea looked at her approvingly. Her sister had a tendency toward plumpness that made Dorothea fear she would never find a husband. But she looked very fine in a gown that fit her correctly. Sophia was ravishing as usual.

The door opened, and Dorothea looked up. It was not Turton as she'd expected, there to announce their guest. It was Everard. She frowned at him and gave a shake of the head as he walked into the room, his grin showing clearly he knew she would have something to say about his appearance in the drawing room. The problem was that he didn't listen to any remonstrance she made.

"Everard," she began, but she could say no more for their butler appeared in the doorway, followed by Miss Stanley and three gentlemen. All three were dressed in the modish attire of the *ton* and had youth on their side. The surprise caused Dorothea to momentarily forget about her brother and turn a smiling visage to their new visitors. This was a change, indeed. Three gentlemen!

"Miss Maryann Stanley, Lord Throckmorton, Mr. Weathering, and Mr. Pollard," the butler announced. She recognized Mr. Weathering as the gentleman who had been in Mr. Shaw's company outside of Gunter's.

Dorothea curtsied and gestured at her side. "This is my

96

mother, Lady Poole. These are my sisters, Lady Sophia and Lady Camilla, and—" She turned toward her brother, suddenly remembering his presence and her full displeasure at it. "And this is my brother, Lord Poole. Won't you please sit?"

She glanced at the butler as she did so, knowing he would communicate to the servants to bring the tea tray. Miss Stanley had taken the seat closest to her, so she smiled at her as she resumed her own. Mr. Pollard, of an ordinary-looking countenance but fashionable, attempted to draw Sophia out in a painful process that bore little fruit. Miss Stanley struck up a lively conversation with Mr. Weathering on her left while Dorothea, her mother, and Camilla sat there as though struck dumb. Why couldn't they be more interesting?

She looked across at Lord Throckmorton, the most promising of this morning's visitors in appearance and in title, and he seemed to be assessing her curiously. She wondered what he thought of her. Did he find her pretty? Poised?

When she met his regard, he smiled and shifted in his chair, then turned to her brother who was seated beside him.

"Lord Poole, where do you attend school?" He placed his elbows on the armrests and steepled his fingers.

"Eton," her brother vouchsafed.

"You keep your instructors busy, I imagine?" he said.

"I do my best, sir," Evo replied, wearing a sapient expression, his twinkling eyes evident to Dorothea who was ready to strangle him. They must have been evident to Lord Throckmorton as well for he returned an answering grin.

"He has not yet been sent down from school, but we are every term in anticipation of it," Camilla said placidly from the sofa next to their mother. Dorothea suffered a shock and glanced at her sister. She could almost accuse her of flirting, but Camilla did not have the capacity for such a thing. Was she truly in expectation of their brother being sent down?

As she knitted her brows, Lord Throckmorton tilted his head back and laughed, showing that he at least had not thought her serious. Camilla's expression remained unchanged, so Dorothea could only assume she had been. Her sister would never secure a match by being dumb-witted.

The footman and maid brought in the tea things, and the conversation shifted easily as everything was set up, and Dorothea poured the tea for the guests. When everyone had been served, Miss Stanley turned to her.

"I hope you do not mind that I brought some gentlemen with me this morning," she said. She tilted toward her as though they were great friends, and against her will, Dorothea responded to the gesture. She was desperately short of friends. There was no time to keep any.

"Not in the least. It is always a pleasure to make more acquaintances in London." Dorothea clasped her hands on her lap, too nervous to sip her tea. She feared she might inadvertently dump it in her lap from her stress over the first time receiving callers of consequence. Well, Lord Hastings was of consequence, but he was not as close in age to her as these callers and did not make her quite as nervous.

She studied Miss Stanley, whose rich, reddish-brown curls shone in the sunlit room. She could not help but compare her heart-shaped face and sweet mouth to Sophia's more noble nose and brow. Her sister must be declared the more beautiful, but Miss Stanley certainly had an engaging way about her that Sophia could learn from.

Miss Stanley leaned in again in that confidential way. "Lady Dorothea, I do not wish to be impertinent, but I was wondering if we might dispense with formalities? You may call me Maryann if you wish."

Dorothea knew that such a thing was for her to propose as the social superior, but the thought of snubbing Miss Stanley so soon did not seem like something she could do. And it did seem as though Miss Stanley had been raised to mingle in Society in a way Dorothea had not, and therefore in that way was her superior. Besides, it would be nice to have a friend who was not related by blood.

"Very well. Please call me Dorothea."

She listened as Maryann chatted away about the *soirées* she had been to and the people she had met without seeming to require much in the way of answer. Dorothea did not mind. It took the burden off her to think of something witty to say when all she could focus on was what Lord Throckmorton must think of Everard, who had managed to keep him in conversation, or whether Mr. Weathering must find her family insufferably dull. No, he could not, for he was staring at Sophia in a promising way. She must find out more about his situation. Mr. Pollard had seemed to give up and was happy to intersperse a word with Lord Throckmorton and Everard, while her mother and Camilla looked on in silence.

By the time they took their leave, all Dorothea had managed to learn about Lord Throckmorton was that he was a viscount, but she was not sure if he was one in his own right or if it was a courtesy title. He was handsome, but apart from that first assessing look, he had seemed more intrigued with what Evo had to say than her.

She was beginning to fear she was frightfully dull.

CHAPTER 10

Miles had received the promised invitation to the Answorths' ball, which showed that Lady Milton had found a way of discovering his direction and had enough sway with Mrs. Answorth to ensure he had been invited. The fact that he lived in rented rooms rather than owning a London house had not deterred Lady Milton from securing a potential suitor for her daughter.

He entered the residence and searched the crowds still in the entryway, hoping to spy a glimpse of Lady Dorothea. Although he had come with the full intention of honoring his promise to dance with Miss Milton, his thoughts had begun to turn to Lady Dorothea in increasing measure. He had not —*could* not—forget the sight of Albert's carriage barreling away with her in it, a fault he still laid at his own feet despite the fact that she had dealt with the situation admirably.

Somehow, with the instinct he had for understanding people, he had known she would be capable of handling the reins, and that if she weren't, she would tell him so frankly. But he still should not have put her at risk. Then, to see her turning the carriage and directing the horses to him—her usually cool

100

demeanor transformed by the sparkle in her eye—his profound sensation of relief made way for admiration. She had been anxious to leave his company that day, and he wondered if his admiration had been too obvious. It was only after the opera that he was able to feel they had restored their budding friendship to some sort of equilibrium.

The Answorth residence was smaller than Lady Berkley's but it did possess a ballroom that was not to be despised for a London house. He glanced around at the modest ivory columns that created alcoves and the broad space for dancing with a black-and-white patterned marble floor. Most of the assemblies had only room for an intimate number of couples, but this event could properly be declared a ball.

The dancing was already in progress, so as soon as he greeted his hosts and thanked Mrs. Answorth for the invitation, he entered the double doors and stood looking around at the guests already assembled. There was Gerry Wilmot, who he'd had dinner with since meeting him in Hyde Park. When asked how the young lady had fared after her incident with the runaway carriage, Gerry only grimaced. He had been unable to calm her hysterics and had gratefully deposited her with her guardian. Next to Gerry was Andrew Barrett, whom he had not seen in years. He walked over to him and stuck out his hand.

"You, here! When did you arrive in London?" Barrett asked him.

"A few weeks ago," Miles answered. "And you?"

"Yesterday. I'd only been away since Christmas. Otherwise, I'm practically here year-round. That's why it's such an oddity to see you here at last. I'd begun to think you'd given up all society, save for what you find in Lancashire." He said the last word with disdain, but Miles knew him well enough to know it for jest.

"He's on the hunt for a wife," Gerry said, too loudly for Miles's comfort.

That was another thing they had spoken about at dinner, and Miles now had cause to regret his confidence. Mercifully, he had not said who was at the top of his list or Gerry would blurt that out too.

He glanced around to see if the statement had been overheard, and the younger Miss Milton turned her face his way showing that she, at least, had. Her eyes widened, and Miles—who didn't think he ever blushed—felt his neck heat up.

"Thank you, Gerry," he muttered, but his friend only laughed. His regard snagged on the elder Miss Milton, who was frowning in a corner. Why had he promised to dance with her? Oh, right. Compassion. It seemed like a heavy price now that he was forced to pay it, especially with Gerry's ill-timed jest.

He turned back to his friends. "Have you seen Rock?"

"Not coming," Wilmot said. "He found out about a fight in Islington, and he's hared off to see it."

"Shame," Miles said. He'd been hoping to ask Rock what he thought of Lady Dorothea as soon as he could point her out. He sought her in the crowd of people and found her dancing with Lord Hastings and stood still to watch, wondering if she could be considering the man's suit. Hastings was almost old enough to be her father. Miles frowned as his eyes sought out Lady Dorothea's fresh complexion. They would not suit. Then again, a distinguished age was not an uncommon allure for young ladies, especially when the man was reputed to be rich and was titled.

Miles trained his eyes over to the other end of the room again. Well, he had better get it over with. He would ask Miss Bernice Milton to dance before he lost his will.

"If you'll excuse me, gentlemen. I have promised a dance."

"Of course. There is no time to waste," Gerry said behind him, snickering. Why had he thought this fellow was a friend?

If he weren't so annoyed, he would find it funny. In fact, if the situations had been reversed, he would be provoking Gerry in much the same way. It was what they had always done.

He made his way over to Miss Milton, who was looking plainer by the minute until she spotted him and her face broke out into a smile. Miles hoped she would find someone who would make her smile more often. She seemed to deserve it, even if his own heart was not stirred to take on the role.

"Mr. Shaw, you remembered," she said with a guilty start, then flushed.

"I did," he said, bowing over her hand. He lifted his head and smiled, causing her features to lift. He would have to tone down his charm if he didn't want to give her the wrong idea.

"Shall we?" he asked. She nodded and placed her hand on his arm.

The current set was winding down, and Miles turned to watch Lady Dorothea curtsying in front of Lord Hastings. Before he had any time to regret he hadn't waited to ask her for the next set, Weatherby was bowing in front of her. How the deuce did *he* know her? He soon guessed at the answer. Miss Stanley tugged the arm of her partner up to Lady Dorothea and Weatherby, grabbing Lady Dorothea's arm in an intimate way. *Ah.* It was through the means of the vivacious Miss Stanley that Weatherby had been presented to Lady Dorothea. Miles hoped not all of her dances had been taken for the evening.

The music began and Miles led Miss Milton onto the dance floor, marshaling his efforts to treat her in a way that was worthy of her. He would not allow his attention to wander to Lady Dorothea, although she was wearing a gown the color of a peach. The underbelly of a peach, he corrected himself, then wanted to laugh at the precision. Her smooth complexion glowed, and her eyes sparkled in the candlelight.

"What activities do you enjoy in your spare time?" he asked Miss Milton, conscious of his duty. He expected a banal answer, for what lady did anything but sew or learn Italian?

The dance separated them, but when it brought them together again, she answered him.

"I enjoy grafting plants together to cultivate new species. I am currently working on an apple that retains its sweetness into maturity without losing its crispness."

The dance pulled them apart again, and he could not help but let his surprise show. He would have to introduce her to Rock's friend, Pollard, who was particularly interested in the agricultural aspect of his estate. They must surely find something to talk about.

"How did you come to be interested in such a thing?" This must be the most unusual conversation he'd ever had with a young lady.

"Well, you must have noticed that I am not particularly valued by my mother or sister." She flushed slightly, and after a hesitation, he nodded.

Once again, the dance separated them, but as soon as they were rejoined, she said, "My father is interested in these sorts of things, so I would trail behind him and the gardener. I suppose it was inevitable that I would find the same sort of interests as he did."

In a complacent tone, she added, "Plants are not mean."

It was definitely the most unusual conversation he had ever had with a young lady.

"No, they are not mean," he said. Another member of the *ton* might mock her for her eccentricity, but he could not. There was not enough authenticity in London society.

That was what kept drawing him back to Lady Dorothea—

besides her portion, of course. She was undeniably authentic, for all she attempted to show a mask to the world. He just feared that if she married the wrong man, the mask she wore would become impossible to remove.

DOROTHEA FINISHED her dance with Mr. Weatherby—another introduction courtesy of Maryann, even if he did also know Mr. Shaw. She appreciated the introductions, of course. To date, it was her most lively Society event since arriving in London. That said, she did not always enjoy her conversations with Maryann. It seemed that she had no thought beyond what sort of attention the gentlemen were paying them—and Dorothea soon understood she meant what sort of attention they paid *Maryann*. Even for Dorothea, who was accustomed to being the less-pretty older sister of Sophia, being thrust in the shade grew wearisome.

She had noticed Mr. Shaw's arrival but tried not to. He danced with Bernice while she was paired with Mr. Weatherby, and despite herself, it touched her that he had remembered his promise to her. It spoke well of him to remember a promise to a woman he was not interested in. Or...perhaps he might be interested in her, but such a thing was difficult to fathom. It was not that Bernice was not attractive. She was. It was just that she did not seem to pair well with Mr. Shaw.

Behind her, Dorothea recognized the unmistakable voice of Abigail Milton.

"Mr. Shaw's friend spoke of his being on the hunt for a wife, then he immediately went over to ask Bernice to dance. Is that not the most outrageous thing you've ever heard of? *Bernice!*"

Not wishing to be discovered eavesdropping, Dorothea held herself still and was privy to the waspish giggles that erupted over this announcement. Abigail was surrounded by a circle of young ladies she appeared to have some influence over. Perhaps she was like Maryann in that way, although undeniably more unkind.

Then the weight of what she had just said settled upon Dorothea. So Mr. Shaw *was* considering Bernice for his wife? That couldn't be. They were nothing alike. She felt a strong inclination to try to go and talk some sense into him. But that would be ridiculous, besides being highly inappropriate.

The Miltons were wealthy, and Bernice likely had more than a substantial dowry. In fact, Dorothea herself had a respectable portion, but it was not what one might call brilliant. Besides her desire to sit at the head of Society, this was one of the reasons she sought a good match. Her own dowry would not save any gentleman from being a pauper. It was fortunate that Mr. Shaw had assured her he was not searching for a wealthy wife, for she did not think she misread his intentions in her regard.

She quite thought she should be happy for Bernice and Mr. Shaw, yet the idea of the two marrying each other was impossible to imagine. Mr. Shaw was a force of nature with his charming ways, and Bernice was too retiring. Dorothea could not convince herself it was a case of opposites attracting one another, for they were *too* opposite.

The musicians had taken a pause, and she looked around the room, hoping for a glimpse of Lord Throckmorton. To date, he was the most promising catch of the season, and she had thought about him more than once since he'd left her house in Maryann's wake. He was almost as handsome as Mr. Shaw and much more eligible. It was not that she had been given any reason to hope for interest on his part, for he had shown her none apart from that one assessing gaze he'd sent her at the beginning.

She supposed it was for the best. Lady Dorothea Throckmorton would be *much* too much for anyone to say without fumbling.

She was pulled out of her reverie by Lady Berkley's goddaughter appearing in front of her.

"Good evening, Lady Dorothea. I hope you do not mind my greeting you, although we were only briefly introduced by my godmother. I am Anne Kensington," she added with the hint of a smile when she saw Dorothea's slightly blank look.

"Of course I remember you," Dorothea rushed to assure her. "It was only that I couldn't recall your name." She strove to recover from her lapse in memory by engaging her in conversation. "I see that my sister has gone back to my mother's side. May I introduce you to her?"

"Please," Miss Kensington said with a smile. "I am not very fond of dancing and would prefer conversation."

"Oh, not I," Dorothea replied, smiling. "I could never grow tired of dancing."

She brought Miss Kensington over to Sophia and her mother and presented her to them. Her mother responded to her curtsy with a nod and some murmured greeting. Her sister curtsied as well and whispered something unintelligible.

Dorothea was disappointed by the colorless reaction of her mother and the shy one of her sister, but she endeavored to draw Sophia in nevertheless. It would do her good to have more acquaintances. After several attempts to include her sister, and even her mother, in their conversation, she gave it up. She and Miss Kensington drifted toward a more intimate conversation between the two of them.

Dorothea learned that Anne had grown up in Essex, the second child of five, four of whom were still alive. Although her mother had married an impoverished gentleman, their family had always been a happy one—made even happier when in a tremendous reversal of fortune, a spinster great-aunt left her entire fortune to Anne's father. This led her to embark upon a season under her godmother's wing without feeling like an encumbrance.

In their short conversation, it did not take long for Dorothea to feel an affinity for her in a way she had not with Maryann. It prompted her to propose they use Christian names, to which Anne instantly agreed.

As the break drew to an end, with the musicians settling into their seats, Dorothea spotted Mr. Shaw walking toward the two of them with what she thought—hoped—was determination to dance with her. He looked too focused to have idle intentions. Again, her mind went to what she had overheard. Surely, his heart could not have been caught by Bernice. She should not care—she knew it. But everything felt wrong about his marrying her.

Before she could summon a measure of good sense, her heart gave a wild thump at the sight of him walking toward her. And it did not cease to thump when he stopped in front of her with that smile of his that was so impossible to resist.

"Lady Dorothea, good evening. And, if I am not mistaken, it is Miss Kensington?" He lifted an inquiring brow as she confirmed it. "I was wondering—"

His words were interrupted by the untimely arrival of Lord Hastings. Dorothea should have been deeply gratified. After all, Lord Hastings had sought her out to tell her—in a way she could only consider to be significant—that he had postponed his journey and would be in London for an indeterminate length of time. And he had requested this second set so close upon the heels of the first. But his presence fell flat next to Mr. Shaw's. His lacked the spark that Mr. Shaw seemed to elicit in her without trying.

She clamped down on the unreasonable turn of her

thoughts and gave Lord Hastings her most welcoming smile. "Is it time for our dance again? I am quite ready."

She nodded to Anne and Mr. Shaw before stepping away at his side. And if she could congratulate herself on her will of steel in pursuing her course to marry a man worthy of her position, she could not quite keep herself from casting longing glances at Mr. Shaw as he danced with her new friend, drawing from her all the smiling rejoinders Dorothea could hope for—if she'd wished for Anne to attract a suitor who must be so beneath her station.

Throughout the rest of the evening, Dorothea passed from one partner to the next. Nearly every invitation had been someone Maryann had introduced her to, and she delighted in presenting her as Lady Dorothea, and then addressing her quite pointedly as Dorothea to show the intimacy of their connection. It had, at least, the desired effect of giving Dorothea a slew of suitors who had begun to show her the attention she longed for—an attention she felt was her due as an earl's daughter. If only Mr. Shaw's words had not stuck with her and caused her to doubt her quest. He had said her worth as a friend, and she supposed, as a prospective wife, did not depend upon her status and title. The unspoken part must be that a gentleman's worth did not depend on that either. Perhaps that was true...but it could hardly be a factor in matrimonial considerations.

Her only unclaimed dance was the last one, and she was mulling over Mr. Shaw's words again when the man himself appeared before her. It took every ounce of her strength not to show him how glad she was to see him. As a result, she gave only the tightest smile.

He appeared not to notice her reserve. "Please tell me this dance is unclaimed, for it is the last one, you know."

She shook her head and softened when she looked at him. She could not help it. There was something trustworthy in him that seemed to be missing in all the court the other gentlemen paid. With them it was pretty compliments meant to please, but which felt empty when heaped on. Or it was polite conversation that did not stimulate her in the slightest. But Mr. Shaw seemed to come to life before her whenever she appeared.

"My dance is still free," she replied.

His answering smile set her heart beating again.

"Come, before there is no more room for us. If the Answorths had not suggested a closing hour for their ball, we would still be here until the sun came up, I believe. As it is, we must make haste."

Mr. Shaw led her to the floor, and they took their places for the dance called the Hole in the Wall. She remembered once again how much she loved dancing with Miles Shaw. Although it was a line dance, her heart bubbled with happiness when she turned around him and met his gaze as they turned back. It seemed that she floated at his side rather than danced. And when their hands joined, it sent a shock through her arm each time. When their eyes met, he smiled at her in an intimate way he did not reserve for others.

Time spent reflecting on this as they danced brought her clarity at last. When she was with him, she felt *seen*. She was not another face to him. She was Dorothea. And that was something she had never known before.

Oh, heavens. She would truly have to guard her heart.

CHAPTER 11

Miles walked along Bond Street, tipping his hat to the few acquaintances whose paths he crossed. It was an effort for him to wear his usual carefree look. The smiles cost him, for he had just received the most unwelcome letter from his mother. In it, she stated that the entire roof of their rambling house had caved in. The worst of the disaster had thankfully occurred in the guest wing, she wrote, but even in her bedroom she had needed to place a dish to catch the drips from the melting snow that had seeped through from the attic above her. And if he'd harbored a secret hope that perhaps his mother might have overstated the case, he was quickly disabused of the notion upon opening his steward's letter, which listed in greater detail the extent of the damage and the estimated cost to repair it. It was not an amount his scant coffers could cover. Not by any stretch.

He had seen Lady Dorothea at times since the Answorth ball, but they had not been given a chance for a deeper connection. At one point, they crossed paths in Hyde Park, but she had been riding with her groom and he was on foot, which made a prolonged conversation impossible. On another occasion, they'd met at a musical *soirée*, and he was almost certain her gaze had followed him as he went to greet the hostess. But when he went to greet her, she was already seated, with Lord Hastings beside her. The sight of them together once again had almost induced him to give up his suit. How could he compete with Lord Hastings?

But then they met at the theater the next night and had a brief exchange during the intermission before they were interrupted. He'd felt the strong tug of attraction that was always between them and suspected she felt it too. She froze as he drew near, her lovely eyes widening at the sight of him and her cheeks growing pink.

With his downturn in fortune, it would behoove him to set about wooing Lady Dorothea on an accelerated path. He knew this. It made perfect sense. But he felt increasing hesitation over the idea. She would never believe that he liked her for herself when he needed her dowry this badly. If at one time he'd had the noble idea to offer for her without touching her dowry, that hope was now as futile as a puff of smoke. He was forced into a position of needing her portion more than ever.

He could try his suit elsewhere, Miles reasoned. There was no need for him to marry into the peerage, he argued to himself. Especially since he strongly suspected his absence of a title would be a stumbling block to her accepting the offer of his hand. It should be a simple matter to turn his attention to an heiress who was less...discerning. It would certainly bring the matter to a successful resolution more quickly.

Miles transformed his expression of furrowed brows into a smile as he lifted his hat to a passing matron he knew. As soon as she walked by, a frown settled back on his features. He liked Lady Dorothea too well to give another woman a thought. He liked the tiny glimpses beyond her façade she'd afforded him. They were by turns vulnerable, playful, and intrepid. She was capable—an incredible woman, really—and yet she seemed to open up to him in a way she did not with other men. Surely she was not indifferent to him. But was non-indifference enough?

"Miles!"

He looked up and saw his cousin almost upon him. He had been too consumed by his own thoughts to notice. They shook hands, and Miles forced his usual cheer.

"How was the match?"

Rock tucked his cane under his arm. "Jem's protégé, Henry Pearce, acquitted himself well, but not as well as Cribb. I lost a monkey. Might have been more except I happened to see Cribb warming up and thought I might limit my losses."

"You do not seem overly put out by your loss." Miles pushed the corners of his lips up at his cousin's unconcerned cheer. How nice it would be not to cavil at the loss of five hundred pounds.

Rock shook his head and turned to join him. "Such a great match must be considered worth it. Where are you going?"

"For the moment, nowhere. I am just enjoying a day that shows no signs of rain or a biting easterly gale." He slipped his arm through his cousin's, attempting to shake off his dismals. "And you? Let us go together."

"I was on my way to White's hoping to find you. I've met your Lady Dorothea."

"Did you?" Miles glanced at him from the side, adopting an attitude of nonchalance as though the news did not affect him. "And how do you find her?"

"You've understated her beauty. I've half a mind to make an attempt for her hand myself." Rock trained his eyes forward, a grin settling on his face.

Miles knew he was joking, but he slipped his arm out of his cousin's. This was pressing on a wound. Rock was the better catch of the two—at least he was to someone of Lady Dorothea's ilk. He had both title and wealth.

"No, no. Don't give me the cut." Rock was laughing. "By Gad you must be in earnest to take my joking so seriously. And you promised no theatrics."

Miles gave a weak grin. "I know you are joking, but... Deuce take it! You've caught me in a wretched mood. My mother wrote to say that the blasted roof on my house has caved in, and Fripley confirmed that the damage is as bad as she says. I've scarcely enough funds to make it through the spring, much less repair a seven thousand square foot, four-gabled roof."

Rock's expression turned grave. "That *is* serious. Must you find a new situation for your mother? Will Penworth take her?"

Miles shook his head, then shrugged. "I cannot let her stay where she is, and I cannot say with any certainty whether my brother-in-law would welcome her. Perhaps Mary will cry, and he will then be only too eager." A bitter attempt at humor.

"Let me help—"

"No, Rock." Miles pulled him to a stop. "It would injure our relationship if I were to be beholden to you. I know you say it wouldn't, but it would."

They walked in silence for a ways, easily dodging the pedestrians since the street was not crowded—a surprising fact for how beautiful the day was.

"Propose to Lady Dorothea," Rock said, glancing at Miles to see how he took the news, unexpectedly attentive. "She must have funds enough to save your estate. Go over the rough ground lightly. A surprise attack, you know. Perhaps such a thing will do the trick."

Miles didn't answer, and he added, "Do you think you have made any headway into gaining her affections?"

The fact that his cousin was willing to humor him on the subject of marriage when he himself was not ready to take the step touched Miles.

"I believe to have done so, but in all honesty can only claim to have scratched the surface of the image she presents to the world. I am far from certain I have scratched the surface of her heart. She does not willingly reveal much of herself."

He fell silent as they walked to their club, realizing that although this was true, there was more. Lady Dorothea...no, Dorothea—he would have to stop addressing her as "my lady" in his head or he would not be able to cross the divide—did not respond to his attention at all in the usual way. It was as though she were unused to being considered the object of a man's regard and possessed no ability to flirt. She was so serious all of the time, as though she carried a weight on her shoulders. And when he managed to make her smile, it caused his own heart to—

Blast. I'm getting carried away. What if she says no?

"So. Surprise attack, you say?" he asked, lifting his eyebrows at his cousin, attempting to lighten the mood.

"Yes. You call upon her, or take her to the park. And not Hyde Park—too many people. You declare your undying devotion and how you've never been so blindsided by love and in so short a time, even if it's not true—"

"Actually, there is some truth to it," Miles admitted, compelled to honesty.

"Well, all the better! A sincere proposal of marriage beats all. You lay out your claims. You are a gentleman. You're heir to an earldom should something happen to me."

"Rock, I beg of you." Miles did not find that funny.

"It is no less than the truth, if only you would play that card." When Miles shook his head, his cousin continued. "You have a considerable-sized estate—"

"—desperately in need of funds, thus the rush to marry into wealth. How soon after declaring my undying love do you suppose I can ask her for the details of her man of business, so we might come to an agreement?" Miles spoke with heavy irony, already despising himself.

"You have always had an effortless charm." Rock slapped a heavy hand on Miles's shoulder causing him to wince. "I have the greatest faith in you."

"*Hm.*" Miles needed time to reflect on how to proceed. He was hopeful of his suit, even though she had not given him vast encouragement. But she was not unaffected by him, of that he was sure. And he knew women.

He quite thought he would do it. He *must* do it. What had he to lose after all?

"So...White's?" Miles slipped his arm through Rock's and directed their steps the short distance that remained to their destination.

HAVING DECIDED to press his suit without delay, it was left only to decide how to go about it. Miles had not caught a glimpse of Dorothea in the three days that were needed to gather his courage to take the monumental step. It was not marriage he was afraid of. It was the potential look of disapproval—which Dorothea would have every right to show him when he proposed after promising her he was not on the hunt for a wealthy wife. It was the rejection that he was half expecting that almost caused him to abandon the idea were he not so desperate.

His first attempt to find her at her home failed, for the women of the house had all gone out, he was told.

Thwarted, Miles set a hand on the iron gate of Grosvenor

Square and watched the traffic as horses and carriages rattled by on the cobblestones. He had come on foot and was tired but did not relish the idea of flagging a hackney. He began to walk to Bond Street before it occurred to him that he had neglected Lady Berkley, to whom he'd promised a morning call. She was one of the few remaining friends from Society his mother had retained. Not only that, but he owed his connection with Dorothea to her. The Berkley residence was not far from Dorothea's, and he decided to walk there.

Upon sending in his card, he was admitted into the drawing room. At first glance, he thought he must be *de trop*, for there did not appear to be a single seat unoccupied. Lady Berkley was not one to turn anyone away, nor did she make people wait in the entrance until some of the guests had left as some did.

Then, a swift glance around the room revealed that Dorothea was *here*, along with her mother and sister. He nodded his head in her direction and waited to receive her acknowledgment. A brief smile flashed on her face before it disappeared and she averted her eyes. He took that as a good sign. It was not often he won a smile from her, especially with a public acknowledgment.

His first step was to greet Lady Berkley and her goddaughter, Miss Kensington, and he presented himself as soon as there was a clearing in front of them.

"Miles, I had thought you'd forgotten about me," Lady Berkley said.

"Never," he responded, smiling at the kind woman. Her welcome soothed his nerves, and her answering smile, his heart. It was never his intention to be false, even when he was teasing, coaxing, or gracing the old and young with a flirtatious smile. He liked when things were pleasant around him, and he liked to contribute his part to making his surroundings agreeable. Surely this could only be a point in his favor for Dorothea.

"I am sure you will find someone here you wish to converse with." Adopting an unstudied air, Lady Berkley added, "Lady Dorothea is here, with her mother and sister."

"Indeed? I shall have to greet them." Miles then turned to her goddaughter. "How do you do, Miss Kensington?"

"I am very well, I thank you." She smiled at him, but she, too, glanced at Dorothea as if she wished to release him. Uncertain, and fearful of making a gaffe, he stayed for a moment longer, but she did not attempt to hold him in conversation, so he turned.

Dorothea had just finished a conversation with one of the gentlemen, who was taking his leave. He knew she was aware of him by the way she studiously did not look at him. He went first to greet her mother.

"Lady Poole, your servant." He bowed before her, and the older woman murmured something in reply. She seemed rather forgettable for a woman who was mother to Lady Dorothea. Perhaps there was some hidden depth to her, for how was it her daughter could have so much character and she so little?

"Lady Sophia," he said next with a bow and his most charming smile.

If he could charm the shy sister, he might make inroads into Dorothea's heart. At least he hoped so. In the few times they had danced or conversed, Lady Sophia's timidity had not managed to bore him in the same way it did with other women. He rather thought it was because she was as eager to talk about her family as he was to learn of it. He had gained a much better idea of what sort of man Lord Poole had been from Lady Sophia's artless conversation, which helped him to understand Dorothea. They had reached a sort of understanding that way— almost a friendship.

He gave Lady Sophia a mischievous grin now, as Dorothea

continued to studiously avoid him. "How is your rapscallion brother...er—I beg your pardon—the earl?"

He accompanied this with a look of feigned regret and it caused her to laugh. The sound of Lady Sophia's laughter brought her sister's head around in surprise. Miles did not waste the opportunity.

"Ah, Lady Dorothea. I am gratified to find you here. I had stopped by your house earlier, but your butler said you had gone out. It is the veriest chance that I have run into you at Lady Berkley's house."

"The veriest," she murmured. She bit her lip and looked down, and he was at pains to understand what she was thinking. How could he propose to her if he did not know whether she liked him even a little bit?

"However," she continued, "I beg you will excuse us as I believe my mother expressed a desire to return home." A startled glance from Lady Poole made him question this and he lifted a brow, which caused Dorothea to avert her gaze.

Why was she so hot and cold with him? One minute she smiled and the next she was running in the opposite direction. It was exceedingly frustrating. For one, he was quite sure she would be falling at his feet if he'd had a title and fortune. For another, he longed to win her for her own sake and nothing else. He detested that his need for money infiltrated any part of his suit.

"Well, I shall accompany you if you do not mind it," he said, shoving these unpleasant thoughts down. He had come on a mission, and he intended to fulfill it. "Have you come on foot?"

"We have," Lady Sophia said. "It would be nice to have your escort, wouldn't it, Mama?"

That surprising young lady stood, and he sent her a grateful smile, after which he directed his gaze to Lady Dorothea. She seemed resigned, which did not bode well for what he wished to say to her.

He gulped. Rather, it was what he wished to *ask* her that was difficult.

When they had collected their effects from the butler—Miles having invented some excuse to Lady Berkley why he couldn't stay—they exited out into the fresh air.

"Mama, let me walk alongside you," Lady Sophia said, slipping her arm through her mother's.

"Very well, my dear, but you needn't hurry us along. I fear I shall slip and turn my ankle at this pace."

"Oh no, I shall not let go for an instant, and it *is* chilly out," Lady Sophia said, moving her mother at a quicker pace than he could have thought. What a surprise it was to have an ally in the quiet, shy Lady Sophia, for he was certain she was giving him the *tête-à-tête* he so clearly desired with her sister.

He offered his arm to Lady Dorothea and set out at as slow a pace as she would allow.

"I have not seen you since the theater on Wednesday night," he observed.

"It is true, our paths have not crossed," she replied in a noncommittal tone.

Despite that, he felt little tremors from her at his side. She would not be trembling if he left her entirely unaffected. It gave him courage. He was considering how to begin when she paused her steps, causing him to stop and look at her.

"I am sorry, I—" She did not continue.

"What is it, my lady?" Surely she couldn't have divined what he wanted to ask her.

"I seem to have a rock in my shoe, and it is making it difficult to walk."

From Dorothea's flushed countenance, he guessed the admission embarrassed her. A wild image of sweeping her into his arms and carrying her home was dispatched as quickly as it entered his head.

"There is"—he looked around—"there is the public garden there. Do you think your mother would allow me to escort you into the park so you might remove it?"

She looked pained—frustrated. After a minute she glanced ahead at her sister, who was well out of earshot. "Will you explain the situation to my sister and mother? I fear it is the only option I have, for I certainly cannot take off my shoe on a public road, and I cannot walk."

"Stay here," he said, with a light touch on her arm.

He jogged forward as quickly as he could to where Lady Sophia and her mother were and explained the situation. They turned back to look at Dorothea, who stared at them with an indecipherable look on her face that he was beginning to be able to puzzle out. She did not like being in a vulnerable position.

After receiving permission for the brief detour in the garden, Miles jogged back to Dorothea.

"Your mother is fretting that you do not have your maid with you, but your sister reasoned with her that it is not likely to cause people to talk. Not in such an open, public place."

Dorothea breathed out. "I hope not."

She turned toward the garden he had indicated that was really just a short distance away. It was only now that he noticed her slight limp. He gave as much support to her arm as he could, enjoying the occasion to draw her near. They approached the black iron gate to the garden that cut across to an opposite street. There were stone benches inside, and plants and trees placed artfully throughout. The park proved quite private, actually, for a public garden. It was the perfect setting for discreetly removing a pebble from one's shoe.

It was the perfect setting for a proposal.

Although Miles could not believe his luck, he would have been heartily relieved if he could be sure she felt the same way about him as he did about her. He would have waited to be sure if he could, but his circumstances did not allow it. It was indeed a trouble to go about his courtship this way, but continue he must. Now, if only she might be induced to accept him.

CHAPTER 12

Dorothea was in perfect misery as she limped into the public garden at Mr. Shaw's side. Her body had betrayed her. Her heart betrayed her. No matter how much she wished to wrestle into submission her reaction to seeing this man in keeping with the decision she had made for her life, her stomach *would* quiver, her heart *would* thump, her face *would* blush. And she was furious about it.

If she had not precisely been able to keep Mr. Shaw from her thoughts in recent days, she had at least convinced herself that it was all for the best. His absence would allow her to focus on her matrimonial goals. On her future.

Not that she was actually given time to do any of that, for Tilly had caught another cold, and this time had passed it on to Miss Cross. As for Evo, rather than listening to any of her remonstrations, he had only caused her more headaches. His latest devilry was to threaten not to return to school, stating that he knew his father had dropped his education early but that everyone liked him so much more than a bore like Mr. Sands. Then, Joanna had walked out alone on the streets of

London without a maid as though she were a common scullery girl.

That last bit brought Dorothea back to the present. How ironic that she found herself in the same position for which she had taken her sister to task. Here. Alone with Mr. Shaw without a maid. She was now seated on a bench in an empty public garden, staring at his back.

He had turned, allowing her to untie her half boot and remove the offending pebble—*how had a pebble made the leap into a laced half boot?*—giving her the privacy her delicate situation required. She tried not to stare in front of her for too long, but one glimpse of his athletic set of thighs and she was reliving the memory of him leaping onto the runaway carriage. And her admiration took flight once again.

What if he sat on the bench next to her? What if he pulled her close? What if he put his arms around her and tilted his head down and touched his lips to hers—

"I am finished."

He turned and held out his hand to assist her to rise, but for a brief instant she was too frozen to take it. The warmth of his proximity brought home the intimacy of the moment and how vulnerable it was to be in his presence. She looked up at him reluctantly, and he smiled, his eyes crinkling, oblivious to her warring internal thoughts.

She placed her hand in his and allowed him to help her up. He did so, pulling her with enough strength so that he had to place a hand on her arm to keep her from stumbling into his chest. She looked up at him, startled as he froze in place, his eyes wide.

"Thank you," she said, turning to break the spell. She cleared her throat very quietly. They had been so close. If she had not turned away, what would he have done? This occupied her mind as she moved forward.

After a couple of steps, he held out his arm. She slipped her hand around it and subtly breathed in whatever it was that made him smell so good. They directed their steps back to the street, but his steps were slow, as though he was in no hurry to leave the green haven in which they found themselves.

He cleared his throat. "Dorothea."

She shot him a look of surprise at his intimate use of her name, but found she liked it on his lips too much to protest. He amended it nevertheless.

"Forgive me—I mean to say, my lady. I wished to tell you how glad I was to see you today. I have... I've been hoping for a sight of you these three days past, if you must know. In fact"— he glanced at her almost nervously, which caused her pulse to race—"I could not help but look for you everywhere I went and endured no small frustration that our paths never seemed to cross."

Dorothea breathed out, her heart beating a wild flutter to hear him all but admit to having a *tendre* for her.

This would not do. It would not do! She must not allow him to go on.

"I don't know what you would have me say to that." The words were out, and it felt an eternity before they had a response.

"Say you will align your path to mine." It seemed to her that he swallowed hard.

She slowed her steps and met his gaze, forcing her expression to show an unyielding front she did not feel. Perhaps he would not force her to the point. *Please, please, do not ask me what I fear you will.*

"What exactly are you asking of me, Mr. Shaw?"

He pulled her to a stop and turned to face her as close as when he had all but pulled her into his arms. He settled his blue eyes on her and she had only to tilt her head up a very little bit to meet them. In his gaze she saw uncertainty and nervousness.

"I am asking you to accept my proposal of marriage. Allow me to express—"

No, no, no! Dorothea wrenched her arm away, turned and marched forward, forcing him to hurry at her side. She set a pace that would not allow him to speak to her, and he did not attempt it as he strode with her.

They exited the park and were on the street, but her house was still another block away. An entire block in which she had to suffer from the discomfort of refusing a man she liked all too well. But she had to put an end to this now and somehow make it to the safety of her room where she could attempt to still the whirlwind of emotions that had stirred in her breast. If only her voice could be steady when she spoke.

"I am most sensible of the honor you do me in offering your hand in marriage," she said, her voice even but breathless. She refused to look at him, continuing to walk at as rapid a pace as she could without exciting any curious glances. It was torture. Wishing to put as much distance as she could behind them before the final knell tolled, she marched on. Eventually, she could not continue to keep him in suspense, even if they had not quite reached her house.

"I am sorry, but I cannot accept it, Mr. Shaw."

"No?" His voice cracked on the word, which made her feel more guilty than anything else. It felt odd to be so far from him when she had grown used to taking his arm. When he spoke again, his soft tone almost broke her remaining will.

"I understand that in my eagerness I have rushed my suit. Can you give me any hope at all of changing your mind?"

Their house was now in sight at last, and Dorothea's steps drew quicker to her destination. She refrained from answering him until they had arrived at the bottom of the stairs.

"I am afraid I cannot give you any hope." She turned and held her hand out to him. "My answer is final, Mr. Shaw."

There was a look she could not entirely decipher, something else in addition to the hurt and disappointment it contained, as Mr. Shaw bowed over her hand.

"Well, then, I must bid you good day, Lady Dorothea." He had reverted back to her title, and when he lifted his head, there was none of the playful charm she was used to seeing.

"Good day," she replied softly, wondering if she would see it again.

Hesitating only an instant, she hurried inside, gulping back an inexplicable desire to cry. She had most certainly made the right decision to refuse his offer of marriage. Even though she didn't think he had proposed because he was in need of funds —she trusted his assurance that he was not looking to marry for wealth—the fact remained that he was impoverished. And besides that, he could do nothing to elevate her position in Society. He would not be instrumental in bringing her sisters into fashion. There was nothing that recommended him to her.

Nothing except attraction and feelings, and those were fickle things, were they not?

Inside, she gave a tight smile to Turton as she walked past him. Noises filtering down from the stairwell indicated the presence of more than one of her siblings upstairs. It would be impossible for her to meet them with any semblance of placidity, and she would not reach her bedroom without having one of them spot her and require something of her. She turned instead into the drawing room and inside found blessed silence at last.

Dorothea crossed over to the chairs in the middle of the room and sat. After a moment, with only the company of the ticking clock and the muffled sounds of household noise in the rest of the house, she untied the ribbons to her bonnet and laid it beside her. Then, she removed her gloves and set them on top of the bonnet and leaned back to think.

Mr. Shaw had been disappointed, and she hadn't calculated how much it would hurt her to have to disappoint him. His eyes had lost all signs of their humorous sparkle, and his face became somber. In his own gentlemanly way, he'd attempted to have her reconsider, but he did not insist.

She had done right to refuse, so why did it feel like she had made a mistake?

No. Mr. Shaw would go on to marry another woman who was more suited to him, and she would marry a peer. It did not matter that she liked how she felt around Miles—that she'd wondered what it would be like if he had sat on the stone bench beside her and leaned over to kiss her... *Kissing him must be nice.* He was the first man to inspire her with a desire to try it.

The door opened, interrupting her moment of quiet, and she forced a smile as she greeted her mother.

"I am glad to see you've made it back. Was Mr. Shaw all that was proper when he escorted you home?" Lady Poole came over and sat on a chair near Dorothea.

"Yes, Mama," she replied, surprised that their mother cared enough to ask about such a thing. She had never voiced any concerns over Dorothea's protection, and she'd almost thought she had none.

Yes, Mr. Shaw had been all that was proper. His proposal had been properly delivered and his rejection properly received.

"Well, I am glad. I did not like to leave you, but I was too fatigued to wait."

Her mother leaned her head back on the sofa, and for the first time Dorothea wondered if she had cause to be fatigued. She had always taken it for granted that it was in her mother's nature to complain or to try to escape doing anything that required her to exert herself. But theirs was not a relationship to ask such a question, so she kept silent. It was unusual for her mother to sit beside her and not seek the quiet of her own room, but stay she did. And just when Dorothea needed her privacy the most.

A knock resounded on the front door, and Dorothea's heart performed a somersault despite herself. Could it be Mr. Shaw returning? Would he sit her down and insist that she listen to his suit? *Would he sweep her into his arms?* She felt wretched enough over having said no that she was almost tempted to reconsider. If he did come—

The door opened and Turton entered.

"Lord Hastings."

Dorothea's heart plunged in dismay. Of all the people she did not want to see at that instant, it was Lord Hastings. Carrying on a conversation with him was like pulling teeth. Each word was wrenched out of him painfully, after what seemed like an interminable wait.

Her mother stood, and Dorothea followed suit, attempting to bring her expression into that neutrality she had so often practiced.

"Lord Hastings, welcome," her mother greeted.

Dorothea forced a smile to her lips as she dipped into a curtsy.

He bowed before both and sent an uneasy glance at Lady Poole before clearing his throat. "I had hoped to have a private word with Lady Dorothea if I may."

Lady Poole's face registered understanding, and after glancing at her daughter, she nodded.

"Of course, my lord. My daughter is old enough that she may speak for herself in answer to anything of a confidential nature."

Don't leave, Dorothea thought desperately, but her gaze followed her mother out of the room. Then she was alone with Lord Hastings. The moment had come for her to receive what she had always wanted. Before having met Mr. Shaw, she would have been crowing with victory at this moment for it could only mean one thing.

"Will you not sit?" she asked him, and took her own seat so he might take his.

He folded his hands together comfortably, absent of any of the nervousness that Mr. Shaw had seemed to exude. It came as something of a disappointment. His would not be an expression of ardor.

Allow me to express...

"My lady, I think you can have no doubt about why I am here today." There was a lack of questioning in his voice but he looked to her for confirmation. She nodded.

"Allow me then to come to the point without delay. I wish to offer you marriage. As Lady Hastings, you will be comfortably situated at my estate and will have a small but delightful society at your disposal there. I confess that I do not spend a great deal of time in London, but your encouragement has led me to believe this is not something you would object to. May I assure you that I am in a position to offer you every comfort you might wish for."

How had she led him to believe she would be happy living in Northumberland?

His speech done, he met her regard. "What answer, then, would you give to my proposal, my lady?"

Dorothea felt cold inside. He hadn't even attempted to take her hand or say her name the way Miles did. This was what she was supposed to want, but she didn't want it at all. And it was not just because he had whisked away any hopes she might have of taking an elevated place in London society. It was that he had laid everything out in clinical terms.

Mr. Shaw had not been consumed by passion either—he had not permitted himself a single liberty. But he had stirred something in her. He had provoked in her a desire to say yes, even if her reason forbade it. She could not say the same for Lord Hastings.

She could delay her response no longer, but she was no closer to knowing what to do.

"I am most obliged for your offer, my lord." She moistened her lips. "Would you grant me some time to think over my answer?"

"Ah." Lord Hastings looked away for a moment before bringing his eyes back to her. "I had been hoping that you would know your heart by now. I have plans to return to my estate at the earliest opportunity. I have already put it off."

"I am sincerely sorry to cause you to put off your visit. I...I will have an answer for you by next week. I appreciate your understanding."

"Well." Lord Hastings stood. "Of course you must have time to be sure of your decision. I will call upon you Thursday next. If you arrive at a decision before then, be so good as to put me out of my suspense, I beg of you."

She curtsied and thanked him, allowing him to leave the drawing room on his own. Turton would see to him. Then she sat down and breathed out.

Her mother would want to know what had happened—would expect that she was now a betrothed woman. Dorothea would have to face her siblings and possibly wait until this evening to have a few moments of peace in the quiet of her chamber. Until then there would be no time to sort through her feelings about having entertained two proposals on the same day, one of which she surely must accept and was yet strangely glad to have put off the inevitable—and another she did well to refuse and could not help but regret she did not accept.

She collected her gloves and bonnet and walked slowly toward the door, listening on the other side of it. The sounds had quieted upstairs, and she deemed it safe to leave the drawing room. Perhaps she might just find solace in her room without needing to wait until evening.

CHAPTER 13

Miles had paced the floors of his room enough to wear down the wood. He knew his priority must be seeing his mother safely settled with family. He could not consign her to living next to a dripping basin. Besides, what was to say the ceiling above her would even hold? The house was centuries old. He knew this was where his attention should lie, but he could only focus on the dull pain in his chest that came from dwelling on Dorothea's rejection.

It was supposed to have been a proposal to save his estate. He should easily be able to move on and woo another woman with a fortune at her disposal. But the mysterious workings of his heart had caught onto Dorothea and could not be transferred to someone else. How could she be so shallow as to wish for an advantageous match rather than one based on affection? She felt the current of attraction between them as much as he— he knew she did. She was denying her own feelings just so she could marry some gentleman of consequence.

And yet, you were trying to marry her for wealth.

Grimacing, Miles sat at last and looked at the plate of cold pork chops that had not been cleared from his table. He should call a servant to do it. Now, with the money he must send to Fripley for the most urgent matters, he was beginning to wonder if he would even be able to pay his shot.

He needed to speak to Albert, needed to write to his mother. Rock had sent a note around asking if he had been successful in his endeavor, and Miles hadn't been ready to respond. He would need to talk to his cousin eventually. And he would have to work up the courage to begin a new courtship with some woman he didn't care about.

He leaned his head on his hand and stared at the fire in moody silence. Today had been warm enough that the fire hadn't seemed as necessary. Soon it would be spring in earnest. It was a shame that feelings for another woman couldn't pop up like new buds in a thawing earth.

A knock came on the door.

"Enter," Miles called out, suspecting that it would be his cousin and was therefore unsurprised when the man walked through the door.

"You've been ignoring me."

Miles shrugged, not bothering to defend himself.

Rock came in and set his hat and cane on the side table, then tugged off his gloves.

"Brooding never solved anything."

"No. That requires money," Miles answered bitterly.

"Turned you down, did she?" Rock asked in sympathy and sat across from him. He looked at the nearly full decanter of brandy at his side and poured himself a glass. "At least you're not drowning your sorrows."

"Can't afford to," Miles grumbled.

Rock raised an eyebrow, and Miles knew he was taking his disappointment too far. It was bad *ton* to be overly gloomy. But what his cousin didn't understand was that it wasn't really about his money troubles. Not entirely, for he had always struggled to keep his ancestral estate afloat. That was nothing new.

This was about Dorothea. She had essentially told him there was no hope she would ever reconsider his proposal. He hadn't realized how much he had begun to imagine himself married to her until he'd asked and was turned down. She was the first woman he had ever met who wasn't waiting to be led for every small decision. If something needed to be done, she did it herself. Their conversations had revealed as much. For him, the necessity of being the strong one in his family had become natural, but how nice it would have been to have someone at his side who was capable. Someone who would be a partner.

It was this loss that disappointed him as much as the desire he attempted in vain to suppress, that of sweeping her into his arms and kissing her senseless.

"She turned me down," Miles confirmed at last.

"If it's your estate you're worrying about, you know I'm good for whatever you need. We're family." Rock sipped his drink, keeping his eyes on him.

Miles shook his head. "You know I couldn't take it. I need to go and talk to Albert about taking in my mother, however. I will practically have to beg the man." He rubbed his face in his hands. "It shouldn't be so difficult for him to wish to care for his own wife's mother."

"He'll do it. Just threaten that Lord Throckmorton will wonder quite vocally about town why Lady Isabelle Shaw is forced to live uncomfortably, when her son-in-law might easily welcome her into his home."

Miles chuckled. Albert was excessively concerned about his image, and he most assuredly would not like that.

"Let's go culp a few wafers. There's nothing like shooting at something to lift your mood."

"Or punching something." Miles sent him a feeble grin.

Rock didn't usually fare well when they met at the boxing saloon.

"No, you may go punch someone else, thank you very much. Bring your pistols, and let's go to Manton's. Something will come to you that will pull you out of the River Tick. I am sure of it."

Miles gave a grunt in reply. It was easier to go along with Rock than to explain that even if he could pull himself out of poverty, he wasn't sure anything was going to pull him out of his lovelorn state.

It took another day before Miles had the fortitude to face anyone else. At last, he ventured out and went to Mary's house, where the butler informed him his sister was out. However, he found his brother-in-law in an amiable mood when shown to the study.

"Miles." Albert got up to shake his hand. "How goes your suit with Lady Dorothea?"

The question caught Miles entirely off guard, and he had the most unpleasant sensation of taking it like an arrow to the heart. He could only guess that Mary had shared her speculation regarding his courtship of Lady Dorothea, for Miles had said nothing to him on the matter other than to explain his request to borrow Albert's carriage that one time. Mary had also witnessed him dancing with Lady Dorothea on two different occasions, and his sister's penetrating eye missed nothing. He had not expected the rumor would reach his brother-in-law's ears, however, much less have the man put the question to him in such a blunt way.

"I am afraid you must be misinformed. I am not pursuing Lady Dorothea. I believe she has her sights set on…"

He almost said *on someone higher than myself*, but thought it unfair to present her in such a cold and calculating light. "On someone else," he finished lamely.

Albert seemed to take this disappointment to heart. After a period of wondering, and exclaiming that he understood, and another spell in which he voiced his regret, he finally finished with, "Shame, shame. Here, have a seat. It has been an age since you've come to visit."

His brother-in-law continued in this jovial tone, despite having learned of Miles's failure in his pursuit of Lady Dorothea. As they'd never been particularly close, he was at pains to understand what had come over Albert. It could only have been some piece of good news unrelated to Miles's worries.

"You seem to be in a good mood," he said at last, taking a seat. "What's toward?"

Albert sat and crossed one leg over the other, the picture of satisfaction.

"I have been asked to take a seat in The Commons, and I have enough support to believe I will win it. As this is a life's ambition of mine, I cannot help but think it is owing to the connections I have fostered in Parliament—and to the advice I give, which several members have been at pains to follow."

"I must offer you my congratulations. That is good news indeed."

Miles let his brother-in-law fill him in on the circumstances of having his name proposed while he thought of how to shift the conversation to what he'd come to say. He feared it would not be easy.

When an opening came, he knew no other way than to come right to the point.

"I'm afraid my visit is not an idle one. I've come to tell you that I've suffered a misfortune on my estate."

"A misfortune! Of what sort?" Albert looked wary as though he feared Miles was going to ask something of him, which of course he was.

"The roof—or at least a large part of the roof of my house has succumbed to the elements, and for the time being, I fear that the house is not quite inhabitable. At least, it is far from comfortable to live there. I have come to ask if you would have the goodness to welcome Lady Isabelle here in London until I sort the situation out and figure out how to rectify the problem."

"You wish to rectify your estate's problem, how?"

Leave it to Albert to ignore his question. "I am not sure as of yet. I am working on a solution. But I fear my mother—our mother, Mary's and mine—is left quite uncomfortably situated. As I cannot host her myself, I have come to request that you allow her to live here until something can be sorted out."

Albert frowned. "It is most regrettable, but the request comes at an unfortunate time. I must see to my election and can't be distracted by domestic matters. Surely you must understand the importance of this period."

"I fully understand you," Miles said, attempting to keep all traces of sarcasm from his voice. He paused while he gathered his arguments.

"But how might it look to your constituents if they were to become aware that your own mother-in-law was living in dire straits while you do nothing to assist her? Do you think they would be eager to elect a man to care for his district when he has allowed such neglect in his own family?"

Miles's voice held a hint of steel. He had come prepared. He had nothing against his brother-in-law, but he would do anything to protect his mother, and he knew his sister felt the same way.

"Are you threatening me?" Albert asked, his face growing red.

"Of course not, Albert. I wish you every success with your election. How could I not when my sister's happiness is at stake?" he replied smoothly. "But others, such as my cousin Lord Throckmorton, will surely learn of the situation. He and our mutual friends are quite attached to Lady Isabelle, and I cannot be responsible for what public observations they might make."

His threat seemed to work, for of course that was what it was. He would not reach his brother-in-law any other way.

"I see your point," Albert said. "Very well, I will tell Mary to send for Lady Isabelle, and she may stay here while you sort out your estate matters. Do make haste, though. You are a reasonably attractive option for many women on the marriage mart, and you should easily find someone to marry who has enough of a dowry to set your estate to rights. I can't allow any distractions to hinder my political career. I'm counting on you."

"And so you might." Miles stood. "Well, I thank you for your forbearance and appreciate your efforts in caring for our mother. I do not wish to trespass upon your time any longer, so I will bid you good day."

"Of course." Albert stood, and they shook hands. Miles left, feeling relieved of the immediate concern, at least. His mother would not have to be subject to leaky ceilings and moldy walls.

He had not liked pushing Albert into the corner in that manner, but he was desperate enough to do so and didn't think it fair to force his sister to bear the entire burden of trying to cajole him into acting honorably.

A full week passed before Miles saw Dorothea again. He hadn't precisely been looking for her, as he knew this first glimpse was something for which he would need to fortify his heart. When their paths crossed at last, it was in the unlikely place of the Pantheon Bazaar. He had let down his guard, thinking that she wouldn't be found in a place like this, so filled with common people.

He had come in an attempt to distract his mind and lose

himself in watching the motley set of people and looking over the accessories that could be bought for shillings. As he gently elbowed his way through the crowds of people standing over tables and examining the articles on offer, Lady Sophia turned and spotted him, causing him to stop dead in his tracks and turn his eyes to the figure next to her, his heart pounding.

Lady Sophia's eyes lit with a smile, and she nudged her sister, who was talking to Miss Kensington. Dorothea turned with a startled look then turned away again just as quickly. When he arrived in front of them a moment later, she pivoted back to face him. Her face was flushed as she dipped into a curtsy.

"Good day, Lady Dorothea." Miles bowed, wishing their meeting could have some of the ease they had had before. If he had not found her entirely forthcoming at the beginning of their acquaintance, now he felt entirely out in the cold.

"Lady Sophia," he added, bowing to her sister. She smiled and dipped her eyes. Last, he greeted Miss Kensington.

She returned the greeting and said, "I am afraid I was just bidding Lady Dorothea and Lady Sophia farewell. I have a prior engagement with my godmother and must not tarry."

Miss Kensington handed her package to her maid. "I will see you both tonight," she said with a small wave and nodded to Miles before leaving them. He stood, almost motionless, unable to move on but unsure what to say.

"Mr. Shaw, how good it is to see you," Lady Dorothea remarked in a colorless voice. He wished he knew if she found this meeting as difficult as he did. If she did, it would allow him to feel hope.

"It is indeed a pleasure," he replied.

Although the pleasure he spoke of was more akin to torture. In the week that had gone by—even when it had included two intimate *soirées* dancing with very lovely young ladies—he had not been able to convince his heart that his proposal was a mere practical one. He had tried, certainly. But his reluctance to enter into any other suit, no matter how desperate his situation, had proven him otherwise.

They might have stood like that, immobile and awkward, were it not for the unlikely assistance of Lady Sophia.

"Would you care to walk with us? Or..." She stopped and looked at her sister, as though hoping for help. Dorothea remained silent. "Or perhaps you have other things you might wish to do."

If Miles had wanted a perfect excuse handed to him to escape their company and lick his wounds in private, this was it. Furthermore, it would be a chance to send a sharp message to Dorothea that if she did not wish for him as a husband, she might not have him at all. The loss would be hers. He would find someone else who considered him worthy.

For, despite his state of relative poverty, Miles had never doubted his own worth. He had never struggled with thinking that it came from wealth or position. It would be gratifying to send her that message and hope that the next time their paths crossed, it was while he was escorting a very beautiful woman —one who happened to appreciate him.

However, there was something in the way Dorothea looked at him, as though she expected him to refuse. He thought he saw regret there. It was the glimpse of this more vulnerable emotion that caused him to shake his head and smile at Lady Sophia.

"If my company is agreeable to you, then I am happy to give it."

He knew he had made the right decision when he saw a tiny smile light on Dorothea's face. Even if she were not interested in marrying him, it appeared she did not wish to sever their ties entirely.

Lady Sophia nodded once. "If you will excuse me, I wish to look at the ribbons here, for I believe I spied a blue one in just the shade I need." She did not wait for an answer but tucked herself into the crowd of women around a table displaying ribbons. Miles and Dorothea looked at each other.

"I did not expect to see you here," Miles said.

Dorothea lifted her eyes then dropped them to his cravat, where they remained fixed. She was far from the haughty woman he had met that first night.

"And would not have come if you had known you would find me here, I suppose."

Miles glanced at the crowds. Although people circulated around them, it was noisy enough that he thought he could risk saying what was really on his mind. After all, he was rather sure he perceived a hint of regret over her refusal.

"I am not quite as mercenary as you must think me." Miles leaned in slightly to make sure this was not overheard, adding softly, "I am disappointed. I will own to that. But I wish to be a friend. I like you, you see."

To his surprise, Dorothea's eyes took on a sheen of moisture. She breathed in and looked away. After blinking and controlling her features in a manner he was coming to recognize as a desperate attempt to keep her vulnerabilities hidden, she turned back to him.

"I appreciate your friendship, Mr. Shaw, and must tell you that I am glad not to lose it altogether."

"Then call me Miles, please," he said, offering her the first smile of the day. It was probably the first smile he'd given in a week, and the unused muscles made his cheeks feel like they were cracking. By way of answer, Dorothea gave a barely perceptible nod.

Lady Sophia returned with her treasured ribbon. "I have

found the very one, and it was only two shillings. Can you believe it?"

"That is a good deal," Dorothea said. She inhaled deeply, as though she had forgotten to breathe before. "Was this all you needed?"

Her sister nodded. "And it is growing more crowded here by the minute. I know you will think me foolish, but..."

"You are ready to return to the carriage," Dorothea finished with an understanding smile, then glanced at Miles.

He held out an arm for each of them. "Allow me to escort you then. I shall see that no one crushes a single fold of your gown."

"An impossible promise to fulfill, but a noble one," Dorothea said, smiling in a way more akin to the woman he had just been coming to know before he had rushed his proposal.

He was relieved that she was not completely lost to him, but it was also something of a sweet torture. That he needed a wealthy wife was indisputable. That he wished to win her on fair and open terms was no less so. But with Dorothea so near, he was not sure he was going to have the heart to pursue anyone else.

"Impossible, you say? Ah, but my lady, I am nothing if not ambitious," he replied laughingly, then he cut it short.

Really, Miles. Ambitious? He felt like groaning over his poor choice of words, but summoned another smile and sought another topic of conversation, which he soon hit upon. After all, it was what he did best. He charmed and entertained members of the *ton*.

That's what poor gentlemen did when living on the fringes of Society.

CHAPTER 14

After leaving the bazaar, Sophia was content to look through the window of the carriage and keep her own counsel, which left Dorothea in blessed silence to think over what had just occurred. She had seen Miles for the first time since she had turned him down. She was still certain she had done the right thing—fairly certain. It did not change a thing that the sight of him made her the happiest she had been in a week. Yes, he was reassuringly solid in a mass of people one might easily get crushed in. Yes, he smelled divine. Not overly perfumed, but rather simply clean and inviting. And yes, the offer of his friendship was a balm to her heart. She had thought it too late for any such thing.

But the fact remained that he was ineligible. Absolutely nothing would change that. She had not been raised her entire life the daughter of an earl just to settle down with a plain Mr. Shaw (who was really not very plain at all) who had no connection to the peerage. With her father gone and her mother dependent on her for everything, she was for all intents and purposes the head of the family. She needed a husband who could assume that role.

Dorothea had been given a reprieve in answering Lord Hastings, for he had sent word that he was obliged to visit one of his holdings. He would return in a fortnight in anticipation of her answer, which he hoped would be favorable. With a man like Lord Hastings at her side, she could take her place in Society and help her sisters all find the right husbands. It was the most logical step to take for a woman of her position.

But with Miles, she might enjoy his friendship without guilt. And she would certainly reward such faithfulness when she was married by continuing to invite him to her *soirées*, thus elevating his position into her orbit. It was the least she could do.

What she could not do was to marry him.

It was a most unfortunate thing that her heart would not obey the dictums of her mind, for it foolishly fluttered and flopped about when near him. Why, she had been at the greatest risk of bursting into tears when he had said he liked her. Had anything ever been so ridiculous?

"I was thankful Mr. Shaw came when he did," Sophia said. "The bazaar was beginning to be too crowded for my comfort."

"And mine," Dorothea said. She wondered if he would be at the Grenvilles' ball. Anne Kensington had told her she had also received an invitation, and she was glad they would enjoy it together. Anne was the closest thing she had to a female friend. In many ways, she thought just as Dorothea did. And as it was Anne's second season, she also knew more people in the *ton* than Dorothea did.

In the meantime, there must be Almack's to get through, and the ongoing search for a man who was her equal in every way, in case she decided Lord Hastings would not suit. The pickings had been surprisingly slim. Besides Lord Hastings, she had been passed over by Lord Peregrine, had been briefly assessed by Lord Throckmorton—and, she supposed, to have been found wanting, for he did not follow it up with an invitation to dance—and had danced once or twice with Sir Barrett. As for the rest of the *ton*, she had yet to form any meaningful connection with a single gentleman of note. It was as though she were invisible to them.

It was her third time attending Almack's, and as she had never seen Miles there, she could only assume his status in the *ton* was not high enough to be awarded a voucher. It was probably for the best. At least she knew her nights at Almack's would be free of fluttery distraction in her quest for matrimony.

On Wednesday night at the peak fashionable hour—none too early, but well before the doors would close to any late arrivals at eleven o'clock—Dorothea led her sister and mother through Almack's hallowed doors. She gave a quick glance around and spotted faces who were familiar to her. The Miltons were present, as were the Berkleys, and she was now on nodding terms with four of the patronesses. A few of the gentlemen who had been introduced to her and could be depended upon to ask her to dance were present. Even Maryann Stanley had been given a voucher, showing that she had more than simply wealth to recommend her.

Dorothea cast a casual gaze at the entourage around the heiress and sucked in a short breath, her heart beginning to race as soon as the sight impressed itself upon her mind. It could not be! *Miles was here!*—standing in Maryann's circle of swains, next to Mr. Weatherby and Mr. Pollard. Dorothea quickly turned her face away before he could see her. How dreadful to be caught looking.

Next to her, Sophia and Lady Poole were caught up in conversation with Lady Milton, as Anne Kensington spotted her from her godmother's side and moved forward to greet her.

"You are here at last." She smiled conspiratorially.

Dorothea slipped her arm through Anne's, happy for an

excuse to escape Mrs. Milton. Desperate to hide from Miles for reasons unknown to herself.

"Indeed I am. You cannot think I would miss a night at Almack's." She darted the quickest glance again at Miles, then turned away with determination.

"I know. The match that must be made in your very first season," Anne teased. She knew Dorothea's feelings on the matter and had even seemed to understand, although she professed herself in no hurry to become riveted. That, in fact, was the only point upon which they disagreed.

They discussed who had already arrived and who was likely to come, and Dorothea was proud of herself for studiously not looking once in the direction of Miles Shaw.

"Did you hear that Lord Throckmorton has become the Earl of Pembroke?" Anne whispered, pulling her closer. She glanced over to where Maryann stood, and Dorothea knew why. That was where his particular friends were. She would likely have wondered at Lord Throckmorton's absence if Miles had not been there distracting her.

"Indeed? That is fortunate for him," Dorothea said. She wished she could summon more interest over the matter and think about his potential as a suitor, but the news felt flat.

"His grandfather died two days ago, which is why he is not here," Anne added. "He will be in mourning now, which takes him out of the sphere of eligible bachelors for this season."

"Do you know if he was close to his grandfather?" she asked, testing her heart. No, she felt nothing for Lord Throckmorton. She did not care whether he pursued her or not, despite being handsome and supremely eligible.

"I do not know. I hope the loss will not weigh on him too heavily. And you know, of course, what that means?" Anne waited until Dorothea shook her head and met her gaze for enlightenment.

A crease appeared between Anne's brows. "Do you not? I was sure you would, as you and Mr. Shaw are particular friends, I believe. It means that Mr. Shaw is now the next heir to the earldom should anything happen to his cousin."

The shock was too great for Dorothea to comprehend. "Why...what can you mean? Mr. Shaw? Miles Shaw?"

Anne pulled away to look at her. "Of course! Did you not know, then, that he and Lord Throckmorton—that is, Lord Pembroke—were cousins?"

Dorothea swallowed over a dry throat. "I did not know it. He never mentioned such a thing." It shouldn't have come as such a shock that he would withhold the information from her, but she had thought them better acquainted. It was...disappointing to know they were not.

"Are you quite sure?" she asked.

"Quite. I understand he has an aversion to boasting about his relations and does not think a great deal of the peerage." Anne pulled her away from a woman who had drawn near, seemingly for no other reason than to eavesdrop.

"My godmother has told me everything," Anne leaned in to whisper. "Apparently she and his mother were quite close when they were younger. His mother was the Earl of Pembroke's daughter, and she married an impoverished gentleman for love. Her father cut her off without a groat. Can you imagine such a thing?"

Dorothea had trouble finding the words and just shook her head as she bent to listen, so Anne went on. "Indeed. It was the talk of the town. Lady Isabelle Shaw disappeared from Society. By all accounts, Lord Throckmorton could have given Miles the cut at Harrow when he discovered they were related. Instead they became inseparable. You must have noticed that they are forever in each other's company."

"I have never once seen them together," Dorothea said in

little more than a whisper. She glanced at Miles now. He was the grandson of an earl. How could she not have known it? So their station was not so very removed after all. This must be why he seemed to have such an ease in Society, and why he appeared to know everyone. But why had he not told her as much if he was so bent on winning her heart?

Would it have made a difference? she asked herself.

The fact that it would have done so filled her with shame, for Miles was no longer a faceless peer—or heir to a title—that she was attempting to win. He was a gentleman she esteemed, though she had not considered him suitable as a husband. He was still impoverished, she reminded herself. But the conditions and restrictions she had imposed upon herself for what she declared suitable were becoming increasingly difficult to remember.

At that moment, Miles glanced her way. She could not take her eyes off him as he came over to them. Had he been laughing at her when she refused him over his supposedly low station?

"Good evening, Lady Dorothea, Miss Kensington. I shall hope to persuade each of you to dance with me, if I may."

Dorothea held her breath. At last they would have a chance to talk about this amazing development and what he thought of it. She might be tempted to give him a piece of her mind.

Miles pulled his gaze from her to Anne. "Miss Kensington, are you free for the next set?"

Anne sent Dorothea a quick, hesitant glance. "I am."

She set her hand on his arm and allowed him to lead her over to where a few couples were waiting for the next set to begin.

A stab of pain went through Dorothea, and she swallowed, turned up the corners of her lips, and lifted her chin. She pasted an artificially bright smile on her face and looked around for her sister. All that was needed was a little time to recover, and everything would be well. It was natural that he should wish to dance with Anne when she had turned down his proposal. Of course he had every right to set his sights elsewhere.

It was only that the rejection of being overlooked by Miles was compounded by the fact that his promise to dance at some point in the future seemed more an attempt to appease than a real desire to dance with her.

There was Sophia. She would go to her and steady her nerves in her sister's quiet company. *Ah!* But no. Sophia was being led over to the dance floor. With nowhere to go, Dorothea's smile faltered, and she had the terrifying sensation of being on display.

A few feet away, Maryann Stanley was—surprisingly—not dancing and had just dismissed one of her suitors. After a second's hesitation, Dorothea went over to join her.

Maryann fanned herself vigorously. "Dorothea, are you not dancing either? I made up my mind that I shall not dance tonight, but now that I have turned the gentlemen down, I am already beginning to regret it."

She seemed to be waiting for a response, so Dorothea obliged. "Why is it you are not dancing?"

"I wanted to do a little test to see which one of my suitors would be the most distraught over my refusal. But my ploy has fallen flat." She stamped a little foot and laughed. "I had most hoped that Mr. Shaw would wish to stay by my side, but he has taken Anne Kensington to dance. And she is so plain!"

Dorothea wrestled with displeasure over Maryann's wish for Miles's attention and also disliked the dismissive way she spoke of Anne. She could not voice any objection to the former, but she did address the latter.

"I am afraid you must not say such things in my presence. I am attached to Anne and don't wish to hear ill of her."

Maryann slipped her arm through Dorothea's. "Oh no, I

don't mean anything by it. But have you heard the news about Mr. Shaw? The grandson of an earl! I could never have guessed such a thing. I had been at pains to discourage his attention, but now you may be sure I shall do no such thing."

"Why had you discouraged him?" Dorothea asked, a funny buzzing beginning in her head.

"Why, the man has not a farthing to his name. My father warned me about him."

Maryann directed Dorothea's gaze to a man on the far side of the room with a florid complexion. He appeared to be deep in conversation with an attractive woman well out of her first blush of youth. His eyes were firmly fixed below her face.

"Papa has come tonight, as he does not trust my Aunt Florence to find me a suitable husband. He detests these social gatherings."

"You said once that your father knew mine," Dorothea said. She had not dared to ask before, and she supposed it was from an odd fear of what she might find out. Tonight, she was feeling reckless. "In what capacity?"

"Oh, you know gentlemen." Maryann's eyes flitted about the room as though in search of a more interesting companion than Dorothea. "You know what sorts of things interest them. I believe they frequented the gaming clubs together, as well as establishments with women of low repute. The two of them were quite favorites there, I assure you."

Dorothea's eyes went wide, and she couldn't stop the heat from stealing into her cheeks. "Maryann, I am surprised you know of such things, much less will speak of them—and of your own father, as well."

Maryann darted a surprised look at her. "Oh, are you shocked? I had not taken you to be quite such a... Quite so particular. Your father certainly wasn't."

She dropped her fan to her side and looked at Dorothea as though explaining something to a child.

"Why, this is the way all of Society acts, although I suppose you are being wise in pretending to know nothing of it. One must feign ignorance until one is married. However"—she lifted her lips in a smirk—"once one is married, one might not only admit to knowing things, one might also be more free in the company she frequents." Her knowing smile left no doubt in Dorothea's mind as to what she meant.

She had heard of occasions when even women were unfaithful to their vows, but she suffered a shock to hear it spoken of so openly. And this from a girl who was no older than she was herself. Her father's infidelity was also the greatest reproach she'd had against the late earl.

She knew she should not be so transparent but could not seem to help herself when she asked, "And you—did you know my father?"

Maryann sent her a saucy look. "Of course I did. He was not above flirting with me, although he was an earl, and my father a mere gentleman. Papa invited me to his dinners whenever it suited him, because he said I made everything much more interesting for his guests. I suppose he did not raise me in the usual way, but I do not care."

She shrugged. "My father is accepted everywhere in Society, and he sets no store by walking the straight and narrow, as he calls it."

Dorothea began to feel ill. "I cannot listen to this. You will please excuse me," she said, turning away.

"What?" Maryann whispered in a sharp tone, stopping Dorothea in her tracks. Against her judgment, she turned.

"You think to judge me, but you had better think twice. It matters not that you are the daughter of a peer if your own father did not bring you into Society. Lord Poole cannot have cared about your place in it if he did not trouble to bring you to London. But he spent plenty of his evenings at our house when he was here."

Dorothea turned and walked away—disappointment and hurt leaving a bitter taste in her mouth. It would be impossible to leave Almack's this early without raising conjecture, even though all she could think about was the sanctity of her bedroom. But Sophia was dancing, and her mother was still in conversation with Lady Milton. And Miles, of course, was dancing with Anne.

She found a seat near the wall and held herself rigidly upright, her hands placed in a deceptively casual position on her lap. She might not be able to remove the flush from her cheeks, but she *could* refrain from crying or giving Maryann the satisfaction of thinking she had any power by running out of the room.

The rest of the set was the most miserable stretch of time Dorothea remembered enduring. A few gentlemen walked by but none of them knew her or seemed to look at her twice. Young ladies walking arm in arm sent her a pitying glance. To be sitting quite alone was the pinnacle of wretchedness.

What Maryann had said about her father was true. He could not have cared about her at all. She knew deep in her heart he had not.

She swallowed and lifted her chin a notch. Miles and Anne talked together in between sets and looked completely at ease, as though they belonged together. Anne would surely fall under his spell. Who could not? And even if Miles did not end up seeing Anne for the woman of worth she was, Maryann had now set her designs on him. Dorothea could see that a woman like Maryann would be difficult for a warm-blooded male to resist if she decided to turn her full attention on him. There was a fullness to her that men must be particularly drawn to. And of course, her victim would not discover her true nature or suspect that she might play him false until it was too late.

If only Dorothea could warn Miles about this. She glanced at him as he led Anne back onto the floor for a second dance. No. It was impossible. She had lost her chance to do that. Had lost all claims to anything more intimate than friendly acquaintances when she turned down his offer of marriage.

It was beginning to become more difficult to remember why she had.

CHAPTER 15

B y the time Miles wished to ask Dorothea to dance, he could no longer find her. He had meant to do so right after asking Miss Kensington, and the only reason he hadn't asked her first was to save his pride. But when he led Miss Kensington back to Lady Berkley, she then introduced him to a young maiden who had only been solicited once, and of course Miles had to do the honorable thing and stand up with her. He had already given the two dances after that away, so by the time he was ready to ask Dorothea, she and Lady Sophia were gone.

Miles hired a hackney to take him back to the hotel. It would be foolish to walk as parts of the path back to his rooms were subject to footpads. He sank into the squabs and thought about Dorothea as the carriage drove him over the rough road. He had seen a stricken look in her eyes when he turned to Miss Kensington first, and that was what he could not get out of his mind.

This was also how he knew he still harbored feelings for her. He could not yet say if those feelings were love. How could he, when she was so reserved with him? His feelings were only based on what he suspected was there, and that was all he had to go on. Perhaps they also sprang from the desire to see her come out of her shell, and to know she had done so at his coaxing.

However, as much as he tried to convince himself that his feelings did not run so deep, he tossed in his bed that night because of her stricken look. Should he try again?

No! Miles could no longer stay in bed, so he got up and paced. No. He was resolute. His intentions were not entirely pure in her regard, for he still needed her dowry. Never mind that she had been proud. He had been grasping. He would not attempt to win her again until he could do so on his own merit. And that meant never.

The next day, Miles went to visit Rock in his old quarters as he would not be taking up residence in their grandfather's London house until the testament had been read.

His cousin was sitting in his study, unusually somber, sifting through papers of some kind. He looked up when his servant announced Miles, then came over to shake his hand. He was wearing the stark black of deep mourning, and his greeting was more subdued than Miles had ever seen it.

"When is the reading of the will?" Miles asked him.

"Tuesday next. I don't suppose you got summoned." Rock peered at him with curiosity. "Or your mother? I have been wondering about that."

Miles chuckled softly. "No. But then I did not expect it, so it did not come as a disappointment."

"Sit," Rock said, indicating a plush leather chair. His London house was infinitely better than Limmer's. He poured two glasses of brandy and handed one to Miles. "You will think me naïve, but you see, I *am* surprised. I had always hoped that your mother would be remembered at the very end."

"Mother is wearing mourning. She has written to tell me of

it, but I will not be hypocritical and wear it myself. I never met the man, although he was a blood relation."

"Besides," Rock added wryly, "how are you going to be able to woo an heiress if you are unable to dance with her?"

"Precisely," Miles said and lifted his glass. His sense of humor was of a bitter nature, however. The weight of having to marry a woman for her wealth felt increasingly wrong to him. Besides, after finding one he liked, anyone else would be a poor substitute. To continue on that path would make him truly mercenary. He shook off the black thoughts.

"So what will you do now?" Miles asked him.

"I suppose it will be a good excuse not to have to dance at every assembly. But I don't see myself precisely keeping from the clubs because of mourning." Rock set his glass on the polished round table next to him. "But I will miss the old man. I am sorry to say it. I don't like to talk about it with you, considering you did not have quite the same relationship." He glanced at Miles.

"It is not an altogether happy subject to dwell upon, I suppose," Miles said. "But you at least had your grandfather—our grandfather, if you must—while I was able to grow up with my father, which is something you did not have. I suppose it all works out in the end, although it would have been nice to have at least met my grandfather once."

"I think he loved your mother and felt betrayed," Rock said. "I suspect he was so shocked that she went against his will that he just decided she no longer existed for him. If she had been a son, he might be able to cut him out of part of his inheritance, but he would not have been able to touch the earldom."

"And if my mother had been born a son, I would not be here, and you would likely be a barrister."

"So I suppose in the end it is better for both of us." Rock took another sip of his drink. "And Lady Dorothea?"

Miles breathed in and folded his arms. "I saw her last night at Almack's. I asked her friend to dance right in front of her. Miss Kensington." He twisted his face in a grimace. "And then Lady Dorothea left before I could ask her."

"Spite, do you think?" Rock asked. "After all, she turned you down."

"Perhaps there was some of that," Miles admitted. "Perhaps I just wished to show her what she was missing by not having my undivided attention as she once did. I would not be unhappy to have my mind free of her if such a thing could be done. As I suspect it cannot, I would not be unhappy to have a small fortune. I don't suppose you have any knowledge of how to raise funds on the 'Change?"

"Do not gamble your nonexistent fortune away, I beg of you," Rock said. "I have an aversion to Newgate and would not relish having to soil my hands to enter it and bail you out."

"Ah, it was just an idea," Miles said.

THAT WEEK, he refrained from going anywhere he thought Dorothea might be in an effort to remove her from his mind and allow her to find the husband of wealth and position she so clearly desired. He had grown up with the knowledge that his mother had been completely cut out of her father's life, but it was not until she was cut out of his will that he began to shift in his understanding of Dorothea's situation.

It was difficult for his mother to endure a life of relative poverty. She was on the fringes of society as the daughter of an earl, but she could not frequent society without her impoverished state becoming evident to all. Gentlemen might be able to get away with a coat cut from a less fine cloth, or boots that didn't quite possess the sheen of those whose valet was a master of the trade. But a lady must have a change of gowns for every occasion. If he truly pursued Lady Dorothea in earnest and attempted to wear down her resistance so that she accepted his offer, he would be sentencing her to just such a life.

She was suspected to have a decent dowry, but she did not come with independent wealth. It might be enough to fix up his estate, but it would not be enough to keep her in comfort. He could not do that to her. He would not.

One day, in an effort to distract his mind, he went to a traveling show in Peckham. Apart from the cost of the hackney to get there, he would not be tempted to spend more than a few coins. And it would pull him firmly out of his usual sphere so he could try to free his mind from the endless cycle of desire to pursue and reasons not to pursue. The main traveling theater event did distract, and when it was over, he walked by some of the stalls that had been set up. The sights only depressed him, and he decided it would be better to return to his hotel than to continue.

A crowd formed out of nowhere in the crossroad ahead, and they seemed to be cheering over some sort of mill in the center of it. For no other reason than idle curiosity, Miles stepped forward and leaned in to look. He was tall enough that he was able to get a glimpse of the middle, once he had edged his way through. The fight appeared far from an even one, for on one side was a street urchin who fought without any science but with incredible viciousness. On the other was the son of a gentleman. Even if his clothes had not labeled him as such, his demeanor and manner of speaking must have.

"I'll teach you," he yelled out before getting hit in the eye in a way that made him stagger.

He had more courage than he had skill, and Miles had to admire him. He glanced around the crowd, looking for the boy's friends who must be egging him on from the sidelines. But there was no one that he could see. That was unusual.

The urchin hit him again in a way that caused the boy to topple to his seat. That was enough. Miles had to intervene. The stripling was going to get himself killed if no one stopped it. He pushed forward, and that was when he caught a glimpse of the boy's face.

It was Dorothea's brother.

"Move out of the way!" he yelled, pushing through the crowds in time to catch the urchin by the waist, just as he was about to kick the earl's stomach who was now on the ground.

"Let me go!" The urchin was as vicious as a rat, and Miles set him down and gripped him by one shoulder, easily catching the fist that attempted to reach his midsection as soon as the boy was loose.

"Oh no, you don't. I'm not a lad you can easily take out. I've had my share of fights, and won my share too."

He leveled his gaze on the urchin. "If I release you, will you be gone?" The street urchin glared at him, then gave a nod. Miles let him go, and the boy ran off. He turned to look at the crowd that had gathered, noticing belatedly how ungenteel the fairgoers all were.

"This show is finished. I propose you all go and look at the entertainment that is here for your benefit." He went over to help the Lord Poole to his feet as a uniformed officer arrived on the scene, grumbling about the disturbing of the peace.

"I am responsible for this young man, and I will take it from here," Miles said firmly, gripping Lord Poole's elbow. It took a little more effort and a discreet coin to win the officer over before Miles was allowed to leave with his charge.

Lord Poole spit from the side of his mouth, then wiped it with the back of his hand. "You had no need to get involved. I didn't ask for help."

Miles took no offense at his surly tone, especially since he could hear the hint of tears underneath it the boy valiantly clamped down.

"You certainly didn't, my lord. You were doing a fine job on your own. However, I don't think Dorothea would like to see you come home bloody, bruised, and your fine suit in tatters."

"You know Dorry?" he replied in surprise, his voice suddenly sounding much younger. The boy looked at Miles more closely with the one eye that was fully open. "Ah, yes. You were at our house, although I don't remember your name. I apologize."

"No matter," Miles said, tempted to smile as he remembered the boy's cocky words when he'd been in the earl's drawing room.

They walked on a space and Miles handed him his handkerchief. "How is it that you are here on your own?"

Lord Poole scowled at him. "In case you haven't noticed, I'm not exactly in short coats. I'm old enough to do anything I please."

Miles shook his head with a patient smile. "No, that was not what I meant. Where are your friends? It's not common for a young man of a certain...*milieu* to be wandering around a place like this without friends."

"Oh. I came here with Arthur. He's not precisely one of my friends, but we met at the cock fight last week. He invited me to go around with one of his chums who knows how to sneak into the Royal Menagerie, and I was keen to see what it looks like inside. But then we couldn't get in, and he talked about how there was a woman who had an actual beard at the Peckham traveling show, so I decided I would just come with him this once. We didn't get to see the lady though."

Despite a sort of nasally tone to his voice, the young earl

had started to sound more cheerful. Miles attempted to bring him back to the fight.

"So, how did you end up fighting this... I assume it wasn't Arthur you were fighting?"

"No." Lord Poole's face took on a look of disgust. "He introduced me to that lout who said his name is Rufus. And Arthur had only brought me to meet him so he could pick my pockets, knowing I was a green'un. I know it was so. Except I felt him do it, and when I reached in, I no longer had the half-guinea. So I challenged him to a fight so I could get it back."

Miles absorbed this with an air of serious contemplation. "Only, you realize he has grown up fighting on the streets. It's much dirtier fighting than you'll find at Eton. I'm surprised he didn't pull out a knife."

"Oh, he did. Went right for my gullet, too," the earl said. "But I grabbed it from him and threw it. Told him he needed to fight fair."

"Well done," Miles said, torn between admiration for the boy's gumption and horror at what had almost happened to Dorothea's brother. She would never recover if she lost him. Not only that, Miles had no idea who was set to inherit should something happen to Lord Poole, and he could not be sure she and her sisters would be taken care of.

That led him to wonder if this could have been a planned attack, but he dismissed the idea from his mind. Perhaps, but the most logical thing was for it to be a simple matter of targeting a boy who—despite his courage—was a bit of an innocent and relieving him of his purse.

"Why don't I flag down a hackney and take you home," he said. "There's one just arrived whose passengers are alighting."

"I don't need you to take me home," Lord Poole said. "I will be fine on my own."

"What if I told you I wished to call upon your sister and that since we are going in the same direction, I am offering you a ride?" Miles turned to him with a lift of the brow.

"I would wonder why you didn't have your own carriage and are in need of hiring a hackney," the boy shot back. Dratted boy.

"And you would be wise to ruminate on such a thing, but your manners might be improved by keeping such thoughts to yourself and simply thanking me for the gesture." Miles led him over and negotiated the fare. "In you go."

"Thank you." Lord Poole sank into the seat and leaned his head against the side of the carriage. "I had no more money."

Miles hid a smile. The earl was just as proud as his sister. He quite liked the boy.

"But if you are calling upon my sister, you will need to do better than hired hackneys." Lord Poole folded his arms and closed the other eye.

He *had* liked the boy.

"Right you are. You warned me that should I aspire to any one of your sisters' hands I should not find you unreasonable. But I suppose hired hackneys go beyond what might be considered reasonable." Miles leaned back in the other corner, suddenly feeling tired himself.

"You would be correct, Mr.... What was your name again?" His eyes remained closed.

"Mr. Shaw. But you may call me Miles if you wish."

"Miles. You may call me Evo when it's just us, and Poole when in company."

At this, Miles looked at the earl in surprise and saw that his one eye was open again regarding him. "You did save me back there, and you didn't make a fuss about how I should be grateful to you. Nor did you read me a lecture."

Miles turned his head, and this time he did smile. They rode on for a distance, and he wondered if Evo was realizing as he was just how long it would have taken him to get home had he not found someone to take pity on him. Although, as Miles was coming to know Dorothea's brother, if anyone was able to turn any and all situations to good account, it would be him. He would probably charm, argue, or evoke pity—anything to get a ride.

When they arrived at Grosvenor Square, Miles accepted Evo's invitation and followed him into the house. It had not been his intention to call upon Dorothea—he'd only said that to convince the boy to accept his ride. Now that he was here, he found he could not resist seeing her. He waited in the entryway until the butler could introduce him properly. But in the end, Dorothea, Lady Sophia, and one of the younger sisters came out of the drawing room at the sounds of their arrival.

"Evo, you scared me half to death," Dorothea said. Then she looked up suddenly and saw Miles. The blood seemed to drain from her face. "Oh!"

The two other sisters took over scolding when Dorothea stopped, flustered. But she was only quiet for a moment before turning her attention to her brother and giving him her share.

"I know you think you are quite old, but you cannot forever be leaving the house without telling a soul where you are going." She glanced at Miles, her brows furrowed. "Did...did you have something to do with his leaving?"

He shook his head and gestured for Evo to speak up. The boy got himself into trouble, and he could get himself out of it. He could cover his tracks better than Miles could, at any event.

"You mustn't fuss over me," Evo said, pulling away from Lady Sophia's ministrations, though not unkindly. "You are treating me as though I'm still in leading strings."

"How did you come by the black eye?" Dorothea asked him, glancing again at Miles.

Once again, he held his peace. He wouldn't alienate Evo by

stirring up trouble, but *by Gad*, he could only imagine the palpitations if Dorothea knew everything.

"Come with me," Lady Sophia said. "I will get you cleaned up. Camilla, will you help?" she asked their younger sister.

Miles was now beginning to be sure he had indeed an ally in Lady Sophia, for she always managed to put him and her sister together. It was a shame that her efforts had come after he had decided not to pursue Dorothea. For he had definitely decided not to pursue her. It wouldn't be right.

Or at least he was attempting not to pursue her.

When the hall was quiet, Dorothea looked at him for a moment. She was wearing a gown the color of an autumn leaf that had a gold shimmer to it. She still looked shaken, and he longed to pull her into his arms.

"Would you like to step into the drawing room for a moment? I am sure my mother or one of my sisters will not be long in joining us."

So there was no one at present. Miles did not like the way his heart sped up again in anticipation, but he was powerless to resist the invitation.

"With pleasure."

He followed her in, and she sat on one end of the sofa before silently gesturing for him to sit on the other end. It seemed she had softened toward him, to allow him to sit so near. This was new. More intimate.

"I ran into your brother quite by chance," he explained. "He was at the traveling show in Peckham and had got into an altercation, so I got involved and invited him to return home with me."

She absorbed this, then sent Miles a worried look. "I do not know what would have come of him if you had not been there."

"I am glad I was there." He wouldn't be giving her too many details about what had happened. It would frighten her. "But I must say that your brother seems to have a remarkable way of landing on his feet."

That made her smile, but it didn't reach her eyes. She looked at him, somber.

"I am sorry for your loss."

"My loss?" Miles had trouble following, but all at once he understood her meaning. "Ah. My grandfather."

"You have decided not to go into mourning, I see." Her words were curious and without judgment.

"I am not such a hypocrite." He leaned back and rested his arm on the back of the sofa. She was still far enough away that he would not be importuning her by the gesture.

"My grandfather cast off my mother when she married my father, and he had never had the least interest in meeting me. I will not wear mourning for a man such as that." He glanced at her, wondering if she would understand. Hoping she would.

She nodded. "So Lord Pembroke is your cousin, then. Why did you never tell me?"

He lifted an eyebrow in surprise. "I didn't know you knew Rock. That is—Lord Pembroke."

"No. I mean about all of this." She waved her hand at him. "About you being the grandson of an earl. It seems like it's the sort of thing one would talk about to...friends."

A smile touched his lips, and he held her gaze for a long moment. She considered him a friend. She did have feelings for him—he knew it now. He also knew he liked her too well to exploit them.

"It isn't though," he corrected her. "Friends don't care overly much about position or titles when it concerns someone they care about."

She blushed and looked at her hands, a smile touching her lips. "That's giving me my own again."

A small laugh escaped him. "Truly, though. I would rather

have you like me for who I am rather than who I am related to."

"I—"

He was not to know what she would have responded. The door opened, and one of the Rowlandson sisters—the youngest perhaps, although not Lady Matilda—walked through.

"Dorry, did you hear—" She stopped short and looked at Miles, then back at her sister as he stood.

"This is Mr. Shaw. And this"—Dorothea indicated her sister —"is Lady Joanna."

"Enchanted." He stood and bowed over her hand. She dropped into a curtsy, and a brief smile clamped her lips shut.

"Will you stay for tea, Mr. Shaw?" Dorothea asked him.

Although the temptation to say yes was great, Miles knew it would not be a wise thing to do. The more he stayed near Dorothea—*Dorry*. She did have a nickname—the more he was tempted to remain. And he had made the decision to let her go. His feelings for her had run too deep to pick up his flirtation again, when the fact would not change that he could not support a wife. If he did marry, the woman would have to go into it with open eyes. And he would have to begin the courtship with honesty.

"I'm afraid I cannot stay, much as I would like to. I shall take leave of you now," Miles said. It cost him. He was not sure he would be able to continue to resist pursuing her the more time he spent in her company. Therefore, he would have to curb that tendency.

"I will walk you out then," Dorothea said. She brought him to the door, where her butler was stationed. "Thank you for bringing Evo to us."

"Of course." With a quick glance at the butler, he bowed, bid her farewell, and left. He would do everything he could to keep her at a distance. But he would do it without wounding her by making her think she was unimportant in his eyes.

CHAPTER 16

M iles arrived at his sister's house, having come as soon as he'd heard the news that Lady Isabelle had reached London. After handing his hat and cane to the butler, he told him he would announce himself, then opened the door to the drawing room where his mother and sister were sitting over cups of freshly poured tea. The two women did not look alike, as his mother had passed on her dark hair to him and his sister had inherited the coloring of their father. His mother was still young and pretty in his eyes, and although she must have been tired, she turned her bright gaze to him.

"Mother." He walked over and pulled her into an embrace, only now allowing himself to acknowledge just how worried he had been over her at the manor house. He'd imagined her getting sick from the cold and wet, or worse, getting crushed when the ceiling came crashing down upon her.

"How are you, Miles?" She lifted a hand to his cheek and laid it there, staring into his eyes as though to see the truth there.

"I am well, now that you are here. Good morning, Mary." He

slipped out of his mother's embrace and went over to kiss his sister's cheek.

"Will you take some tea?" Mary poured it without waiting for his answer. She knew he would, of course.

"When did you reach London?" he asked, reaching out for the cup of tea with a nod of thanks. "The note didn't say."

"I arrived last night, but we both thought you might otherwise be occupied. Gentlemen don't generally sit at home in the evenings."

His mother smiled at him over her teacup, and he returned it before leaning forward to take a small cake.

Lady Isabelle was further from the truth than she knew. He had been sitting at home the night before in a most deliberate attempt to avoid temptation. It was the weekly evening for Almack's and he was afraid that if he attended, he would ask Lady Dorothea to dance. He was afraid he would try to make her laugh and pull her close as soon as her arm was in his. But he had already decided he must do no such thing.

"The question that Albert and I have both been asking, and for different reasons"—Mary added wryly, with a subtlety Miles could guess at—"is what are you going to do now?"

He glanced at her, then sipped his tea to gain time. She continued without waiting for an answer.

"Mama and I were attempting to think of a solution, but we cannot do much without your input on the matter."

Miles set down his teacup and put his chin in his hand, rubbing it. He spotted a tuft of cat hair on his pantaloons from one of the animals Mary kept about and rubbed it off.

"The truth is, I do not know." He glanced at his sister, then his mother. Their family was close. They had to be to survive the years after his father's death. Close enough for him to admit he had arrived at *point non plus*. "I have been going over many scenarios in which I might save the estate, and none of them seem to be enough. I don't have a ready solution."

"And your plans for an advantageous marriage?" his sister asked him, exchanging a glance with their mother. They had been discussing it before he arrived.

"I have not found anyone I wish to marry at present." This was a complete falsehood, but he preferred that than to bare his soul, even to the two people he loved best in the world, along with Rock. It came too close to a wound he was attempting to dress.

Mary and his mother exchanged another look, and he was nearly certain Lady Dorothea had been at the center of their conversation. He was thankful they did not say so.

"I trust you to sort something out," his mother said, finishing her tea and folding her hands in her lap. "You have always been a resourceful young man."

He glanced at her gown, which he could see was a refurbished one, although she wore it well. It goaded him that he could not provide her with anything better.

"What are your plans today? I hold myself perfectly ready to escort you wherever you wish to go. It has been too many years since you have been in London."

"We had thought to visit Lady Berkley," Mary told him with a glance at Lady Isabelle. "Mother has written to say she will be in London, and Lady Berkley has expressed the desire to see her as soon as it might be arranged."

"Well, let us go there then." Miles uttered the words with a false bravado, as he was putting himself in the same sphere as Dorothea. She lived nearby, and the last time he met her there he had ended up proposing.

Would she be there today? How often did ladies pay social calls on the same people? He supposed it did not matter if she was there, for it only required him to be polite. And if she was not there, he would enjoy watching his mother back in London society, frequenting the company she had grown up with rather than being stuck in a moldy house, alone in the country.

On the way to Lady Berkley's house, they discussed how the wool carding was going and which tenants were going to remain despite not yet having their houses redone for added warmth. The women of the family had always been interested in the tenants and the people in the village. It was a small enough holding for them to be personally involved in their lives.

When they arrived at Lady Berkley's house, the butler led them to the drawing room, which was less packed than the last time he was there. It came as a shock—though he had half expected it—to find Dorothea present. She was sitting with Miss Kensington beside her, and her mother and sister in two chairs on the other side of the sofa. Miss Kensington leaned in to say something to her, then crossed the drawing room and opened the door.

Miles wrenched his eyes from where Dorothea sat. At the way his pulse raced, he began to fear he would not so easily put Dorothea out of his mind. When he cast his gaze to Lady Poole, he noticed Evo standing beside his mother. The sight surprised him, and he wondered if his presence was forced or if the earl had come of his own volition. He looked bored, but when he caught Miles's regard, he stood straight and nodded.

Lady Berkley took both of his mother's arms and held her at a distance to look at her. She then kissed each cheek, exclaiming how well Lady Isabelle looked, while his mother blushed and disclaimed and turned the compliment back to Lady Berkley. They fell into conversation even before they were seated, and Mary took his arm, steering him over in Dorothea's direction. The two women were not acquainted, so he supposed her goal was to get him close enough so he would be forced to greet her. Then Mary would learn where his heart lay.

She was good at getting what she wanted. At the moment, it was what he wanted too, although if he were wise, he would think the better of it.

"Good afternoon, Lady Dorothea." He bowed and repeated the greeting to her siblings and mother. "May I present my sister, Mrs. Mary Penworth?"

Mary curtsied, and Dorothea regarded her with interest. "It is good to meet a sister of Mr. Shaw's. And"—she knit her brows and glanced at Miles—"is that your mother speaking to Lady Berkley? You are her likeness."

"That is Lady Isabelle Shaw, who is indeed my mother."

Miles glanced over at her as she smiled and spoke to Lady Berkley as though they had never left off. He was proud of her noble bearing and kindness and was glad to present her to Dorothea. "I will introduce you as soon as they allow for a pause in their conversation."

"It does not look like they will," Dorothea said, watching them with a smile. "They seem to be old friends."

"They are." Miles glanced at his sister, who was being surprisingly circumspect. She was usually loquacious, but today it seemed as though she was willing to let him do all the talking. He guessed it was because she still thought he was pursuing Dorothea. He would have to disabuse her of the notion, little though he liked speaking of his dashed hopes.

"May we take these seats?" He rested his hands on the back of one of the armchairs and gestured to the other beside him, happy to be in her presence despite himself.

She nodded and gestured for them to sit, and there didn't appear to be any reserve in her bearing. Perhaps she was perfectly content with their friendship now that the subject of marriage had been summarily dismissed. The thought of it dimmed his happiness.

"Miss Kensington was sitting here," Dorothea added, "but you've just missed her. She has gone to see about tea being brought."

There was still a place on the sofa beside her, and Evo came around his mother's chair to sit in it. Miles wondered again what brought him here, but was unwilling to ask. The crowd in Lady Berkley's salon had begun to thin, and the only other guests present were settled in groups of two or three, deep in their own discussions.

A silence fell among the party, and he strove to fill it.

"How have you been?" He could not be near her without wishing to learn what she was thinking, to see her grow animated.

"Well. I—" She looked at her mother and sisters for assistance. "We are all well."

Lady Poole remained silent, and Lady Sophia was not meeting anyone's gaze, seeming to keep her eyes permanently fixed on her hands. Evo cleared his throat.

"Dorothea is *particularly* well, you might say, for she has received an offer of marriage from Lord Hastings." Evo leaned back and lifted his arm to lay it along the sofa, grinning up at her.

So that was why her brother had come to take part in the conversation. To cause trouble.

"We are every day in expectation of the announcement appearing in the *Gazette*."

Miles felt like he had been run through and he perceived Mary's sharp glance at him from the side. He gripped the armrests of his chair as his eyes went from Evo to her. Dorothea blushed a more fiery red than he had ever seen on her.

"Evo, that is a most inappropriate subject of conversation."

Her words came out strangled. "I have neither given my acceptance, nor have I given you leave to talk about it."

"Well, it is nothing short of the truth. I heard you telling Mama," he retorted, his grin just as wide. "It's going to be public knowledge soon enough."

"That is enough, Poole." Miles couldn't bear her discomfort any more than he could bear the news he had just heard. His tone was pleasant but firm.

Dorothea looked at him in surprise. She didn't know her brother had given him leave to address him intimately, he supposed. Or perhaps she was shocked that he had reprimanded her brother as though he were a family relation. But honestly, the boy would have to learn to have better manners or someone in the *ton* would teach him. And that time it might be pistols at dawn.

"Why should it matter if I do say it?" Evo insisted. "It is not as though I am telling a perfect stranger. Miles has been to our house frequently enough." Dorothea's wide eyes went from her brother to Miles. He saw the embarrassment, the desperation there.

"We are going to have a conversation, gentleman to gentleman," Miles said, standing and waiting for Evo to rise. "Come."

Evo folded his arms on his chest and looked up at Miles with an air of belligerence. He was most definitely testing every one of them to see who would bring him to brook, if anyone. His sisters, his mother. Miles himself.

"And if I should not wish to?" he asked, a challenging tilt to his chin.

"I think you would prefer to hear what I have to say to you in private," Miles said in just as pleasant a tone, "but I will not hesitate to say it here in front of everyone."

Evo stood and followed him over to the part of the drawing room near the bookcase and tall windows. There were no guests sitting on this end of the room, and Miles made as though he wished to show Evo one of the books on the shelf. He would spare the boy any discomfiture if he could.

"It is not gentlemanly to torture your sister, and I think you know that." Miles dropped his pleasant tone and held the boy's gaze firmly. "Therefore, there must be a reason you have decided to do so."

Evo flushed and looked around, and Miles saw a slight tremor in his arms. It gave him hope. The boy was troubled. Angry, perhaps. But he was not completely lost to them. Evo glanced at his sisters and mother, who had resumed the conversation with Mary.

"Dorry does not cease to ring a peal over my head every time she thinks I am not acting quite as she believes an earl should. It's intolerable. *She* is not the head of the family—*I* am. But I have no space to breathe in that house of females, no liberty."

He brought his eyes up to Miles, a hint of his stubbornness returned. "I am only giving Dorry her own so that she will leave me be."

Miles turned his eyes toward Dorothea, who had sent them a discreet glance. She immediately withdrew her regard and focused on Mary, and now Miss Kensington, who had returned.

"I think you already know your sister wants what is best for you, so I won't belabor the point." Miles paused, struck by his desire to protect Dorothea. To care for her.

He loved her. It sat like a heavy weight in his heart knowing he could not marry her. But he would do all he could to ease her life. He set a hand on the bookshelf and looked down at Evo.

"However, allow me to remind you that a gentleman does not seek to embarrass a lady. He must be above reproach, and avoid anything that hints of vulgarity. A gentleman doesn't provoke or display ill manners, no matter how irritated he might feel. If anything, he will become even more rigidly polite when irritated. A peer even more so."

Miles studied the expressions that flitted across Evo's face, hoping that something he'd said had reached him.

"My father, the earl, was not that way. He cared not a snap of his fingers for the ladies of the house. Why should I be any different?" Although Evo's tone was still surly, something in his question led Miles to think he was trying to sort out the answer himself.

"Do you wish to be like him?" Miles asked softly. Evo shrugged, and when he gave no answer, Miles said, "Think about that, for it has far-reaching consequences. You have your whole life ahead of you, and how you treat others will have an impact on how pleasant your life is. And how long," he added in a wry tone. "In the meantime, if I hear of you embarrassing Lady Dorothea in public again, I am afraid I shall have to teach you a lesson you will not soon forget."

Evo darted interested eyes up at him, arrested by his words, and his face considerably brightened. "Will you? Can you teach me to box?"

"That wasn't exactly the type of lesson I had in mind," Miles said dryly. "But yes, I can teach you to box if you'd like. And I shall do so, if you behave yourself and treat your sisters and mother with the respect they deserve. Do we have an understanding?" He held out his hand.

Evo nodded and shook it. "Perfectly clear. You have no need to fear I shall step out of line again." He turned and moved toward his sisters.

Miles followed, impressed by the quick turnaround in the boy's mood. If this was any indication of the heart that lay underneath, Evo would make a fine earl. He had a heart and conscience underneath the momentary displays of bad manners. And furthermore, he did not appear to hold grudges.

Miles was not sure he could have boasted such humility at the boy's age.

As Miles regained his seat, Dorothea glanced between him and Evo with curiosity. He gave her a tiny smile, just as Lady Berkley brought his mother over to their circle. They all stood for the introduction.

"Lady Isabelle, allow me to present you to the Earl of Poole's family. This"—she gestured, smiling—"is Lord Poole. Lady Poole is the late earl's widow, and this is his eldest daughter, Lady Dorothea, and his second-eldest daughter, Lady Sophia."

Turning to Lord Poole's family, she added, "And this is Lady Isabelle Shaw, who, I am sure you will not be surprised to learn, is Mr. Shaw and Mrs. Penworth's mother."

They exchanged greetings, and Miles looked for signs from his mother to see what she thought of Dorothea. Lady Isabelle's eyes rested on her the longest, and he was now sure Mary had spoken of her.

"Anne, I shall need you to pour, if you will," Lady Berkley said to Miss Kensington.

Mary and Miss Kensington had struck up a conversation, and his sister followed her over to the tea table. Lady Berkley gestured for Miles's mother to sit next to him, while she went to join Lady Sophia and her mother.

His mother smiled at Dorothea, sitting across from them. "I knew your father a very little, although I have not met your mother before today."

Dorothea swiveled in her seat to face Lady Isabelle more fully. "Will you be staying for the rest of the season, my lady?"

His mother looked hesitant and glanced at Miles. "I am unsure. It will depend upon whether Albert—my daughter's husband—will find it convenient to have me stay."

"Oh!" Dorothea sent Miles a confused look. "But if he does not find it convenient, you will be able to stay with Miles—that is, with Mr. Shaw." Her voice was inclined upward as though she was stating the obvious and waiting only for it to be confirmed.

Miles shifted in his chair. It was the least he should be able to do—to provide for his mother. How uncomfortable that he could not. He was unable to bring himself to answer her, and it was his mother who shook her head.

"I am afraid it is not possible. Miles is renting a room in a gentlemen's hotel."

Dorothea didn't exclaim outwardly this time, but her face told Miles all he needed to know. The fact that he could only afford to rent a room, and not even a house in the unfashionable quarter showed, if nothing else did, the extent of his poverty.

"That is a shame," Dorothea said, turning back to Lady Isabelle. "It is fortunate, then, that you have a home to return to in Lancashire. I imagine it must be quite comfortable. Mr. Shaw had said it was of a snug size." She looked at him, a smile touching her lips. "Or you said something along those lines."

Miles was frozen. What could he say? He had never purposefully deceived her about his house or its condition. In fact, he had not even been aware of the extent of its condition when he had spoken of it. But this was getting dangerously close to the truth he longed to have out but dared not reveal.

"Snug." His mother looked at him, startled, and laughed. "I suppose it was quite snug. At least, I have always loved it, especially in those years I shared it with Miles's father. But I am afraid it is far from snug right now, as we have suffered a setback. Nearly the entire roof has caved in, and the rain water is pouring onto already damp walls."

She shared a look with Miles that included a wan smile. "We are hard-pressed to find a means to repair it, are we not?"

He stared at his mother, trying to hide the sensation of

horror. Was she trying to put him to the blush by describing their situation so openly?

"We...I..."

He turned his eyes to Dorothea, whose full regard was now on him, her lips parted in surprise, and her eyes glittering.

"Are you?" she asked, directing her question to him in a voice that was as civil as it was cold. "Are you hard-pressed to find the means? There is always the possibility of marrying an heiress. That would solve all of your problems at once."

"Oh dear," his mother said, staring at Dorothea in dismay. "I fear I have been out of Society for too long, and have spoken all too honestly about our circumstances, which is not a thing done. I hope you will forgive me, Lady Dorothea."

"You may be assured of it." Dorothea turned to his mother, her expression controlled, but her eyes livid. "I shall not breathe a word of your circumstances. I should not dream of causing any embarrassment to you or Mr. Shaw."

Miles's heart sank. Any headway he might have fooled himself into thinking he had made in her heart, despite his disadvantageous situation, had been destroyed by this revelation. She would know at once that he had proposed to her out of desperation and not—as he would have liked—out of the love he was now sure he felt for her.

"Mary, would you give me a moment with Miles?"

Lady Isabelle was seated once again in Mary's drawing room, and although Miles had attempted to make his escape after Lady Berkley's house to think through the disastrous disclosure in Dorothea's presence, his mother had gently steered him back to Mary's house, saying she wished for a word with him.

Mary murmured her agreement and left the room, and Miles sat across from his mother. He could not know what she was going to say, but he felt sure it would be something direct and that he would likely wish to evade any questions she might ask. He steeled himself for what was to come.

She sighed and raised her eyes to him, the gentle lines on her face tracing the compassion in her features. "Miles...this Lady Dorothea. You will forgive my asking you such a thing directly, but yours is not a mere friendship, is it?"

His resistance deserted him like a puff of smoke as soon as she mentioned Dorothea's name. He knew his mother would never force a confidence, and—grown man that he was—he had a sudden desire to speak openly. He had been able to think of little else.

"I asked her to marry me."

"And she...?" Lady Isabelle let the word dangle.

"She refused me. She didn't give a reason, but I know her desire is to marry a man of more wealth and consequence than I can boast."

"And yet, she has some feelings for you, I believe," his mother observed tenderly. "She must have, or my disclosure would not have bothered her the way it so obviously did."

"I had once thought she felt something for me." Miles turned his face toward the bow windows of the drawing room. It was a cheerful room, even when the sun hid behind the clouds, but he drew no comfort from it. "Of course, she thought my only motivation for proposing was for her wealth, but that was not true. Now, she is sure of it."

"Of course it was not true," his mother consoled. "I don't believe you could offer for a woman you had not developed a deep *tendre* for. You are very like your father."

Love, thought Miles, then. *A woman I've fallen in love with.*

When his father had died, he felt a grief of the deepest kind.

He could not compare that grief to the pain of watching Dorothea slip from his life. But it was still a crushing thing to lose her. A thing one did not easily recover from.

"I do not regret a single day of my life with your father," Lady Isabelle said, pulling him from his reverie.

Her tone caused Miles to look up at her. He had heard the words before, but this was the first time he'd heard them said with something that sounded like a caveat.

"I do not regret anything, but I am a woman who can be happy with simple things. I am happy in a home where there is bread on the table, and where there is love. It is all I need. I cannot say that every woman in the *ton* can be so content, even if there is love. If you want a truly happy marriage, you will have to look for contentment with little. This, in addition to all the other qualities."

Miles did not answer right away. She was right, as hard as it was for him to hear.

"You are wise, Mother, and I would be a fool not to heed your words." He shook his head. "I will not seek out Lady Dorothea, for I fear she will not be content with the little I can offer her."

His mother made a sound of sympathy in her throat. After a beat, she said, "There is always friendship. It might seem like a poor substitute now, but friendship always has value."

After a slight pause, he shook his head. "I do not believe she wants even that from me."

"I see." Her voice was soft. "I am sorry, my son."

Lady Isabelle did not offer platitudes, and for that he was grateful. There was nothing she could say to improve the situation. Therefore, the sooner he made peace with it, the sooner he could move on.

CHAPTER 17

Dorothea was still enraged when she thought about Miles Shaw's duplicity, even two days later. She did not know quite how she finished her conversation with his mother. Blessedly, it had been cut short because Lady Poole indicated she thought they'd stayed long enough. For once, Dorothea was inclined to agree with her mother.

Miles had lied to her when he said he was not hanging out for a rich wife, she was sure of it. It was one thing to be in a general state of financial distress, as he had led her to believe. When one was impoverished, one might continue to scrape by and attempt to shift one's fortunes over the course of a lifetime. It would not cause a man with any scruples to push a courtship to a happy resolution for financial gain.

However, it was quite another thing to have one's roof caving in on one's mother in a way that could only be resolved through the urgent acquisition of funds—the kind a gentleman could only obtain through marriage. She had compassion for Lady Isabelle, of course, who had seemed like a lovely, honorable woman. Even though she'd spoken with more direct honesty than Dorothea thought quite proper, she was a lady in every way.

Lady Isabelle had not lost the elegant bearing of her youth in all her years of poverty, although her financial state was evident in other aspects of her person, such as her outmoded gown. Lady Berkley seemed to pay no mind to the disparity in wealth, so not all members of the *ton* were quite as particular as Dorothea had been led to believe. She had understood from the things her father said, and did not say, that nothing short of perfection was required.

Nevertheless, the fact remained that Miles had been pursuing her to get his hands on her dowry. It had not been the proposal of passion and love like she'd thought it was—a proposal of the heart that made it difficult to remember why she had refused in the days that followed. It had not been that he'd offered for her against his will and his reason, after having made a point about not marrying a woman for her dowry. No. He was pursuing her with only one goal in mind: her financial worth.

Ooooh. She clenched her hands into fists. The desire to give him a set-down was so strong, she had nearly written to summon him so she might do so without delay. She had refrained, of course, but the desire had been almost impossible to master.

Instead, in the days that followed the revelation in Lady Berkley's salon, Dorothea looked for him in all the places she thought he might be, with the sole object of giving him a piece of her mind. The opportunity had not appeared, despite her efforts, leaving her in a state of constant disgruntlement.

Arguments were stacked against him, and every bit of evidence in her recollection was catalogued to support those arguments. She longed for the opportunity when she could tell him exactly what she thought of him, so she might put him out of her mind and never think of him again.

She was sitting at the desk in the drawing room, sorting through the correspondence and invitations. At last, so many invitations arrived each day, she had to pick and choose and often send her regrets. Dorothea had rekindled some of the relationships with the writers of those letters to her late father, thereby bringing her family into fashion through those old connections. She had done well to keep them, for she could say with something close to honesty that her father had spoken of them in his lifetime. Oh, perhaps it was not so very honest, but he had kept their letters, had he not?

As for the scented letters, she burned those. There was no need to torture herself or dishonor her mother by holding on to them. And when these particular ladies were pointed out to her at the opera, she knew they were to be avoided at all costs. Unsurprisingly, neither did they attempt to seek an introduction. Dorothea was gratified that her popularity had not seemed to dip, despite the distinct cooling in relations between Maryann and herself. Instead, she was busy greeting acquaintances almost everywhere she went. The only disappointment to mar this gratifying rise in popularity was that her mother and Sophia were too reserved to do the same.

A knock on the front door echoed in the entryway, and Dorothea paused in surprise, an invitation in hand. It was not the time of day for morning calls, and they were not expecting anyone to come. When she heard a deep male voice coming from the hall, her heart pounded and she stood suddenly, light-headed as the blood drained from her face. The invitation dropped from her nerveless fingers.

Was it...? She could not resist stepping out of the drawing room to have her suspicions confirmed. Dorothea opened the door, and her breath hitched in her chest. *Miles.*

He went still, greeting her with a hesitant look, a tiny furrow between his eyes. *A guilty look*, she thought.

"Good afternoon, my lady."

At least he did not attempt to use her Christian name after what he had done. Well! It was as well he did not. Her blood coursed with the desire to vent her spleen, especially after days of adding fuel to the fire of her wrath with no avenue for its outpouring.

"To what do I owe the pleasure of this visit?" she asked him at her haughtiest, congratulating herself on how steady her voice was.

"I am here to see your brother." He glanced down the hallway where the stairwell was. "We have made plans to meet my cousin and go to the races."

He has not even come with the intention of begging my forgiveness?

The minute she had caught sight of him, Dorothea had been eager to hear his apology, so she might throw it back in his face. But apparently, apologies were the last thing he had in mind. No! He was here for a pleasure jaunt.

Turton seemed to sense the air crackling between them and murmured, "I will go and inform my lord of your visit."

She nodded and slid her eyes back to Miles. They listened as the butler's steps sounded down the hallway until he turned the corner and climbed the stairs.

"Mr. Shaw, I wish to see you in the drawing room," she said in polite, clipped tones. "It won't take but a minute of your time, and then you may go on your way to visit the races." *Or the club. Or the northern tip of Scotland. Anywhere but here.*

Dorothea swept into the drawing room, sure that Miles would follow. As she strode to its center, the anger inside of her warred with her curiosity over why Miles would be taking Evo with him and Lord Pembroke. The curiosity was unhelpful at the moment, for despite herself, she was grateful Miles was taking her brother in hand. It provided an opportunity for Evo to frequent the company of Miles's cousin—an earl Evo could look up to, and one who had no need to marry for a fortune. What was more, after her brother had come and apologized for his behavior at Lady Berkley's residence, she'd had to work at rekindling her anger toward Miles over his base conduct. Such an unusual apology could only be owing to Miles's influence.

However, none of that changed anything. She had fully trusted him to behave honorably, which was why it had hurt so much upon discovering the true nature of his situation. To learn he had not been authentic was difficult to forgive.

When she'd reached the middle of the drawing room she turned. "Close the door, if you please. What I wish to say to you is of a private nature."

Miles did as she bade him and came into the room to stand in front of her. His bearing was somber and unlike the charming, teasing gentleman she once knew. Dorothea did not offer him a seat, for she did not intend for him to stay long enough. Besides, she was too agitated herself to be able to sit down.

"Did you or did you not propose to me because you needed my dowry, Mr. Shaw?" She held her fists at her side, afraid she would cross her arms—and a lady did not cross her arms in company.

Miles looked away for a brief instant before returning his eyes to her. "I did, but—"

"Thank you," she cried hotly, cutting him off. "That is all I need to know. For all you might have hinted at wishing for a match based on the more tender affections, you have, in the end, acted upon very mercenary ones. You have proven yourself to be exactly like every other gentleman in Society, and I congratulate myself for not being quite so naive as to be deceived by it. Although I was naive, was I not? You must have sensed it and preyed upon me for that reason."

He stepped forward, putting his hands out. "Dorothea, allow me—"

She would not hear it. "Although, you did not precisely speak of any of the more tender affections when proposing to me, did you? I suppose I imagined those all on my own."

To Dorothea's horror, tears traced down her cheeks. She whirled around and swiped at them.

"No, please don't."

His voice sounded in perfect agony as Miles came over and put his arms around her, then turned her gently. With one hand, he wiped the tears from her cheeks and leaned forward until he rested his forehead against hers.

Dorothea was unable to move as his fingers softly caressed her cheeks. Then his other arm encircled her, pulling her close. To be held tenderly was something she had only dreamed of. No one—*no one*—had ever held her in that way. It was more affection than she had ever thought possible coming from a man.

Time stretched, filled only with the sound of their breathing. She grew dizzy from remaining still but not for the life of her could she move. And then he was rocking her back and forth, murmuring something her senses were too befuddled to understand. He leaned down and kissed where her cheek met her temple, and she dared not draw breath.

"I love you," he whispered.

Dorothea's eyes snapped open. After a stunned moment, she pulled away slightly to look at him, her dream coming to an abrupt end. She saw the confusion on his face, but she knew better than to trust it.

He is lying! He did not love her. He had only feigned to, and was pretending still. Dorothea wrenched herself from his embrace and stood back to look at him, her chest heaving. She had been fooled into letting down her guard. It would not happen again—she would be sure of it.

"I never want to see you again." Her teeth clenched, she punctuated each word and watched him receive them like blows.

Then she spun around and hurried to the door, just as Evo was entering it with a broad smile. He looked at her in astonishment as she pushed past him.

MILES WATCHED DOROTHEA RUN OUT, feeling as though he had been punched. He had just told her he loved her. She was the first woman ever to pull such a confession out of him. And that had only made it worse, for she hadn't believed him. There was a moment as the air whooshed out of his lungs, then his shoulders fell.

"What did you say to my sister to make her run out of the room that way?"

Evo walked over to where he stood, and although his question held curiosity, gone was the earl's habitual grin, whether from general insouciance or pure mischief. He glared at Miles, waiting for his answer.

Miles already felt like a cad. He had hugged Dorothea and kissed away her tears. In doing so, he was trying to tell her he was sorry, that he had not meant to make her the object of his pursuit for wealth. But he had breathed in the scent of her hair, had held her in his arms, and it intoxicated him enough to tell her he loved her. What a fool he was.

"I believe you will have to ask your sister about what happened, if she is inclined to answer you," Miles replied at last, in a suffocated voice. "I am not at liberty to discuss what went on between us without her leave."

He wanted nothing more than to quit the premises but held his ground. He had promised Evo that he and Rock would take him to the races. It mattered not whether Evo's sister wished him to the devil; he had engaged to help the boy, so he would.

When Evo stood, remaining motionless and unconvinced, Miles sighed and faced him. "I can assure you, I did not intentionally wound your sister."

Evo studied him critically, understanding dawning at last. "You like her."

"I do," Miles admitted. "But as you know all too well, for you have told me so yourself, I am not a suitable candidate for her hand."

"Ah, well, there is nothing for it but to give her up then," Evo said, reverting to his usual self now that he had solved the mystery of seeing his sister cry, likely for the first time in his life. "Dorry can nag at times, you know, so you are very likely better off without her."

"Is that so? You are probably right then."

It took Miles every bit of his self-control to leave off meditating on the conversation he had just had with Dorothea and to enter into a discussion on the intricacies of racing with a thirteen-year-old who was going to witness a horse race for the first time. He was thankful that Rock would be joining them so he could uphold his end of the conversation.

The day passed more pleasantly than Miles had feared, as he was able to shut off the topic that hovered on the edge of his consciousness at every moment and enter into the enthusiasm for a horse race, which was always interesting. He and Rock allowed Evo to pick the winners, and they lost a tremendous fortune—all imaginary, of course. Afterwards, they examined the various foods and drinks on offer and chose something to eat from one of the stands nearby. Rock drove his phaeton back to Evo's house on Grosvenor Square and dropped him there before riding on with Miles.

"Tell me why you wanted to take the boy under your wing?" Rock asked him conversationally as they headed to the club for an early dinner.

"He needs a father figure, and in absence of that, an elder brother," Miles returned shortly. Without Evo's chatter, his mood had begun to plummet again.

"And you would still like to marry his sister, I suppose," Rock said. He directed the carriage to the mews near his house. They would be walking to the club.

"If the thing were possible, such would be my desire," Miles admitted. He climbed down from the carriage when they reached the stables. "Alas, she never wants to see me again."

Rock handed the reins over to a stablehand and walked around the phaeton to get a look at Miles. "She said as much?"

"Just today in her drawing room, right before her brother walked in to join us." He took Rock's arm and they began walking to the club. "So it matters little whether I desire to marry her or not. It's difficult to bring a woman to the altar who does not want to see you."

"I'm sorry, coz." Rock walked at his side in contemplation. The sky had grown dark, and the warmth of the day was beginning to dissipate. "I don't suppose you're going to be very good company tonight."

Miles returned a crooked smile. "I don't suppose I will."

"Then I shall not keep you." Rock looked up at the sky with a loud yawn, before adding in a deceptively austere voice, "But escort me there so I might find someone whose company I will enjoy more."

Miles gave another glimmer of a smile at the jest. "You may count on me."

He was true to his word—and even though Rock protested

laughingly that he had only been joking—as soon as Miles saw that Rock had all the friends around him he needed to promise a pleasant evening, he bid them good night. He reached his room at Limmer's, stripped off his gloves and dropped them on the table, then lit a candle. He unbuttoned his coat before sitting.

I never want to see you again.

He had no reason to think she did not mean it. There had only been one thing he could truly offer her—his heart. And he had not dealt honestly where that was concerned, because a man in love did not lie to the object of his affection. He should think about what to do next with the disastrous condition of his house and estate, but no idea came to him that did not involve marriage, and he was ready to swear that off forever. If he could not marry Dorothea, he had no desire to marry at all.

CHAPTER 18

Tonight's invitation to Mrs. Matheson's comfortable salon promised to bring together everyone of fashion for an evening of music. It would not be the young ladies of the *ton* displaying their talents which drew the crowds. Famed soprano Mrs. Elizabeth Billington had been invited to sing, and she was the main draw.

Normally, Dorothea would enjoy such a thing. Even if she did not attend for the music, she would go to see *le beau monde* and to show herself as part of it. People had always entertained her more than opera. However, this evening she dressed for the musicale with less enthusiasm than she had ever shown. Any ambition or zeal she had once felt in embarking upon her season had dissipated until there was almost no enthusiasm left. She had come to London hoping to make a brilliant match —expecting to—but she was slowly realizing that she had secretly hoped for some of the more tender emotions as well. And what was more, she had completely deceived herself on the matter.

When they arrived at the Mathesons' house, Lady Poole greeted the hostess then moved over to the seating area so she could choose a comfortable place to sit. Sophia caught Dorothea's look of displeasure.

"Mama is not comfortable in crowds. You know she is not. I cannot leave her alone." With a squeeze of Dorothea's hand, she followed their mother and sat next to her.

Dorothea did know it. Her mother tried to make herself as small as possible when in a room full of people. But that meant that the responsibility for securing their family's standing in Society was given to Dorothea. Why must she be the only one who made an effort to come to the notice of the fashionable world? It was for their whole family's sake, so that her sisters might also find eligible husbands.

As for her brother... Well, she supposed Evo would find his way without her help. For one thing, he was an earl and would one day have all the freedom of a gentleman. Little else was needed for him to take his place in Society. For another thing, Evo had a natural aptitude for making friends, even if he had as much of an aptitude for getting into trouble. She conceded he would be fine even without her help, if only she could keep him from falling into serious trouble.

But what about her sisters? Sophia was too shy to speak to anyone. She would more than likely end up single since she could scarcely utter a greeting to a gentleman, much less a "yes" to his gratifying proposal. Or perhaps, some suitor desiring a timid, biddable wife would woo her with persistence enough to win her, but would he be kind to her?

Then there was Camilla, who had no natural gifts at all to attract a suitor. Dorothea was only assessing the matter in an unbiased fashion. She did not wish to be cruel toward her sister, but one had to admit that Camilla's conversation was not stimulating, and her looks were only just above average. Joanna, she feared, would never learn to employ any of the feminine arts and would likely end up as a bluestocking. Or rather, a horse-mad spinster, because she did not like to read. And Tilly was just as quiet as her mother. Dorothea worried that underneath it all she had nothing to distinguish herself except a pretty face.

Without Dorothea's help in securing a good match for each of them, her sisters would be doomed to a life of spinsterhood or unhappy marriages. After all, who had guided her mother in her marriage? Why, no one! Her mother had no family to speak of, and although she had secured an earl for a husband, she had been left quite unhappy. Dorothea could not bear to see her sisters in the same position.

This quiet fear had driven her quest from the very beginning, but the pain in her own heart was making it difficult to continue striving for the goal of marrying well. It didn't help that every time she thought of Miles, she was plunged into a melancholy mood which swept away any desire to flirt. That she thought it unlikely he would be invited to this musicale was the only reason she had decided to come.

Dorothea was spared from having to follow her mother and sister immediately because she spotted Anne, who gave her a small wave. She went over, glad to see a friendly face.

Anne, remarkably well connected, wasted no time in giving her the latest news. "Did you hear that Maryann Stanley has secured an offer from the Duke of Worley?"

"The Duke of Worley?" Dorothea knit her brows, searching her mind until she hit upon the right face. "But is he not nearly in his dotage?" she said in a low voice. For Dorothea, Lord Hastings was as close to elderly as she allowed herself to consider in a husband. She could not imagine marrying a man who was old enough to be her grandfather.

Anne didn't respond to that, but with a small indication of her chin, murmured, "There is Miss Stanley now."

Sure enough, Maryann had entered and looked around the room, as if in expectation of receiving the acclaim that should be sent her way for having made such a brilliant conquest. As a duchess, she would take precedence everywhere and certainly lead Society.

"I can hardly believe it," Dorothea whispered back. "That she would accept him when he cannot make a comfortable husband. To do so just to secure a position..." She paused, adding, "And that *he* would propose to her when she is not likely to be faithful."

Dorothea stopped, flooded with other thoughts she could not articulate. That she was critiquing another woman for making a match much in the same way she, herself, had been attempting; that a duke had proposed to Maryann, who had nothing in the way of a title in her family line; that the whole affair felt less like something to be admired and more like something to be deplored. The proposal Miles had offered her, dishonest as she later learned it was, seemed to have more value. His, at least, was delivered with some degree of emotion.

Anne turned to her with a keen look. "Do you think she will not be faithful, then?"

"Oh..." She should not have spoken that out loud. Dorothea would not spread gossip no matter how little she liked Maryann. "I beg you will not mind me. I have no idea what she is likely to do. It is true we became a little close, but quickly found we had not much in common and went our separate ways."

Maryann settled her gaze on Dorothea and Anne, and after a moment's speculative pause, walked over to them. "What a pleasure to see you tonight, Dorothea. And you, Miss Kensington. I am sure you have heard my happy news. I am to be the next Duchess of Worley."

"We did indeed." Dorothea attempted to give her a true smile. "I offer you my congratulations and wishes for every felicity in your marriage."

"As someone who will outrank you," Maryann continued sweetly, "I will be happy to assist you in any way you might need to find a suitable husband. I understand it is taking a little longer than you might have hoped?"

When Dorothea only gave her a bland smile in response, she turned to Anne. "And you, Miss Kensington. You may count on me as well."

"You are too kind," Anne replied with a gracious nod, then went silent until Maryann saw she would receive no more adulation and went off to find a more worshipful audience.

Anne sent Dorothea an amused look. "Ah, my dear. You are surprised, but that is the way Society works. The gentlemen scheme to find a woman who will look good on their arms. The ladies scheme to find a gentleman whose title will grant them prestige. It is all very tiresome, and that is why I do not wish to marry."

Dorothea darted an uncertain look her way. She could not dispute what Anne had said, nor did she wish to tell her how close she had come to putting her finger on Dorothea's own situation. "Mrs. Billington is coming to take her place. Shall we sit?"

She had never been gladder for an evening that required listening rather than conversation. She was so troubled by the awareness of her gradual shift in priorities, and what that might mean for her future, she could not have spoken two interesting words if she'd tried.

THE NEXT DAY, Dorothea went to sit in the drawing room before calling hours. She still went there early to see that all was in order and to have some time to compose herself before receiving company. She and Sophia had fallen into a rhythm where they stayed home three days out of the week and went out calling the other three. Sunday was the day to attend St. George's Hanover Square and listen to the sermon. The idea of entertaining morning callers no longer made her nervous, and their drawing room was always filled with a respectable number of people.

A knock sounded on the front door. Goodness! They were starting early this afternoon, and she had not yet spoken to Cook. Dorothea sat up in anticipation as their butler opened the door.

"Lady Isabelle Shaw to see you, my lady."

Dorothea's heart began to thump. Had Miles confided in his mother about his proposal and her rejection? She hoped he had not. She would not like Lady Isabelle to think ill of her for having rejected her son, and she would surely do so if she knew.

She stood when Lady Isabelle walked through the door, thankful for once that her mother was never on time. She wished for a private interview, although she could not quite pinpoint why that was.

"Will you have a seat, my lady?"

"Thank you."

Lady Isabelle came forward and sat on the chair nearest to Dorothea. Her dark hair held some gray in the temples, but otherwise she looked youthful—even more so than the last time they had met. She must have recovered from her tiring journey and difficulties at home.

Lady Isabelle assessed her with a kind smile for a brief moment then folded her hands on her lap. "You must be wondering what prompted me to pay a visit when we are so little acquainted."

"I confess the thought did cross my mind." Dorothea smiled, which ended in a nervous laugh. "But I wish to assure you that your visit is not an unwelcome one."

The way Lady Isabelle regarded her looked so very much like Miles at that moment that Dorothea swallowed hard. Her heart should behave more sensibly than to act as though she missed him. It was more advisable to remain angry and to put an end to all further possibilities for a relationship. And yet, in absence of seeing *his* face, her heart rejoiced in seeing one so closely related to him and with whom he shared such a likeness. The heart was a foolish organ.

"Well, I am generally one who comes straight to the point, so I have come to apologize to you." Lady Isabelle lifted a hand when Dorothea opened her mouth to tell her such a thing was unnecessary.

"Please. Allow me to do so. I believe discussing our circumstances so openly must have been distasteful to you. You see, I have grown accustomed to frequenting a humbler set of people, where owning to some trouble seems to bring one closer, when the fact that I grew up the daughter of a London peer often makes a rift. I've found over the years since being married to Mr. Shaw that I was happiest with the other women of the village when I was speaking simply and without pretense."

She gave a soft laugh. "I seem to have lost the art of dissembling required in London society."

"I thank you for your forthright speech." Dorothea gave her a fleeting smile, then knit her brows as she contemplated Lady Isabelle's words.

It hadn't occurred to her that it would be as necessary to adjust one's behavior when building friendships with women of more humble origins as it would with those of elevated ones. That Lady Isabelle did spoke well of her. Truly, Dorothea would rather have someone like Lady Isabelle as a model than a woman like Maryann Stanley. She decided to meet honesty with honesty.

"It did shock me a very little, I must own. But what you've

said makes perfect sense, and I can only respect you for speaking so openly."

Lady Isabelle dipped her head, looking almost shy. "I ask that you allow me a little more liberty. Miles has told me of your...friendship and the esteem he has for you."

When Dorothea grew flushed, Lady Isabelle put up a hand. "Forgive me, this was more of my forthright speech. I do not mean to pry, I assure you. It is only that I hoped what I'd said has not been the source of any rift between you and Miles. I should not like to think that I have made him, or any friend of his, unhappy."

She was uncomfortable, but she knew Lady Isabelle's words came from a place of kindness. More than anything, she was struck by the fact that if Miles had indeed spoken of their friendship to his own mother, at least some of what he felt for her must be true.

"I assure you, there is no harm done," she said softly. "I am sure Mr. Shaw and I will meet again soon. When we do, he may be assured of my continued friendship."

"I am glad to hear that." Lady Isabelle turned from Dorothea as the door to the drawing room opened.

At last, Lady Poole, Sophia, and Camilla trailed in. Sophia darted a look of surprise at Dorothea. They had not heard the sounds of Lady Isabelle's arrival. But Dorothea was glad for the time to have had this conversation with Lady Isabelle. It settled something in her heart that she had, until now, only vaguely allowed herself to acknowledge.

She had been just as ambitious as Miles had been. Only for her, it had been the ambition to secure a man with a title. What she had condemned in him, she had been guilty of. Yet he valued her enough to speak of her with his mother, and he had said he esteemed her. For the first time in days, rather than wishing to avoid him, she would not be opposed to a chance meeting.

Lady Isabelle stayed for a cup of tea, conversing easily with her sisters and drawing her mother out in a way Dorothea had rarely seen. When she left, no knock occurred to announce another visitor, and in the quiet of the drawing room, Sophia sent a bright smile to Dorothea.

"She is very kind. So much like her son."

Dorothea nodded, still lost in her thoughts. Her mother filled her plate with two scones and reached for the teapot. Camilla leaned forward to take it from her and refilled her cup as Sophia adjusted the cushion behind Lady Poole. Their mother sat back and took a bite of her scone, and Dorothea could not help but look at her in surprise. Her mother had always been frail for as long as she could remember and scarcely ate what was on her plate, much less taking seconds.

"Lady Isabelle is indeed kind," her mother said. "For all she may have slipped into poverty through her marriage, she is every inch the lady still. I should be glad to know her better."

Lady Poole smiled at Dorothea, who could only stare back at her. Her mother had put together three sentences—volunteered an observation about someone else! And she did not look unhappy. What winds of change had swept through their drawing room?

IT WAS several days of going out to Society events, both in the afternoon and evening, before Dorothea saw Miles again. She knew they had not passed each other unnoticed, because everywhere she went, she found herself searching for that familiar swoop of hair—even if she firmly took herself to task afterwards for being so foolish.

When she perceived him at last, Dorothea was walking in Hyde Park in the company of Sophia and Camilla. Miles was in a carriage with one of his friends, arriving from the opposite direction when he spotted them.

He lifted his hand, as though by instinct, then lowered it. Dorothea stopped and looked at him quite deliberately. She allowed her lips to turn upwards, though she trembled at the thought of speaking to him again. Her emotions seemed to fly out of her without anything to rein them in whenever she was in his presence.

He froze when he saw her smile, then put his hand on his friend's arm and leaned in to speak. His friend slowed the carriage, and Miles leapt out easily before striding over to them.

He greeted the three of them with a bow, his earnest gaze lingering on Dorothea.

"It is a fine day, my ladies, is it not? The first day where one might almost grow too warm when standing in the sun."

"'Tis a fine day," Dorothea agreed.

She glanced at her sisters and turned to walk forward again, ducking her head and wondering if he would follow. He did.

Lady Sophia slipped her arm into Camilla's, and Dorothea walked at his side, adjusting herself to his pace. They began with commonplaces and walked in such a leisurely manner, they soon fell behind, out of earshot of her sisters.

"Did you know your mother came to visit me?"

"I did not know of her intention to do so, but I learned of it after she had returned." He glanced at her and offered a lopsided grin. "She was the one who gave me the courage to approach you today after you told me you never wished to see me again." This last bit was said with just a touch of self-depre-cating humor.

Dorothea allowed her lips to curve upwards. "I apologize for lacking restraint in my speech. I was angry."

"You had every right to be, and I am heartily sorry for my part in provoking you to it."

Miles closed the distance between them and offered his arm. She slipped her hand into it, and they walked quietly that way for a space. Dorothea relaxed with the relief of having peace with Miles again.

Miles leaned down for her ears only. "I must say that, although I was not happy to be on the receiving end of your words—words I very much deserved—I *was* glad to see the passion. Society has a way of ripping the deeper emotions out of us at times, and I should not like for that to happen to you."

Her heart began to race as she decided to open up to him about what she had learned. It was an entirely novel thing to bare her soul to someone else, but the desire to do so was strong —a terrifyingly sweet sort of urge.

"I have come to the realization that as much as I have accused you of being mercenary, I am equally so myself. You are in search of a dowry, and I am in search of a title. It really is the same thing, and it was unfair of me to accuse you."

"Now, this has always puzzled me." He turned his head toward her, and his keen eyes seemed to see into her. "You have a title. You are the daughter of an earl, and nothing will change that. Why are you so bent upon finding a gentleman who possesses one as well?"

"Because..." Dorothea struggled to put her reasoning into words. She had always thought it—always known it—but she had never had to voice such a thing. She looked away in order to think properly. "Because I am the oldest sister, and if I don't marry well, then I fear my sisters will be lost. It is my responsibility to pave the way."

"But how is that? Lost in what way?"

He was genuinely confused, so she tried to explain it to him more clearly. "Don't you see? My mother cannot help us find

202

our place in Society. She is too easily cowed to do so, which means it is left to us to care for her. *I* have to care for her."

She looked ahead, then lowered her voice to a near whisper, ashamed of what she was revealing about her family.

"Sophia is sweet, but she's a sweet widgeon, you must own. Without my help, she is unlikely to find a husband who will be a good match for her, for she will likely accept the first man out of pity or refuse them all out of fear.

"Camilla, I am sorry to say, is forgettable as far as looks are concerned, and has the personality of a maid-of-all-work. I have a great fear that she is destined for spinsterhood. Joanna is pretty and has vivacity, but she might as well wear breeches, for she's bent on spurning everything to do with becoming a lady. What gentleman will take her in that state?"

She darted a glance at him to see if he understood, but his face was inscrutable. "Tilly is the spitting image of my mother," she went on, "which bodes ill for the husband who one day takes her on, for she won't lift a finger to run the household. It will fall to him to do so—or their eldest daughter.

"And Everard! Evo thinks only of his pranks and mischief. He'll end up plunking down the entirety of the family's fortune the minute he's reached his majority. I am trying to bring them all on the right path, but I fear I've only failed them."

Miles pulled her to a stop and stared at her, their faces inches apart. He spoke in a very low voice. "Dorry, do you hear yourself? Do you?"

She froze. It was the first time she had heard censure in his voice.

He shook his head. "There are so many flaws in your reasoning, I do not know where to begin."

"What do you mean?" she asked, hating herself for being so vulnerable, so obtuse. But she had to know what he saw that she could not.

"What I mean is that you judge your family unfairly. They are not the sum of what you see, as though your perception leaves them with no hope apart from what you judge. People are complex. And you"—he shook his head, leveling her with his gaze—"you take too much upon yourself. It is more than is good for you *or* for them. Have you asked your mother why she requires so much care? Have you given responsibility to Sophia so she might feel useful? Have you searched for the good in Camilla as thoroughly as you've searched for her flaws?"

She couldn't answer, nor could she break away from his gaze. When she remained mute, he continued in a softer voice. "I won't go on. I believe I have explained myself well enough."

Dorothea felt ill. Crushed by his chastisement. But then he sighed, turning to walk again, and laid his hand over hers. The gesture brought comfort...forgiveness—not for anything she had done to him, but grace for the flaws he had managed to expose in her.

"Your family requires *only* that you love them without condition. They will sort their own lives out for themselves— and much better than you ever could, talented though you are."

Dorothea blinked her eyes rapidly, and when he turned to point out a high-perch phaeton driven entirely too fast by a wisp of a man, that was in imminent danger of toppling over— an effort, she was sure, of setting her at ease again—she could scarcely answer him. To her relief, Sophia and Camilla had realized they had gone ahead too far and turned back to find her.

"Have you seen the high-perch phaeton?" Camilla observed. "I don't believe the horses are aware that anyone is holding the reins!"

CHAPTER 19

Miles turned his thoughts frequently back to their conversation in the park. Dorothea had been subdued after he had taken her to task. Her inherent prejudice was great, even toward the members of her own family. It should have deterred him from loving her and pushed him to keep a distance after hearing it, but it had the opposite effect. She had unwittingly revealed much of herself in that confession—fears over her own worth and her family's acceptability. This was one area in which he found himself on stronger ground. He never doubted his own worth or his family's, and he longed to help her gain such confidence.

She had allowed him to correct her. What was more, she had looked to him for understanding and had accepted his rebuke without demur. A woman with no depth could not do such a thing. At the sight of her turning to him for understanding, he had fallen even more deeply in love.

But just as his affection for her grew, the awareness of his circumstances had become a relentless albatross. It had become a responsibility he could no longer ignore. It was time to move forward on plans for his life and find a proper solution to his difficulties.

He could not marry another woman when his heart was given over to Dorothea. Yet, Albert had been hinting at the difficulties of hosting his mother-in-law while trying to win a seat in the elections. His words had been nothing more than a man fretting about a situation he could not like, but Miles understood. Lady Isabelle was not *his* mother, and it was up to Miles to find a way to care for her.

After weighing all the options he could think of, he reached the unpleasant decision that his only recourse was to sell his ancestral home. It was the last thing he wanted to do, because it seemed to him that a gentleman without land was not really a gentleman at all, but in the absence of all other solutions, it could not be avoided. The estate would not fetch a very large price because of the condition of the house itself. However, the lands were worth something and even the bones of the house itself were solid. A merchant who longed to play at landowner would likely be his purchaser, but why not? In a generation or two, that man's sons would be considered gentlemen. It was the way of life.

As soon as he had come to that decision, no matter how difficult, Miles felt lighter. It was better to take action than to remain in uncertainty, wringing one's hands. He wasted no time in sending a letter to his man of business in Lancashire, who recommended by return post that he meet with his London colleague to avoid any delay.

The attorney estimated that the sum remaining after the sale of the estate would be enough for a truly snug house, about a fifth the size of his current one, but one that required no major repairs. They would surely find an agreeable house in Lancashire, where his mother would be surrounded by friends and all that was familiar. She had told him she no longer felt she belonged to London society.

And perhaps he would look into using the rest of the capital for some business venture. He laughed to himself. *The wealthy merchant becomes a gentleman and he, the grandson of an earl, becomes a merchant.* But really, did such a thing matter when compared to being solvent? It did not. And even if it pained him to bid farewell to a piece of land that had been in the hands of his father's family for several generations, it was not the most important thing in life.

Rock had asked to meet him at White's, and Miles was sitting at one of the tables near the wall, waiting for him. He stood when his cousin walked in, and they shook hands.

"Did you make it through the reading of the will?" Miles asked him.

"Tolerably well." Rock sat and signaled to one of the servants to bring him a glass. "It was about as pleasant as a night at Almack's ensnared by a gaggle of ambitious mamas, but it had to be done. Now, I have the unenviable task of going through a set of papers from the last two hundred years, at least, and learning more about the holdings that belong to me. Our grandfather never was very generous with information about his property when he was alive."

Rock sat back and let the servant fill his glass. "I want to oversee that the bequeathments are handed over properly. There are not many. Lord Pembroke was a tight-fisted man, much as I loved him."

"It must be got through, I suppose." Miles picked up his drink, took a sip, then set it down and folded his arms. "I've decided to sell my estate."

Rock's only reaction to the news was a lift of the eyebrows. "So it will not be an advantageous marriage for you, then, as a means to save your estate?"

Miles shook his head. "My heart's not in it. I must suppose I am like you. Not ready for marriage." He gave a laugh but it sounded bitter.

He hoped he had successfully turned the conversation from what was a sore topic, but in this, he was wrong. Rock leaned in and murmured out of hearing of the other tables, "Lady Dorothea?"

Miles also glanced around in an abundance of caution, but no one was near enough to hear what he said.

"I cannot offer for her, even though there is nothing I would like better. It would be removing her from the life I know she wants to lead and, to be honest, the life she deserves as the daughter of an earl."

"Are you sure it is truly what she wants? Maybe you are keeping her from having the life she desires by *not* proposing to her," Rock argued earnestly.

"It is what I had hoped, as well. I refused to let myself think about how similar her situation was to my mother's, but my mother kindly"—he grimaced—"reminded me of it. Her heart was completely lost to my father, but even with their affection, it is not an easy life she has led. She assures me she has no regrets, but I am convinced I ought not to attempt such a thing with Dorothea."

"I'm sorry," Rock said.

"Thank you." Miles took a large swallow. "I have another fortnight in London while my banker attempts to find a purchaser. Afterwards, I must be off to find suitable lodgings for my mother and myself. In the meantime, I suppose we shall have to find a way to amuse ourselves."

"Now that is something I can help you with," Rock said, lifting his glass.

Lord Hastings had sent a note with the news that he had returned to London and was eager to meet with Dorothea. She could not say she felt the same anticipation that he claimed to have. In fact, she had scarcely thought about him at all since he'd left, which gave her her answer—if one was needed at all.

Her ideas of what an advantageous match entailed had undergone a change. No, she could not marry Lord Hastings, despite his exemplary title and his estate. And for all that his land being situated on the moors of Northumberland had once been an impediment for her, she knew that even if his estate had been closer to London, she must still decline. Even if he were younger, she must decline. His presence simply had no effect on the state of her heart.

At precisely two-thirty in the afternoon, his knock came on the front door. Dorothea gave a nod to Sophia, who slipped out of the door in anticipation of this interview. She'd been fore-warned what was coming and gave Dorothea the privacy she required. Lord Hastings was shown into the room, and Dorothea stood to greet him, hoping he would come to the point quickly so she might put the uncomfortable interview behind her.

"Lady Dorothea, how good it is to see you again." Lord Hasting's expression showed real pleasure and a tiny spear of guilt pricked her. Guilt, but not doubt.

"Welcome back, my lord." She curtsied, then gestured to the chairs behind her. "Will you sit?"

"With pleasure." Upon taking his seat, he faced her in what seemed to her an expectant silence, which she found a little alarming. He did not expect her to broach the subject, did he?

She gave a tight smile with lips firmly shut, and at last he opened his own. "Well, well. I suppose you can hardly begin the conversation we are to have, can you? But as you must certainly have guessed, I have come in anticipation of hearing your answer to my proposal. Will you make me the happiest man alive and accept my hand in marriage?"

The happiest man alive? Where had this sudden infusion of passion come from? She wondered if Miles would consider himself the happiest man alive if she returned a favorable answer. He might, Dorothea thought, but he would be more likely to show it than to say it. The image of Miles holding her in his arms and kissing her temple filled her mind. It forced her words out in perhaps a less carefully controlled manner than she might otherwise have spoken them.

"I thank you for the honor of your proposal and for your willingness to give me the time I needed to think it over." She paused only to take a breath. "I am afraid I will have to turn down your very flattering offer."

Lord Hastings brought his eyes to hers, the initial surprise quickly changing to dismay at her refusal. "I had quite thought you meant to accept me. May I ask the reason for your refusal?"

Dorothea had not planned on having to justify her reasons and didn't think it fair of him to ask it of her.

"I...I did not mean to give you false encouragement. It is only that I did not know my heart earlier and required time to examine the matter more closely. I have come to the conclusion that we won't suit."

Despite Lord Hastings's look of regret, Dorothea felt the most enormous relief as soon as the words were out. Miles might not propose a second time, but at least she was certain of how she felt about Lord Hastings. He would not do for her. Her total absence of finer emotions did not permit considering the matter any further.

Lord Hastings leaned forward, his elbows on his knees, and he brought his fingers together. "I will not hide my disappointment from you. You are certain that this is your final answer?"

"It is. Again, I am sorry I could not return a favorable reply."

Dorothea stood, knowing that he would then be obliged to bring the interview to an end.

He also got to his feet and hesitated before bowing. "Well, I shall not detain you, my lady. Allow me to wish you a pleasant afternoon."

Minutes after the door had closed behind Lord Hastings, her mother came into the room. Dorothea was still unsettled by the interview, for it was never a pleasant thing to disappoint a person. But it was with a much lighter heart that she met her mother's gaze.

"Lord Hastings had requested an interview, and he just left."

Lady Poole took a seat opposite to her and met her eyes. It was unusual for her mother to sit in a way that invited confidence, and it surprised Dorothea.

"Am I to congratulate you, then, on your upcoming betrothal?"

"No, for I have turned him down." She studied her mother's face to see how she would react to the news. Would she be disappointed in her? Did she care at all? Her mother was so difficult to read. "I found we did not suit."

Her mother tilted her blonde-and-silver curls to one side. Her face looked plumper than it had before, and Dorothea wondered when the change had taken place. She looked more youthful, somehow, as she studied Dorothea.

"I must admit that I am glad to hear it, for I could see very well you did not suit."

Dorothea was not in the habit of receiving such frankness from her mother, and she could only ask, "Why is that?"

"I could see he had not touched your heart, and I would not wish to see you in a marriage where your heart had not been engaged."

This was such a surprising foray into honest speech that

Dorothea blurted out the question she had always wanted to know the answer to—one that had some bearing on the topic at hand.

"Did you and my father have a love match?"

Her question sounded plaintive, and as soon as the words were out, she was horrified at both the impudence of her question and what it revealed about her. Whereas she had always prided herself on acting rationally rather than giving into sentiment, she was just as emotional as any of them.

Her mother attempted a smile, but it was pained. "I had developed a great *tendre* for your father, for who could not? He was exceedingly agreeable, paid me the most particular attention, and as you well know, was above my station. For him to single me out from all the other young ladies was a great coup, and I counted myself fortunate. I thought myself very much in love."

Dorothea searched her mother's face for understanding. "I am led by your words to understand that such a sentiment did not last."

Her mother folded her hands on her lap and sighed. "No, it did not last. I never did learn what your father saw in me to induce him to propose, as there were many other girls whose looks were as fetching as mine and whose station was superior. But propose he did."

"What happened?" Dorothea found herself breathless. She did not remember ever having a conversation like this with her mother—one that was so open, although Sophia had frequently mentioned speaking with Mama on all manner of things. It made her think that perhaps if they were not close, it was Dorothea who was at fault.

"Your father lost interest in me almost from the minute we returned from our honeymoon. He did his duty as a husband, but did not cease to remind me of the disparity of our connection."

Dorothea recalled many conversations where her father had told her the same thing, urging her to choose wisely when it came time to select a husband. Of course, he had always presented it as though he would be there to approve the one who would eventually win her hand.

"I was terribly affected by this, as you might imagine, and my only solace was the growing family we had built together."

She turned her eyes to the far end of the room as though she could not bear to bring them to Dorothea. "Your father was not precisely a faithful man, and in my girlhood, I had always hoped I might at least have fidelity in my marriage. I suppose I was not precisely fashionable in that sense, for women of the *ton* are taught to turn a blind eye when a husband's eye starts to wander."

"I would not have accepted it so readily either." Dorothea had the foreign urge to hug her mother, but she could not do it. They had never had that sort of a relationship that she could remember. Her father had not helped the matter when he said such things as how it was more proper that the governess should raise her, since Miss Cross was more equipped than her mother to teach the finer arts of a lady.

"I know you have always been in a rush to marry," her mother said. "But I urge you not to fly into a decision too quickly. It is not a shameful thing to have a second or a third season. Take your time in choosing, my dear. Find a gentleman who will make you exceedingly happy."

Dorothea looked down, blinking away an overwhelming sentimentality. "I will take that into consideration."

She breathed in and clutched her hands together. The urge was great to ask her mother whether the distance in their relationship was due to her. Was it her fault? She opened her mouth to ask it, but then her mother made a move to stand.

"We have not yet had tea this afternoon. I will ring for some." Lady Poole went over to the bell pull and waited by the door for Mrs. Platt to come.

The moment was lost.

CHAPTER 20

Sophia had expressed a wish for a quiet day at home and was happily embroidering while Dorothea held a book in front of her that she was not reading. Camilla had decided to remain in the nursery with Joanna and Tilly because they were making *papier mâché* flowers to glue to a frame and she hoped to become more skilled in the art. Evo was heaven knew where, and their mother was resting in her room.

Dorothea longed to be out where she could distract herself from her thoughts. All she had been able to think about—besides the bittersweet memory that returned, unbidden, of what it was like to have Miles embrace her—was the way he had corrected her. That, and whether she had been wrong about her family all along.

Her mother's disclosure had caused her to think. She could not have had many happy moments in her marriage. It was therefore unsurprising that she should present to the world and even to her children the appearance of a woman crushed by life. Dorothea was beginning to look at her with more under-standing and compassion than she had before.

She had also begun to look at Camilla with new eyes, and

what she observed astonished her. Camilla, she was beginning to believe, was not dull or dim-witted. Quite the contrary! When she bothered to lift her voice, it was to say something insightful or humorous—very often both at once. One only had to listen for it.

And of course Sophia might lack some of the will or courage that Dorothea had, but she was far from empty-headed. Her strengths merely lay in different areas. In her kindness and attention to the needs of others. And she had known before Dorothea did how desirable it was to achieve a love match. How had she gained such insight?

Miles had turned Dorothea's priorities around and challenged her manner of seeing the world. And then, without a moment's hesitation, he went back to treating her exactly as he had before, his affection undimmed despite her flaws. It caused her to want to trust him with her heart's secrets. He pulled confidences from her heart gently and restored them to her with the additional luster of understanding. He was becoming indispensable to her, and it occurred to her in a wondering sort of way whether this was not what love was.

It required no time to have her answer. She very likely loved him back. Yet, although he had said he loved her, he had not returned and proposed a second time. She could only imagine it was because he did not dare. Although they had made peace over his initial duplicity in seeking a wife, they had never reverted to more tender conversations that could allow her to inform him that maybe she was not as opposed to marrying him as she had led him to believe.

His circumstances had not changed. Oh, he was now the heir presumptive to an earldom should something happen to Lord Pembroke, but not only did she not wish for anything to happen to the current earl, she found that his closer connection to the peerage did not weigh with her in the least. His financial difficulties had not changed, and she began to think that it might not be so terrible to allow him the use of her dowry to reverse his fortunes, if her dowry were enough. If it was not, could they not shift together somehow? Two people who could speak openly to one another, to give and receive the forgiveness needed for flawed humans. Two people who loved each other.

Because then she would be married to him. She would have his mother and sister as family to add to her own. She could dance with him as often as she wished, and laugh with him. Be instructed by him and instruct him in turn. They would be friends.

Maybe you should take matters into your own hands. The thought circled around and around in a loop until it filled her mind and became difficult to ignore. Of course, she could not tell him how she felt about him... Women did not do that sort of thing. It was up to the man to declare the state of his heart.

But he said he loved you, and you rejected him.

The door to the drawing room opened, and Turton entered. "Mr. Shaw is here to see you, my lady."

The book slid off of Dorothea's lap and landed on the floor with a thud. She had not heard anyone at the door. She glanced at Sophia, who had apparently not heard it either. Perhaps the butler had discerned movement outside and opened before Miles could knock. They both stood.

"Good afternoon," Miles said with a bow. He brought the scent of spring in with him.

"Mr. Shaw, if you don't mind, I shall leave you to talk," Sophia said after greeting him with a curtsy. "I have a letter I wish to write."

She had tucked the embroidery under a cushion and went to the far end of the drawing room where the desk was and sat.

Miles's eyes registered the kindness of this action, although there was something troubling in his look that concerned Dorothea. He sat at her invitation.

She prepared herself to speak, her heart hammering at what she'd just been imagining she might say to him, but when the time came, her courage deserted her. The silence stretched until it was broken by him clearing his throat.

"I've come to tell you that I've reached a decision concerning my estate in Lancashire." He paused, bringing his fists together, then raised his eyes to hers. "I've decided to sell it, and find another residence for my mother. It is most likely that I will be moving there to assist her in getting settled, and I will need to begin thinking about what to do next."

Miles looked at her, a wealth of emotion in his eyes. "I could not leave London without bidding you farewell."

Little spots formed in front of Dorothea's vision. He was leaving. "So you are moving away? Will you not marry as you once thought?" The sensation of dizziness that overtook her grew as she realized what she had just asked him.

He gave her a steady look, and with a quick glance at the other side of the room where Sophia sat, he leaned in to murmur, "I realized I cannot marry where my heart is not engaged. And as my heart has been captured by a woman it is impossible for me to marry, I fear it will require some time for me to envision taking such a step once again."

He lifted his eyebrow a fraction in significance, as though he wished to tell her who had engaged his heart.

"Oh," she said quietly, wading through the melancholy that threatened to drown her at his announcement. Perhaps she *should* say something. Perhaps she would.

Her heart sped up again at the thought, but she had to try. She could not let him go without telling him of her change of heart.

"And would you not consider marrying for love?" Her voice

was barely audible, but his eyes were on her lips and she knew he could hear what she said.

"For instance," she went on, nearly breathless, "if a particular lady knew that your heart had been engaged but that you didn't have the means to allow her the lifestyle to which she'd been accustomed, and"—she licked her lips—"and if you knew the lady would not object to entering into the match despite the disparity of your situations, would you not change your mind?"

Dorothea's cheeks were scalding. She trembled at the audacity of what she was saying. Never before had she stepped so far outside the bounds of propriety. For heaven's sake, she was practically proposing to the man herself.

Miles looked extremely pained. His mouth was pulled down into a frown, and he reached his hand forward until it settled on hers. He shook his head.

"As much as such a thing would tempt me almost beyond what I can resist, I could not do so to the lady. It would be most unfair to ask her to leave the life to which she has grown accustomed and force her into a life of poverty. My mother has reminded me of that most forcibly."

"Ah," was all she could manage. She wanted to say it would not matter, but she had already said too much.

Her humiliation was now complete. She had proposed to a gentleman, and he had refused her. There was nothing more to say. She could not respond or even look at him, and as much as she wanted to bear her mortification alone, her heart ached at the thought that she would likely not see him again. After a long moment in which she kept her eyes fixed downwards, he pulled his hand back.

"I must leave you now. Although our lives must go in separate ways, I believe I shall always carry a piece of you in my heart, Dorry," he whispered.

She nodded dumbly. There was simply nothing left to say.

She thought she heard him bid her adieu, but she did not lift her head to watch him go.

When the door closed behind him, Sophia rose from the writing desk and came over to her. "Is everything well?"

Dorothea raised eyes brimming with tears. She bit her lip and shook her head. "I don't believe anything ever will be again."

Sophia sat instantly and put her arms around Dorothea as though she were the older sister—as though it was natural that she should carry her burdens. Dorothea put her face in her hands and sobbed, and Sophia held her. She rocked her in her arms, murmuring whispered assurances that somehow penetrated the heartache, empty though they were.

"*Shh, shh*. All will be well. All will be well."

CHAPTER 21

Before the week was over, Miles accepted an offer on his estate that was more than what he had expected. And although he felt relief that he would be able to move forward with his plans, it was like saying farewell to his father all over again. His father had loved that land.

Rock had made every effort to see that their fortnight together was spent in high entertainment, insisting that Miles move out of the bleak hotel he scurried to each night and into his London house in Mayfair. Miles refused him, however, saying that a man's having his own lodging—be it a house in Mayfair or a rented room in an unfashionable part of town—was his last stand on dignity.

Rock dragged him to the races, to every club in London to which they had membership, to the respectable gaming houses —and the less respectable ones. They even rode the twenty-mile circuit required for membership in the Four-Horse Club, although Miles could never afford the fees for it. It was just to see if they could make the time.

He appreciated his cousin's efforts, for it prevented him from mulling over his last conversation with Dorothea in the maudlin way he had taken to doing. She had trusted him with her heart. Had shown him who she really was. Had tempted him with her vulnerable offer that made him swear off seeing her again lest he take her at her word.

The day before he was to leave London, he received a note from Rock to come see him without delay.

"I came at your summons." Miles walked unannounced into Rock's study. He peeled off his gloves and tossed them on the table, then took off his hat and rubbed his head. It was unseasonably warm outside. "So now that you're the earl, you've taken to barking orders that you expect to be obeyed?" He grinned.

"Only when the subject matter is of such importance it cannot wait," his cousin retorted. "A drink?"

"Don't mind if I do." Miles accepted the glass that was poured, drank, then set it down on the table next to him. Rock came and sat with one leg crossed over the other. His knee bounced up and down in excitement so foreign to his cousin's usual cool demeanor that Miles frowned at him in surprise.

"I don't suppose you know why I have sent for you?"

"Taking in the fact that you're about to bounce out of your seat, I can only guess that you have decided at long last to become leg-shackled." Miles took another sip.

"Wrong you are. Unlike you, I have not found the right lady."

"Unlike me?" The reminder felt unkind, and Miles frowned at him again, this time in displeasure. "I believe I was quite clear about the fact that I would not be marrying Dorothea. Our circumstances are too far apart."

"Well, now, that is just the thing that I wanted to speak to you about." There was the bouncing knee again. "Your circumstances are not quite as bleak as you think them."

Miles stilled and looked at his cousin keenly, an unreasonable sprout of hope budding. He trampled it. His path had been set for him.

"What are you talking about? I have received a goodly sum for my estate, but it means...well..." He did not care to spell out that it meant a drop in his standing, and it meant the loss of the woman he loved.

"What am I talking about?" Rock grinned. "Only, my illustrious cousin, that I discovered in the middle of a set of papers from 1772 a document that was not meant to be there. It was from the late earl detailing the inheritance that was to go to your mother and any of her offspring." He gave a crack of laughter, adding, "I am so pleased with myself. It was two o'clock in the morning, and I was just about to snuff the candle when I spotted it."

Miles attempted to follow what he was saying and could only remain silent.

"The attorney destroyed every old copy of our grandfather's will from before you or I were born—he told me so himself. I don't think it was intended for me to see this paper, but somehow it was mislaid with the other documents. Of course, the testament is clearly labeled as outdated and no longer valid."

His eyes twinkled underneath his clear brow. "However, it was of great value to me, for I was able to learn what my grandfather's intentions were toward Lady Isabelle before she displeased him enough for him to cut her out."

Miles continued to study him, striving to glean what his cousin was getting at.

"But as you say," Miles went on slowly, "the testament is no longer valid. And therefore there is no reason for us to be having this conversation—or for you to be bouncing your knee as though you're about to go galloping through Hyde Park."

Rock shot up from his chair and walked over to the desk and

picked up an official-looking document there.

"Wrong you are, coz. I am at liberty to distribute certain unentailed portions of the estate that are unrelated to the earldom as I see fit. And since I've learned that this particular holding of a modest five-hectare piece of land situated in the county of Herefordshire was to belong to you as its rightful heir, I've had my solicitor make it over to you. Here's the deed."

He handed over a sealed, folded paper, and Miles took it numbly, trying, through the fog that had settled over his mind, to comprehend the ramifications of what his cousin was saying.

"There is an independence set aside for your mother, and as the size of your holding is considerable enough, there is not only a dower house situated there, but the estate will bring you a not-unhandsome income of three thousand a year. If you don't object to using my banker, he is expecting your visit."

Rock resumed his seat, his hands clasped together, his smile reaching his eyes. "And the roof on the house is solid. I had them check."

Miles found it difficult to speak over the lump that had suddenly formed in his throat. He looked up at his cousin.

"You shouldn't do this. You should keep the earl's properties as one and not divide them." He furrowed his brows. He had to try to make his cousin understand, tempted though he was to simply take this very generous gift.

"You will not change my mind on this," Rock said more seriously. "This holding was acquired in my grandfather's lifetime. It doesn't touch any of the estates that were handed down to him or any of the holdings attached to my courtesy titles. My future children will not in any way suffer from the absence of this property in their inheritance."

He leaned back in his chair and folded his arms. "Honestly, Miles. It's the least I can do. Just take it."

Miles dropped his eyes to the paper in his hands, broke the

seal, and read its contents. He could scarcely take in his cousin's generosity—or what this would mean for his life. He could care for the land from a position of wealth rather than one of disadvantage. He would retain the status of gentleman. He could care for his mother.

He could marry Dorothea.

Miles held the paper in his two hands and regarded his cousin, a slight shake to his head. "I don't know what to say."

Rock took him by the arm, pulled him up from the chair, and hauled him over to the door. "I believe you are supposed to say, 'Lady Dorothea, will you do me the honor...?'"

He opened the door and pushed Miles out of it. "And don't come back until she says yes."

Miles's heart began to thump and he moved with hastened steps toward the door, then stopped short. "Wait! My hat!"

Rock chuckled and shook his head, going into the study to retrieve the hat and hand it to Miles. "Leave it to you to ruin my forward charge."

"Thank you," Miles said, holding out his hand. Rock reached out and shook it. He clasped him on the arm and met his eyes. There didn't seem to be anything else to say.

"Thank you," he said again.

"Go," Rock replied.

As much as Miles was eager to rush right off to Dorothea's house, he knew he needed to do things properly. And that involved first visiting Mary and his mother to apprise them of this startling development. He was glad to find Albert out of the house so they could have the intimacy of family for him to reveal the news. His mother burst into tears, and tears were streaming down his sister's cheeks as she held her mother.

Mary looked up at him. "Oh, Miles. This is simply the best news."

He stayed with them until they were all laughing and wiping tears, then left them with an encouragement to visit the *modiste* while he set out for his next stops. Weston's for a new coat, Hoby's for boots, and Tattersall's for a pair of horses he would be proud to drive. It was difficult to be patient in the time it took to send for these items and wait to receive them, but everything had to be perfect. Dorothea deserved as much. He then informed Limmer's that he would be staying for a short while longer.

It was not until nearly a week later that Miles was ready. He climbed up into his new phaeton and directed his gleaming pair of black Thoroughbreds toward the cobblestone street leading to Grosvenor Square. Perched behind him was a small, wiry man by the name of Harry performing the role of tiger today as a trial period.

As Miles drew close to the house where Dorothea resided, he spotted a figure he knew all too well walking on the flagway. The last time he had seen the earl was when he had given him a glimpse inside the boxing club before he and Dorothea had parted ways.

"Poole," he called out.

The earl stopped and looked, assessing his new turnout. His coat had begun to be too short in the arms. "It's you, is it? I thought you had forgotten all about me."

Miles heard the hurt behind the words, which he was very sure Evo would not wish him to pick up on, and he ignored it.

"Get in, if you will. I have something I wish to say to you." Miles waited until he climbed in. Before he clicked the reins, he said, "Please accept my apologies for not visiting earlier. I've had my hands full."

"I can see that." Evo swiveled in his seat to look at Harry, then turned back to touch the wood, much in the way his sister had once done with Albert's phaeton.

"Fine carriage you have here. And that is the most beautiful pair of Thoroughbreds I've seen in an age."

"I was hoping you would say so, for they are mine." Miles clicked the reins, and they started forward for the remaining short distance. "I have just had the fortune to learn I've received an unexpected inheritance."

"Did you now?" Evo turned to stare at him, folding his arms. "Such a thing is rare. You must have quite the luck."

"I will know just how lucky I am by the end of today," he said, his eyes trained forward on his destination.

Evo stared at him curiously, but Miles did not elaborate. He merely said, "However, you are right. A sudden inheritance requires either an almost extraordinary stroke of luck or an extremely generous soul. I shall not go into the particulars, but I believe for me it was both."

"I offer you my congratulations, then." Evo looked truly pleased for him. "If anyone deserves such luck, it is you."

"Thank you." They came to Lord Poole's house, and Miles pulled the carriage to a stop in front of it.

"Before you step out, I was hoping I might take your sister for a ride in my new carriage. Have I your approval to do so?" Miles asked, a smile lurking about his lips.

Evo looked confused. "You are asking if you may take Dorry out? Of course you may." Then his eyes lit with understanding and he laughed. "*Ah.* Because you have at last a phaeton of your own."

"Precisely." Miles grinned at him.

"Well then," Evo said, sounding more like his jaunty self. "You may take my sister out driving. *If* she is willing to go."

"Much obliged to you. Will you have the goodness to ask her if she would indeed be willing?"

Miles told Harry to go to the horses' heads while he went indoors with Evo. His heart beat in anticipation as he climbed the steps. He couldn't wait to see her.

"Lady Dorothea is not at home."

He caught the tail end of the words as he entered the house. The butler added, with a glance at Miles, "She has gone riding with a gentleman in Hyde Park."

Miles clamped his lips together. This was not how he'd pictured the scene. He thought her face would light up to see him, and he would help her into the carriage, and they would ride off together with...with some sort of a proposal that she would immediately accept. He hadn't quite thought that part through.

He glanced at Evo, unsure what to do.

"Well then, you had better go and get her then, hadn't you?" Evo prompted.

It woke Miles out of his indecision. "You're right. I had better."

He turned and jogged down the steps to the carriage, where he climbed in and took the reins. Harry caught the back of the phaeton and jumped up as Miles set the horses in motion toward Hyde Park.

Once again, fate was unkind, because they arrived at the peak fashionable hour and Miles was stuck behind a line of carriages that inched forward as people took in the sights and greeted one another. He ground his teeth in impatience.

It took what seemed an age before the carriages started to circulate, and at last, he caught sight of Dorothea. She was sitting in an open barouche with a man driving in front. Next to her was... Was it a gentleman? He strained to see around another figure on horseback who blocked his view.

No—it was Miss Kensington next to her.

He was flooded with relief. This was not a *tête-à-tête* with a blasted suitor from what he could see. There might be hope for him yet. He directed his team across the lane to their carriage.

Dorothea was in mid-conversation with Miss Kensington, but as she turned and caught sight of him, her words died away. Miss Kensington signaled to the gentleman driving, who pulled to stop.

"How are you, Mr. Shaw?" Miss Kensington said, as soon as he drew near. Dorothea seemed too stunned to speak. "Allow me to introduce my brother, Mr. Frank Kensington."

He nodded his greeting and turned his eyes back to Dorothea.

"That's a fine-looking pair of horses," Dorothea said at last. Her glance took in his pair, the carriage, and even the tiger behind him.

"I am glad you approve, for I have just purchased them." He kept his voice light, adding, "And you must know it is an interest of mine to win your approval."

Dorothea's eyebrows rose nearly to her hairline, so astonished was her look at his public expression of admiration. Miss Kensington hid a smile behind her gloved hand.

"Mr. Kensington, Miss Kensington," he said, "I hope you will not take it amiss if I invite Lady Dorothea to ride in my carriage. There is something of particular importance I must relay to her. I know it is most unusual to interrupt your outing in such a way, and I hope you will forgive me for this lapse."

"By all means," Miss Kensington said. "Ours was a pleasure party. You need not fear that you have disturbed us."

"I'm glad to hear of it," he said with a smile, thankful for her ready understanding. He gave a nod of thanks to her brother as well, then turned to his tiger. "Harry, go to the horses' heads."

The tiger obeyed, and Miles climbed down and went over to hold out his hand for Dorothea to alight. She placed her hand in his and stepped down, looking at him in great surprise. But the delight was all on his side. He couldn't wait to tell her everything.

"Harry, you may wait here, and I will circle around and get you when I am finished."

"Yes, sir."

With Dorothea seated at his side, Miles drove the carriage, easily winding around the crowds as they pulled farther away from the congestion. He focused on driving as he attempted to marshal his thoughts for exactly how he was going to initiate the conversation he had been waiting an age to have.

"I thought you had left," she said after a moment, when he didn't speak.

"No. Not yet," he replied with an inward smile, knowing his way of stating the obvious without further explanation would likely not sit well.

She waited for many more minutes, but still he did not launch into what he had come to say. She began to glare at him in expectation. "How lovely that you have a carriage, Miles."

"It is a nice one, is it not?"

Dorothea turned forward with a frustrated laugh. "I don't suppose you intend to tell me what is this thing of great importance you are impatient to relay. Or how it came about that you were able to acquire this carriage, or why you are still here?"

"I do intend to tell you, but I am waiting until I arrive in a section of the park that is just a little less populated than this one. I would not have chosen Hyde Park for our conversation." He glanced at her briefly. "You need have no fear of me or my intentions, of course."

"I know that," she said in exasperation. "I know what kind of a man you are."

"And yet at one time you were not so sure of it." He trained his eyes forward. Oh, he was enjoying this. To know that he came with good news. To know that his heart was hers—had been hers since he had first met her. To hope that her affections remained unchanged. He glanced at her now, deciding he would simply ask.

"Has your heart shifted since the time you thought me untrustworthy?"

She met his gaze, then looked forward again, the obstinate chin tilting up. "You know it has. Our last conversation can have left you in no doubt of that."

DOROTHEA WAS BEGINNING to regret telling Miles she would go with him. His answering smile seemed altogether too smug for her liking. If he didn't come to the point soon, she would order him to stop and would find her way back to Anne and Frank on foot. She turned to tell him so.

Miles indicated the avenue branching off ahead of them as he pulled into it. "I wanted to take you to an area where I might speak more candidly than where every member of the *ton* is gaping at the pair of us in speculation. This should be good enough, for the closest person is at least ten feet away."

Dorothea looked around. Indeed, there was another couple walking about ten feet away, but they were headed down a separate avenue, and there was no one else anywhere in sight. That was when she began to grow nervous. Not from being alone with him, but from *him*. Why was he here? Was he going to break her heart again? She didn't think so, but it did not do to let one's heart hope.

Miles turned, and his knees touched hers. He put his arm along the back of the seat and allowed his gloved hand to rest near her back. She couldn't breathe from the touch. He had always had that effect on her. She was powerless to move until he released her from his spell.

"Dorothea, I want to marry you." His eyes searched hers, and she tried to draw breath before she grew faint. He was asking this of her now? It was impossible to answer him.

"I think I have wanted to marry you from the very first moment I met you, and not entirely for the *wrong* reasons. For although I needed your dowry, I have never met a woman I wanted to be with day after day, every day, for the rest of my life until I met you."

She let out the scant breath she was holding and turned forward, gasping for more. A multitude of emotions swarmed within her. He was saying what she wanted to hear. But was she ready to give everything up for him? Was she ready to believe the truth of his declaration? Would he love her and be true to her always?

"Dorry, say something. Put me out of my misery," Miles coaxed, lifting a hand and tilting her face so she met his regard. He traced his thumb over her lips until her breathlessness turned into a flame of warmth that shot through her.

He stopped suddenly. "*Ah!* But I am getting ahead of myself. I should have begun by saying that I am proposing to you now with honest intentions, for I do not need your dowry. Not a single farthing of it." His eyes danced. "I have received an unexpected inheritance that permits me to come to you on equal terms. I want to marry you for you, Dorothea. Only for you. Not your title, or your wealth, or anything else—just you."

No amount of lifelong training in keeping her sentiments perfectly in check at all times could prepare Dorothea for the assault on her reason and her emotions. She laughed then, which turned into tears. She covered her eyes, but he took her hands and tucked her fingers into his.

"We can give the entirety of your portion away to the church if you would like and still live comfortably." His doubt seemed to grow at her silence, because he coaxed again, "Only do say yes."

She turned to him now, her knees touching his. A smile came to her lips, and although tears still sparkled on her eyelashes, glinting in the sun on its downward path to the horizon, she leaned forward a hairsbreadth.

He seemed to understand. Miles *always* seemed to understand what it was she wanted. He leaned forward too—just enough so that their lips were almost touching... And then he waited. It didn't require further thought.

"Yes," she whispered.

Miles kissed her then. It was not the feathery kiss on her temple or the dry kiss she had always expected she'd be obliged to endure from her husband. This one was leashed passion, as though he had been waiting to do this very thing for ages and ages and had only held back until she gave him leave to do so.

If the feeling of his lips on her temple had destabilized her, the feel of his lips on her own tilted the earth from under her in a dizzying spin. She placed her hand on his chest to steady herself and he covered it with his own, grasping it, not for an instant losing his focus of sweeping her along in a tide of passion and promises of all that would be hers in marrying him.

The horses started forward suddenly, causing him to break away from their kiss. He spared them only a brief glance as he let the team feel his hands on the reins before bringing his full attention back to her. Sounds of voices advancing down a path that cut into theirs signaled an end to their whispered pledge.

He gave the tiniest smile, his eyes still on her. "Yes?" he asked softly, a little crack of vulnerability sounding in his voice.

Her lips were tender in the very best way from having been thoroughly kissed, and she smiled and nodded.

"Yes."

EPILOGUE

S ummer had come and gone, and with it a much-celebrated wedding in St. George's Hanover Square with Anne Kensington, Lady Berkley, Lord Pembroke, and enough of the *ton* in attendance to receive a small paragraph in the *Gazette,* marking it a distinguished affair. Dorothea hadn't cared about any of that. She concerned herself only with her vow to love and cherish Miles Shaw and to hear him vow the same to her. That —and the kiss that sealed their union as man and wife. And then the kiss after that, and the one after that...

The leaves were beginning to fall and the smell of smoke from a farmer burning them in the distance mingled with the crisp air of autumn. That night they would be having their first white soup of the season for dinner, followed by every tasty dish of venison, pike, sweetmeats, right up until the syllabub she had planned for the guests that were set to arrive that day. Lady Isabelle would also be in attendance that evening, her new footman bringing her by carriage the short distance from the dower house and taking her back the same way.

Dorothea ran to the front door as soon as she heard the line of carriages arriving on the gravel path leading up to their house near Kington. She opened the door before any of the servants could come to it and stood waving and smiling. When the carriages stopped in front of the house, she ran down the stone steps and stood in readiness while the footman opened the door to the carriage that carried her family, while other servants went to remove the trunks from the second carriage.

Lady Poole climbed out first, and Dorothea went over to take her mother's arm, reaching in to give her a little hug first. This was relatively new in their relationship, and she had initiated the affection on her husband's encouragement. Her mother seemed to enjoy the embraces, which gave Dorothea the spirit to continue.

"It is a well-looking house," her mother said, looking up to its roof and then turning to take in the gardens that were visible around it. "Just as you said it was."

"I am so pleased with it, Mama. But I am even more pleased you are here." Dorothea turned to greet Joanna and Tilly, who were now standing in front of the carriage. She hugged them both.

"I suppose I shall have to wait for us all to sit and have *tea* before I am allowed to see the stables or the bay mare you have boasted of," Joanna said with an air of exasperation that— knowing her sister—was more true than she would let on.

"Go," Dorothea said with a smile. "I am mistress here, and if I say you may miss tea and see the horses, then there is nothing stopping you."

Miles rounded the corner at that moment and lifted a hand. He was in shirtsleeves, having expected the party to arrive later in the afternoon. He would put on a coat before he joined them in the drawing room, but she enjoyed the sight he presented and grinned at him appreciatively.

"The stables are found around the corner that Miles has just come from," she told Joanna, who then took off—*not* in an unladylike run as Dorothea had almost feared she would. She was maturing.

"Tilly," she said, glancing at her youngest sister with affection. "There are three bedrooms to choose from, and I told the housekeeper I would let you pick first." When Tilly looked at her in surprise, she added, "As the youngest, you never have any choice. I thought you might like to have first pick while you're here."

Tilly squared her shoulders and smiled proudly. "Why, as a matter of fact I would. I think I shall go see them now. After all, we are to stay an entire month."

"That's right," Dorothea encouraged her. She watched as Tilly took Lady Poole's elbow and assisted her up the stairs into the house.

"Dorry, I've missed you."

She turned to receive Sophia's hug and returned it just as warmly. She had never realized how much her sister's gentle presence steadied her until she was forced to keep up their relationship through correspondence. "I've missed you, too," she said, with a tight squeeze.

"And you." She turned to Camilla and included her in their hug.

"My goodness," she added, pulling away to look at her. "Camilla, you are growing into quite a beauty. Sophia, do you see it?"

"Of course I do," the gentle, faithful Sophia replied. "The suitors will be beating down our door for her next season."

Camilla sniffed. "As though I care a button for that." But her cheeks turned pink, and Dorothea was quite sure she did.

"Evo, well met." Miles went over to him and shook his hand. "You celebrated a birthday last week, I believe. Fourteen?"

"As you say." Evo's voice had the slight warble of one yet undecided whether it belonged in the realm of boyhood or manhood. "Good to see you, Dorry." He plunked a kiss on Dorry's cheek, startling her with the gesture. She beamed at him.

"Come in, come in. It is true we thought you would be later, but I am sure Cook can drum up a tea that I shall not be ashamed of. For what else have we to do but to eat, drink, and be merry?"

Her mother and sisters had all gone inside, except Joanna, who was by now likely in alt over the beautiful mare they had just acquired.

Evo took Dorothea by the arm to lead her into the house and called over his shoulder to Miles, "I believe I have you to blame for this unforeseen side to my sister. When has she ever used words like 'merry?' Miles, what have you done to her?" Dorothea giggled at his side.

"And giggling," Evo continued in disgust. "Oh, *please* do not tell me this was a love match. I would never have given my blessing."

"Too late," Miles said, clasping a hand on Evo's shoulder. "But never fear. You have four more sisters to keep from committing such a grave error as to marry for love. We shall count on you to see to it."

"Oh no, we shall not," Dorothea countered. "Every last one of them shall have their love match or *I* shall get involved and see to it. They must settle for nothing less."

"No!" Evo and Miles both protested at once.

Dorothea looked at them in astonishment at the vehemence of their response. She set her hands on her hips, attempting an air of indignation. Miles and Evo took one look at her then both began to laugh, and after an abortive attempt to keep her dignity, she joined in.

"I've picked my room!"

Tilly ran down the stairs and passed them, going straight

into the drawing room. Through the open door, the familiar voices of her mother and sisters sounded as they examined the paintings, the decorations, and the magnificent bouquet of fresh flowers that Miles had placed for her on the large round table at one end. He had given the gardeners instructions to plant freesias, knowing she liked them, and they were currently in a vase along with tall red and white roses.

When the hilarity died down, Miles slipped his arm around Dorothea's waist. "There is only one love match I wish for you to worry about, and it is ours." He kissed her soundly on the lips.

"I cannot bear it!" Evo groaned and threw up his hands as he walked into the drawing room.

"What about you?" Miles asked her, nuzzling a vulnerable spot on her neck that he knew she liked. "Do you think you can bear it?"

"*Hmm.*" Dorothea drew out the response as she pretended to think. "I suppose I can. But only for sixty more years or so."

"Only that?" She heard his grin as he continued to ply her neck with little kisses.

"Not a day more." She pulled away enough to treat him to a look of mock severity. "Everyone has their limits."

ABOUT THE AUTHOR

Jennie Goutet is the best-selling author of twelve Regency romances, including the Clavering Chronicles, Memorable Proposals, and Daughters of the Gentry series. Her books have received first place in historical romance for the New England Reader's Choice Awards and have hit the number one spot in Regency Romance on Amazon. They have been featured on BookBub and Hoopla, and are translated into five languages.

Jennie is an American-born Anglophile who lives with her French husband and their three children in a small town outside of Paris. Her imagination resides in Regency England, where her proper Regency romances are set. You can learn more about Jennie's books and sign up for her newsletter on her author website: jenniegoutet.com or purchase her books at jenniegoutetbooks.com.

* Photo Credit : Caroline Aoustin